I AM WILDCAT

A Jack and Catherine Love Adventure

C. A. Rollie

This book is dedicated to my mom and brother Kent who both passed in 2020.

Acknowlededment

Surprisingly, writing these books came easily for me, but the decision to publish was not so easy. I would like to acknowledge input from my brothers Kevin Rollie and Jeff Engel that helped me decide to share this story and continue with the books following in this series.

I would also like to acknowledge Mo Gawdat's book, 'Solve for Happy' as my inspiration for Jack's philosophical sensibilities.

Can love transcend death? How will God intervene at the 'end of days'? The answer, through a young woman and the man that loves her.

C. A. ROLLIE

CONTENTS

INTRODUCTION

In an apocalyptic world, a young orphan, Catherine, must learn to survive with the help of a man, Jack, that saved her from his sadistic brother. Catherine falls in love with Jack as he teaches her how to survive in a rough world. Jack tries to resist an intimate relationship because of their age difference, much to Catherine's frustration. They both experience an illusion that sets them on the path to bringing back law and order to the 'rough times' they live in.

This story will begin a series of three books that tell the story of survival, love lost, future generations and the restoration of civilization. Readers that enjoy action and adventure combined with a love story that includes hunting, fishing, shooting, and survival will enjoy the trail Jack and Catherine follow.

PROLOGUE

The little boy peeked into the room and said, "Gramma Catherine, watcha' doin'?"

Catherine opened her eyes and said, "I'm listening Little Jack."

"Watcha' listnin' to, Gramma?" he asked.

Catherine smiled and said, "Before I heard a little boy running up the sidewalk and slamming the screen door and then sneaking down the hallway…"

"Sorry." Little Jack interrupted.

"…I was listening to everything." She continued.

"What?" Little Jack screwed up his face in confusion, "How can you listen to everything?"

"It's easy if you stop thinking." Catherine said.

"I can't stop thinking!" he exclaimed.

"Come here and sit on my lap." she said. Little Jack climbed up in her lap and leaned back against her chest. Catherine said, "Now close your eyes with me and listen."

Little Jack closed his eyes and after a second scrunched up his face and asked, "Are you messin with me Gramma?"

"No." she said. "Now close your eyes and listen while I tell you what I hear."

He closed his eyes and sighed. "Okay."

Catherine said, "Now listen. I hear wind rustling the leaves in the tree outside the window. Do you hear it?"

"Uh huh!" he exclaimed.

"I hear a bird singing in the field across the yard. Do you hear it?"

"Uh huh, it's a meadowlark."

"I hear a fly caught in the spider web outside the window. Do you hear it?"

"Uh no. Oh! He exclaimed, "I hear it buzzing now, cool."

"I hear your mother in the kitchen making dinner. Do you hear it?"

"Yeah, she's makin' 'pasketti tonight."

"I hear your sister in the nursery waking up and standing in her crib getting ready to howl. Do you hear it?"

"No." he said, "That one's hard to hear through the walls."

"I know." Catherine said, and just then Jessica let out a howl.

"Wow," he said, "Gramma you can hear everything. How do you do it?"

"I stop thinking and just listen" she said.

"But I can't stop think'n Gramma cause there's a man downtown 'causin' a stir" he said.

"What is the man stirring up" she asked?

"He's some 'porter from Butte, what's a 'porter?" he said and asked in one sentence.

"Do you mean a reporter? We'll get back to that later. Why is he causing a stir" she asked again?

"Well, he's askin' all kinna' questions about someone called Wildcat. Do you know who that is? He says she killed 82 bad men during the Rough Times." he said in a rush.

"I knew her once." Catherine said with a sad look on her face. "And she killed more than 82 bad men and she killed some good men too."

"Woohoo, Gramma, can I go tell the ree'porter that you know her?" he asked loudly.

"Now hush, Little Jack, I would rather you didn't. Can you promise me that you won't tell him or anyone else that I knew her once" she asked quietly?

"Aw Gramma, this is cool. Why can't I tell" he asked?

"I'm serious Little Jack. Promise me!" she said urgently, "When you get older I will tell you all about her. Promise me!"

"Okay" he said reluctantly, "but you gotta promise me you will tell me about her when I get a little older, okay?"

"I promise" she said.

"Now a reporter is a person that tries to tell stories about things that happened, but they rarely every get the story right" she said. "Now that we promised each other and we would both get mad if either of us broke our promise, can you give me some time alone?"

He asked, "Are you goin' to go back to listnin?"

"I'm going to try, now scoot" she said.

Little Jack jumped down and ran into the kitchen yelling, "Is the 'pasketti ready yet mom?"

Catherine closed her eyes and took a deep breath to calm herself, but try as she might, she could not stop thinking.

CHAPTER 1

I heard a girl scream, and knew immediately what was going on. I walked down the hall and opened the door to see a large man holding a young girl down on the bed and taking her clothes off. She was struggling, but the man was too strong.

"Jim, let her go" I said.

"Shut up Jack, and get the hell out of here" Jim said.

Jack thought, *'Jim has changed a lot since the 'World took the Big Shit'.*

I was only sixteen years old when it happened and my brother Jim was ten years older. That was twenty eight years ago. North Korea and Iran destroyed the world. North Korea nuked South Korea, Japan, their old masters China, Australia, the Philippines, Hawaii, and the west coast of the United States. Iran hit Israel, Russia, Europe, India, and with ships disguised as oil tankers took out the east coast of the United States. Those countries with nuclear weapons retaliated and destroyed the Middle East and the Korean peninsula, and then trying to stay in control, hit their old political enemies. Africa and South America were not spared. Over three billion people were killed in the initial attacks, and then with the sun covered by radioactive dust, we braced for the long winter.

Another three and half billion people that lived in the urban cities and suburban areas died over the next three years due to lack of resources and an inability to create their own. Only a few areas were untouched. Parts of Canada, Scandinavia, the southern tip and west coast of South America, some of the north central United States, and many small islands around the world were spared. People moved out of the cities and into the country, only to find that without oil and power, the agriculture industry had turned into an agrarian, subsistence economy. Money was worthless, unless it was silver or gold. Small towns closed in on themselves for mutual protection, but roving bands of thieves and beggars chipped away at them.

Jim and I set out to protect the small villages in our area from these marauders. We formed the Raider Protection Association and hired men not afraid to fight.

Jim was in the military when the 'Big Shit' happened and he was stationed at a small base in Alaska when all hell broke loose. Jim had never excelled at anything, because of his temper. He had made Sargent in the Army, only to be busted down to Corporal for fighting. In the end, he was a Private and shipped away to Alaska.

Jim was feared by the men that worked with us. He was also feared by the people in the towns we protected. I knew it was only a matter of time before he snapped. He was always complaining how the 'Big Shit' had ruined his life and working for a little hard currency, food and lodging was a worthless way to live. Well, I guess the time had finally come.

I loved my brother. He hiked from Alaska to northern Idaho to find me, and I will never forget that. Our parents didn't last the first three years after the attacks. Mom went first from radiation sickness. After that, Dad didn't have the will to live. I went up into the mountains and learned to live off the land. It was through my trading with the towns, that Jim found me. We stayed up in the mountains for the next ten years, hunting and fishing, then trading our surplus in the small towns that sprang up in the valleys that had good water. Almost all of the older folks had died in the first few years, so the population was much younger and inexperienced.

As the towns repopulated, they started looking for protection. That's when Jim decided that we should come down out of the mountains and make our way by providing this protection. That's what we had been doing for the last fifteen years. But, as we cleaned out the thieves and marauders, and the towns became safer, the towns' people needed us less. It was looking like we had worked ourselves out of a job. I told Jim that we should go back up into the mountains, but he had gotten lazy living in the valley.

◆ ◆ ◆

"Jim, I said let her go."

He yelled, "I said get the fuck out of here and mind your own business."

I pulled my .357 Colt Python and pointed it at him. "I'm not going to ask you again, Jim."

"You're going to pull a gun on your own brother?" he spat angrily.

"Jim, regardless if you're my brother or not, this is not the kind of people we are."

"Fuck that kind of people." he said. "We have been protecting those people from raiders for fifteen years, and what has it gotten us. 'NOTHING'. Well I am going to get what is coming to me, like it or not, so put the gun away."

"No," I said as I cocked the revolver. "Let the girl go now."

Jim looked at me with surprise and could see that I was not going to back down. He let the girl up and as she wrapped her clothes around herself and edged away from him, he said. "You and I aren't done girl. I will find you again after I settle up with my brother."

"There is nothing to settle between us. I am packing my stuff and leaving."

Jim smiled and said, "After everything I've done for you, you're just going to leave. Come on, man. We can work this out. I'm your only brother for God's sake."

"Jim, I appreciate what you went through to find me after

the 'Big Shit', but you've changed, or maybe I've changed. I can't become a taker and prey on people just trying to survive."

I looked at the girl and said, "Leave girl, now. No harm will come to you." She scurried from the room, and ran down the hall. I heard the door slam behind her, and decocked the Colt and looked at Jim with sadness. Jim had always been my big brother and even though we grew up separately, I still loved him. He was all I had.

Jim looked at me with anger and said, "If you're leaving, go. If I ever see you again, I'll kill you."

"No you won't Jim, this is not you speaking."

"You bet your ass it's not me speaking." he said, "I'm going to start taking what I want from this miserable, fucked up world."

I sighed, turned and walked out. I went to my room and packed up my stuff and then went to the corral and saddled my horse, Betty. I loaded my gear on my pack horse, Zack, and headed out of town to the west. Jim stood on the porch of the house we were staying in and glared at me. I stopped and said, "Bye Jim, I hope you don't do what you intend."

Jim said, "Fuck you, you're dead to me."

The other guys in our group stood around whispering and confused about what was taking place. Jim and I had always backed each other up and this was a new situation for them. They feared Jim because of his temper, and they respected me because of my fighting skills. I was also the most experienced tracker and hunter. My even temper held Jim in check whenever there was conflict in our group. I feared that now Jim would bully them into doing whatever he wanted and I wouldn't be there to stop him. I smiled to myself and thought *'this really is a fucked up world we live in'.* I was choosing to walk away from helping others. I felt in my gut that I was wrong for leaving, but I wouldn't be a part of harming innocent people. I didn't realize the challenges that lay ahead of me.

CHAPTER 2

I was about two miles up the trail, and I knew she had been following me for the past half hour. She was about as quiet as squirrel running through the dry autumn leaves. I turned off the trail and tied the horses up about twenty yards in. I snuck back and sat against a tree just off the trail. I didn't have long to wait. About ten minutes later she came stumbling down the trail until she lost the horse's tracks. I stayed still as she looked around in panic. She ran up the trail sobbing, and then ran back to where the tracks ended. I was surprised she found the bush I had slid behind to lead the horses off the trail. She started racing through the trees in the direction I had gone and stumbled on a root and face planted right in front of me. She was a pretty thing underneath all the dirt and sweat from trailing me. She had medium length straight black hair, a snub nose, and dark brown, almost black colored eyes.

I said, "Where you going girl." She yelped and jumped back on her butt and then noticed me sitting against the tree.

She looked me up and down. I was about 6' tall with short medium brown hair, blue eyes and slim but with a muscular build. To her, I was an old man, but everyone over twenty was old to her.

"My names not girl." she said defiantly. She stood up with her hands on her small hips and glared at me.

"I don't care what your name is girl. I asked where you are going." Just then I heard shots echoing through the canyons from the direction of the town. I stood up and more shots echoed from that direction.

The girl said, "That big man is..."

"My brother." I interrupted.

"He is a fucking asshole." she said. "He's gathering all the townsfolk in the corral and his men are stealing everything from our homes. I was living with my dad's sister and snuck out the back before they knocked in the front door."

Jim had his men round up all the people of Elmira and moved them into the corral. There were about twenty five men, no older than forty, but most were younger, and thirty women, some older than fifty. The rest were children from toddlers to teens. There was about seventy five townspeople total.

The town leader, a man named Charley stepped out of the group and said, "What are you doing Jim? We had a deal. For food and lodging and what currency we could afford, you said you would protect us."

Jim laughed, "I am protecting you."

Charley asked, "Protecting us from what?"

"From me!" Jim exclaimed. "We are going to take what we want and leave, and if you all play nice, no one will get hurt."

Jim looked around at the group of townspeople and frowned. "Where is the black haired girl?"

Everyone looked at each other and could see she wasn't among the group.

Jim yelled at a couple of his men, "Go search the houses and find her. She is coming with me."

Charley and a couple of men stepped forward and said, "You're not taking anyone, Jim. She is an orphan and has the protection of the town."

Jim laughed, "I'm the protection of Elmira; now get back in the group." Charley took another step forward. Jim pulled his 1911 and shot him in the chest. Everyone panicked and starting running from the corral. Jim shot the other two men, and the some of his men started shooting into the crowd. Women and children dropped to the ground covering their heads. Then the townsmen tried to rush some of Jim's men. More shots rang out as the unarmed townsmen dropped in a bloody heap.

Jim yelled loudly, "Stop shooting." His men slowly complied, as a few more shots rang out. When the smoke cleared, there were twenty nine dead or wounded. Most of them were men.

Jim paced in front of the townspeople and said, "I said if everyone played nice, no one would get hurt."

"We are all unarmed and you murdered us. You bastard." the oldest women in the group yelled.

Jim smiled and turned towards her. "Bastard, am I?" He raised his 1911 and shot her in the forehead. Everyone screamed and dropped to the ground again. "I said play nice. Now if anyone else has something to say let's get it over with." A whimpering hush settled over the rest of the townspeople.

Jim turned to his men and said, "Take everything of value from the houses, and someone find me that girl. All this killing has made me horny."

His men scurried like rabbits, not wanting to piss Jim off. A couple men watched over the townspeople, while the rest took wheelbarrows and carts from house to house. They filled them with whatever they thought might have trade value. They also took as much food as a wagon they stole could carry.

A short while later, one of the most trusted of Jim's men, Brian, slowly approached Jim. Jim was sitting on the porch of the community center drinking a homemade beer. Jim was a big man, about 6'4", with the same medium brown hair and blue eyes as his brother. He was going to fat in his midsection, and he always had an angry scowl on his face.

"What?" Jim asked.

"We've looked everywhere and can't find the girl."

Jim bolted to his feet and Brian jumped back. "My fucking brother Jack took her. I knew he just wanted her for himself, the greedy son of a bitch. I am going to kill him the next time I see him."

Brian thought, *'Fuck, I should have left with Jack.'*

The next day, Jim and his men headed south towards St. Maries, Idaho. They took some of the younger women with them. His plan was to take what he could from St. Maries and then head to Lewiston to trade what they stole. Jim and his men had gone from protecting to preying on the people.

CHAPTER 3

"**I** said where are you going girl?"

She looked at me and with a sob said, "Aren't you going to do something? People are dying because of your brother."

I looked at her and said, "I am only one man. Jim has twenty men and they are all loyal to him. Do you want me to throw my life away for a few farmers?"

"I thought you were a good man, but I guess I was mistaken." she yelled, turned and started walking back to the trail.

"I said where are you going girl?"

She turned back and ran up to me and started hitting me in the chest and yelled, "My names not 'girl'.

Relenting, I grabbed her by the wrists and said, "Easy there. I'm sorry. What's your name then?"

She dropped to the ground crying. I sat back down against the tree again and waited. As I waited, I listened. I stopped thinking about what was happening in Elmira, and took in all the noises around me. I heard the horses behind me shuffling and pulling up grass. I heard the wind blowing through the tops of the trees, birds chirping and fluttering by; insects buzzing through the warm air. I heard all this, but what I was listening for was anyone coming up the trail.

After about a half hour, the girl stopped whimpering, snuffled, wiped her nose and red swollen eyes on her sleeve and looked up at me. "My name is 'Wildcat'." she whispered.

I smiled at her and said, "That's not your name girl."

She got a stubborn look on her face and said, "Yes it is. Everyone calls me 'Wildcat'."

"They may call you that," I said, "but that's not your name. What's your name girl?"

"Quit calling me 'girl'." she yelled angrily.

"I will quit calling you girl when you tell me your name."

She glared at me and said, "My names Catherine but I don't like it. They started calling me 'Cat', and that changed to 'Wildcat'."

"I think Catherine is a beautiful name, Catherine." I said.

She stood up and stomped her foot, "You're impossible."

"I may be. Where are you going Catherine?"

She ignored the question. "Your name is Jack, right."

"Yes it is. Where are you going Catherine?"

"Stop calling me that. My name is 'Wildcat'."

"No people call you 'Wildcat', your name is Catherine. Your parents gave you that name."

She sighed sadly and looking down said, "I didn't know my parents. They died when I was a baby. Raiders came and hit Elmira and killed them. My dad's sister took me in and raised me."

I remembered when I lost my parents, and how difficult it was for me, but I was nineteen at the time. At least I had many good years with my mom and dad. This poor girl was born during the 'Rough Times'. She lost everything to Raiders, and now she has lost everything again to my brother.

I had a decision to make. I sat back against the tree again and closed my eyes. I cleared my mind of all thoughts except one. *'What should I do with her?'* I listened to everything around me. I heard her sit down and I knew she was staring at me. Thankfully she stayed quiet. I reveled in the harmony around me, while still running that question through my mind. *'What should I do with her?' 'What should I do with her?' 'What should I do with her?'* Then it was all clear to me. I would bring some peace and happiness into her life. I would teach her how to survive and find her a good man to marry and settle down with. I was at least thirty years older than her, so I would be the father she never knew.

I opened my eyes and stood.

She said, "You've made up your mind I see."

I glanced at her and said, "You have good intuition."

She stared at me and asked, "What's 'intution'?"

"Not 'intution', intuition. It's being able to read other people and tell what they are thinking. If you like, we can go to Priest Lake. We will stay in a cabin I know and I am going to teach you how to survive on your own."

"I don't want to be on my own. Can't I stay with you?" she pleaded.

"You can for a while, but you will have to be on your own someday. I am a lot older than you and won't be around forever."

We traveled west the rest of the day, and made camp that evening. I told her to gather firewood and went hunting for dinner. I was able to shoot a couple grouse and gathered some wild tomatoes and potatoes that had seeded from an old garden. This area had been an old farm area when people used to leave the city and think they were getting back to nature. *'Ha'*. They had no clue what getting back to nature actually was. When I got back to the camp, Catherine had a small fire going. I cleaned the area around the fire and told her in the future she must always make sure the fire couldn't spread. I showed her how to clean one of the grouse and had her clean the other. She said 'yuck' when I pulled the guts out and saved the heart, gizzard, and liver. She said 'yuck, yuck, yuck" when it was her turn to gut the second grouse, but she did it. I told her to gather more firewood because it was going to get cold before dawn. She gathered a big pile while I cooked dinner.

After we ate, and were sitting around the campfire, Catherine asked, "Why were you sitting with your eyes closed against the tree when you decided to bring me along."

I smiled at her question and decided it was time to start her training. I said, "When I have something important to decide, I like to listen to everything around me and clear my mind of all thoughts. When I hear the calmness around me, it removes all negative thoughts because there is nothing negative in the present. This way I can make a clear decision."

She frowned and asked, "Why is there nothing negative in the present? We just heard your brother killing people in Elmira."

"Yes," I said, "but what we heard was already in the past and I couldn't let that affect my decision. I had to let the calmness of the present replace the negative things that already happened. I can't tell the future, so I had to decide what to do in the present."

She smiled for the first time since we were together and said, "Thank you."

A little later, I set up our bedrolls and climbed into mine. She crawled over next to me and said, "You can lay with me, I'm not a virgin."

I sat up shocked and said, "WHAT?"

She hurriedly said, "I'm not a virgin, Billy Pee took care of that four months ago."

Not knowing what say, I changed the subject. "What does the P stand for?"

"Not P," she said, "Peeee, cause he always smelled like piss. It wasn't very good and it hurt some cause all he did was hump me, so you can lay with me 'cause I'm not a virgin."

I changed the subject again and asked, "How old are you, Catherine?"

She looked down shyly and said, "I'm 15."

I was still scrambling to take control of the situation which I knew was getting out of hand. Catherine wasn't a little girl, she was a young woman. She was probably 5'5" already and around 105 pounds and starting to fill out nicely. I quickly put a brake on those thoughts and said, "I'm forty four, which is much older than you, and I am a virgin when it comes to little girls. So there will be no laying or humping between us." She looked disappointed and I thought she was probably still in shock with the events of the day, so I said, "You can lie next to me, but that's all, okay." She smiled for the second time and quickly grabbed her bedroll and dragged it over next to mine. I lay back down and she snuggled back against me. I tried to clear my mind and listen to everything, but curse it; I couldn't get to sleep for a long while.

CHAPTER 4

T he next morning I was tired from not sleeping well. I got up quietly and didn't wake Catherine who was snoring softly, bundled up in her bedroll. I walked over to a ridge facing east, sat down and closed my eyes. As the sky lightened to the east, I sat and closed my eyes and listened. Thoughts of Catherine kept popping into my head, and I would have to quell them and focus on the calm morning and the forest waking up. I listened to the birds waking up and chirping at each other. I heard Zack swishing his tail, and Betty shift her feet. I could hear a stream gurgling below me and a squirrel climbing down the side of a tree. Time disappeared and calmness spread over me.

I have no idea how much time had passed, when I heard Catherine sneaking up behind me. The sun was already above the mountains to the east and was warm on my face. I was smiling at the peace that had spread over me and the world around me. Catherine eased down beside me as quietly as she could and hugged her knees to her chest. I turned to her and said, "Good Morning." I could tell she had been crying again from her swollen eyes. I asked, "Are you all right?"

Catherine snuffled and said, "I thought you left me when I woke up and saw you were gone. Then I realized you wouldn't leave your horses too."

"If I am going to leave you Catherine, I won't sneak away. You can count on that."

A small smile crossed her face and she took a deep breath and shuddered. "Thank you, I was scared." She said. "And would you call me 'Wildcat'."

I looked at her and smiled, "No, I will not call you 'Wildcat'. You are not an animal. You are a beautiful young girl. Whether you like it or not, I will always call you Catherine."

Catherine sighed and asked, "Why were you smiling with your eyes closed?"

"I wasn't thinking." I said.

"You weren't thinking? That's crazy. I can't stop thinking all the time."

"Were you thinking while you were asleep?" I asked.

She laughed and said, "I don't know, I was sleeping. Were you asleep when I came up?"

"No, I wasn't asleep, but I stopped thinking and just listened to everything around me."

"How can you listen to everything? That's stupid." She said.

I laughed and asked, "Would you like to try it?"

"I guess, but I'm hungry."

"It will only take a few minutes to start with, and then we'll eat, okay?"

She scrunched up her face and said, "You're not messing with me, are you Jack?"

I said no, and told her to close her eyes, take a deep breath and relax while I told her what I was listening to. She peeked out of her half closed eyes to see that I was doing the same and finally closed them.

I said, "I hear the stream below us burbling over the rocks. Do you hear it?"

"Yes," she said, "that's easy."

I said, "Don't think about it and just listen." "I hear a Blue Jay in the tree tops across the canyon. Do you hear it?"

"Yes."

"I hear Betty and Zack moving around back at the camp. Do you hear it?"

"Uh, no... Oh, I just heard one of them sputter."

"That was Betty; she does that when she's hungry."

"I'm hungry too." She said.

"Stop thinking about your stomach and listen. I hear a bumblebee buzzing around the wildflowers in the clearing beside us. Do you hear it?"

"Uh, okay, I hear it when it's flying."

"Yes," I said, "that's the only time a bee makes sound that you can hear. I hear a large animal, probably an elk moving through the trees below us to the stream. Do you hear it?"

"Uh, no," she said concentrating hard.

"Keep listening, it stopped when it heard our voices."

A few seconds later she heard a couple light footsteps and a small rock rolling into the creek with a splash. Then she heard some slurping sounds. "I hear it." Her eyes shot open as she yelped. Then there was a loud crashing below us and the sound of an animal running through the trees.

"You have to listen quietly or you will disturb the peace around you." I said. "Now close your eyes again, and listen to everything we just heard. Don't focus on any one of them or think about them, just listen." I watched her out of the corner of my eye as she took a deep breath and relaxed again. After a few minutes a small smile started forming on her face. She cocked her head a few times at a new noise, and her smile grew larger. When about a half hour had passed, I asked, "Are you still hungry?"

She looked at me with shock and said, "I wasn't thinking about it."

"Good," I said, "Then let's go eat."

We stood, and she looked up at me and said, "That was strange. It was almost like I was part of everything around me. It only seemed like a couple seconds, but I know it was much longer."

I looked at her and smiled. "We will practice this every morning, until you can feel when there is a change in the world around you."

"What do you mean?" she asked.

"Do you remember when the elk ran away? That was a change in the peace in world around you because it was startled by your voice."

"Sorry." She apologized.

"No, that was an important lesson in survival." I said. "When you listen to the world around you and you hear a sudden change in the sounds you hear, you have to pay attention in that direction."

"Oh, like when a flock of birds takes off suddenly when you scare them, right?" she asked.

"Yes, that is another example, but how about when everything in a certain direction goes real quiet?" I asked.

"That could mean that they are hiding, right?" she asked excitedly.

"Yes, very good. That means you need to know what made them hide." I said.

"This was fun." She said with a big smile.

"It's fun, yes, but it is also very serious if you want to stay alive in these rough times. Let's go eat."

We went back to camp and I let Betty and Zack loose from their hobbles so they could browse while we ate the leftover grouse. We cleaned up the campsite and repacked and then I showed Catherine how to load the packs onto Zack. I left a small area in front of the packs for her to sit. Then I showed her how to saddle Betty. She had difficulty lifting the saddle onto Betty's back, so I helped her. I knew with practice she would find it much easier to do.

CHAPTER 5

It took Catherine and me about two weeks to get to Priest Lake taking our time. We had to follow game trails because of the thick forest growth in the area. I had her practice listening every morning. I noticed a new calmness start to show in her behavior. She stopped crying about the past and started living in the present. She didn't quite get over asking me about what we were going to do tomorrow, and I always replied, "We'll find that out tomorrow." I did take some enjoyment telling her this, because she believed I was just teasing her. She thought I always knew what we were going to do and what was going to happen. I didn't want to shred her budding confidence by telling her that I didn't have a clue what would happen tomorrow. Worrying about it today wouldn't change what would happen anyway. My philosophy was to live in the present. Thinking about the past or worrying about the future wouldn't change what has already happened or what was to come. I preferred to be happy now.

To my surprise, traveling with Catherine made me very happy. Happier than I had been since the 'World took the Big Shit'. Catherine was always curious and asked me about everything and where I learned it. I told her that I read a lot of books when I can find them, and when I was her age I would watch movies. She didn't know what movies were, and she laughed hysterically when I tried to imitate the voice of 'Yoda' from the 'Star Wars' movies. Whenever she said she would try to do something, I would say in a silly approximation of Yoda's voice. "Do or do not, there is no try." We enjoyed each other's company immensely. We lived in the present and had no conditions about our relationship.

Every evening, she would pull her bedroll next to mine and snuggle against me before we fell asleep.

We reached the southern tip of Priest Lake, and I stopped. I could smell smoke. I looked at Catherine and she said, "I smell it too." She saw the indecision on my face and with a smile said, "If they ask, I'm your daughter, Dad." I can't quite explain the warm feeling I got in my chest when she said that.

I said, "I was hoping we could avoid people for a while. Well, nothing for it. Always forward."

We continued down a well beaten steep trail and came upon three cabins on the lake shore. A large boy saw us and ran into the first cabin yelling. We stopped and I leaned forward in the saddle, waiting and listening. A large woman came out of the cabin with a shotgun with the boy behind her. She shooed him back into the cabin and said, "What do you want? We don't have anything."

Catherine smiled at her and moved Zack forward a couple steps. The woman raised the shotgun and said, "Stop right there."

"Ma'am, my dad and I are just passing by and smelled the smoke. We are heading to the northern part of Priest Lake. We don't want no trouble and we'll cause no trouble."

Coming from a young girl, the woman relaxed a little. She called the boy out and said, "Bo, go down to the lake and get your Pa." The boy shot off like a rocket, not that many people know what a rocket is anymore.

We waited a short while and saw a large man, bigger than my brother Jim, coming up from the lake. He had dark brown hair with a bushy brown beard and had to be at least 6'6" tall. I figured him to be about thirty years old. The boy was behind him and had obviously told him what Catherine had said. He had a big smile on his face and said, "Marge is that anyway to treat guests? Put the gun away and invite them down off their horses."

Marge looked at her husband and slowly complied. I noticed a couple other women coming out of the other two cabins with small children as soon as the large man showed up. We got off the horses, and the large man came forward with his hand outstretched. I shook it and almost got my hand crushed.

He said, "Hi, I'm Big Bo Jenson, that's my wife Marge, and that's our son Little Bo."

I said, "Howdy Bo, I'm Jack Anders and this is my daughter Catherine."

Big Bo was a boisterous fellow. He slapped me on the back almost knocking me down and said, "We ain't had no visitors here since we came down from Calgary."

I asked how long ago that was, and he said, "Oh bout a year ago. Where y'all comin from?" I glanced at Catherine, and she gave me a slight smile. I knew she would follow my lead.

"We came up from Lewiston, and passed through Elmira a couple weeks ago."

"Elmira," he said, "that's the little place just east of here ain't it. They got any trade goods that would be worth the trip?"

I didn't know what to say, so I went with the truth. "After we passed through, we were a couple of miles west of there when we heard a lot of shots. Not wanting to get shot ourselves, we hightailed it out of there."

Bo looked concerned and said, "We heard there were still marauders around these parts. Calgary has set up some law and most of the bad men have been pushed out of the area. Heck they even started a school for kids and a college as a matter of fact."

I changed the subject and asked Bo if he had any farrier's tools. Our horses needed their hooves cut back and cleaned and then re-shoed.

Bo lit up and smiled at me. "We got a couple of sets of farrier tools, but none of us are any good at it. Would you be willing to trade caring for our horses and mules too and teaching me how to do it for one of the sets?"

I thought about it for a few seconds seeing how he was open to trade. I said, "I will be happy to teach you how and take care of your horses, but I also need something else."

He put his dickering face on, frowning and thinking slowly. "What might you be asking for?"

I glanced at Catherine, smiled and said, "Well we were crossing a river a ways back and my daughters pack wasn't tied on properly." I glared at her like a father would at an errant child, and bless her heart she looked contrite and said, "I told you I was sorry dad, I thought I tied it tight."

I looked at Bo and then at Marge. I said, "What I need is some clothes for Catherine. She only has the one set she's wearing."

Marge bolted forward and said, "Come with me missy, Janice lost a son about your age on the trip down here and he was about your size." She dragged Catherine over to one of the other cabins.

Bo looked at me and said, "There will be no need to consider that part of the trade. It's the neighborly thing to do."

I took care of the horses, taking their saddles, packs and blankets off. Then I wiped them down. I placed our stuff by a shed.

Later, I thanked Bo and looked around the cabin. It looked like most of the wood to build it had been taken from other construction and the furniture looked like it came from some of the farm homes that had been in the area.

I asked, "Are many of the old homes that used to be in this area still standing? When I was a kid, my parents used to bring us up here every summer from Spokane. We had a cabin on the northwest shore. That's where we're headed."

Bo said, "A lot of the homes were ransacked and some burned down by idiots, but there's a few still intact. We got most of our stuff from some of those still standing. Thieves don't want to move furniture or haul wood. They just take the little stuff."

"I hope our old cabin is still okay." I said.

As we were talking, a couple men and some eleven or twelve year old boys walked in. "John, Ben I want you to meet Jack. Him and his daughter are just passin' through to the north part of the lake. Jack these are my partners in this little venture."

I stood and shook their hands, and everyone sat down, except the boys. They heard 'daughter' and headed for the door.

Bo yelled, "Hold on boys. You go sniffing around Jack's daughter and you are going to have to deal with my wife."

The boys skidded to a halt and returned to the table. All the men laughed at the boys.

I said, "You boys can meet her later. I am sure she would like some company closer to her own age." They smiled at that and sat down in the living room whispering.

Bo turned to John and Ben and asked, "How'd the fishing go?"

John said, "We netted about twenty Northern and fifteen Walleye, and the boys caught four Lake Trout with their poles."

Ben joined in and said, "I see you finished the dock and the fish house while we were out. Now if we can get the smoke house finished we can stock some smoked fish for trade."

"Yeah," Bo said, "Jack here told me that Elmira was hit by marauders a couple weeks ago, so we may have to trade with Bonners Ferry instead or that Indian village we passed through north of here."

John and Ben sat up straight and I saw the boys stop talking and started listening to our conversation. They both started throwing questions at me. "How many marauders? Did they kill anyone? Which way did they head out?"

I didn't want to tell them that it was my brother and twenty of his guys and have them think I was a part of the attack, so I stuck with the story I told Bo. "My daughter and I had already passed through from Lewiston and were already headed west when we heard the gun shots. I believe they probably headed south, because we didn't travel very fast and they didn't catch up to us. Besides no one thinks there is much up here anyway."

All the men looked relieved and the boys went back to whispering. I thought I need to be careful and bring Catherine up to speed on my conversations.

At that moment, Marge and Catherine came through the door. Catherine was in boys clothing, but they fit her well. The boys perked up and I noticed Catherine eyeing them. The clothes weren't new, but well cared for.

"Marge, I don't know how to thank you." I said.

"Oh shush," she said, "it's just the neighborly thing to do." I immediately knew where Bo got it from.

CHAPTER 6

We stayed in Boville for a couple weeks. I had a conversation with Catherine the first night and we got our stories straight, in case there were any uncomfortable questions. True to Boville's easy going nature, the people didn't ask many questions. I helped build the smoke house and trained Bo and Ben how to take care of the horses and re-shoe them. Catherine and the boys ran around and helped where they could. It was peaceful and we enjoyed the company.

One evening after a couple days, I was hand loading some .308 brass with some powder and bullets I had previously traded for, when Catherine asked me if I would teach her to shoot. I had two rifles; a scoped .308 Remington 700 bolt action, a generic AR15 in .223 and a 20 gauge Mossberg semi-auto shotgun. I also had 3 pistols. My Colt Python in .357, a Caspian Custom 1911 in .45, and a Sig Sauer P226 also in .357.

I considered how to train Catherine and figured the AR15 had the least recoil, so I started there. "Tomorrow." I said.

Catherine gave a huge smile and couldn't sit still the rest of the night.

The next morning, we went out along the beach and a ways away from the town, where I found an old log lying next to an embankment. I sat on the log and closed my eyes and started to listen.

Catherine said, "I thought you were going to teach me to shoot."

I opened my eyes and smiled at her. "I am, but there you go

again, thinking about the future. You need to be calm and in the present to shoot properly."

She sat down next to me and closed her eyes, but I felt her fidgeting. After a few moments, I asked, "Where does the bullet go when it leaves the barrel?"

She opened her eyes and asked, "Into the target?"

I said, "Okay, where does it go after it goes into the target?"

She thought and said, "It stops?"

"Sometimes, but not always." I said. "It depends on your target. If the target is solid, it may stop. If the target is metal, it may ricochet. If the target is soft, it may go through. It the target is thin like paper it will keep going well beyond the target."

She thought for a couple seconds and said, "That makes sense, 'cause it's moving real fast."

"It may seem that because it is moving real fast that it makes sense, but the target that slows it down is what you need to be aware of. You don't want to hit something behind the target you didn't intend to. Or even to the side of the target in the case of a ricochet. Does that make sense to you?" I asked.

"Yes, so can we start shooting?" She asked impatiently.

I said, 'Okay, but first I want to get some targets and show you how to aim."

We scrounged around the beach and I found some small stumps, some old thin boards and an old piece of sheet metal. Catherine squealed and held up some small wild melons. We gathered the targets and set them up on the log. I purposely put a thin board behind one of the wild melons and turned the sheet metal at a forty five degree angle. I took a pencil and drew a one inch circle with a five inch circle around it on each target. I paced off twenty five yards and laid a blanket down. I placed a backpack on the blanket and laid the AR15 across it pointed at the targets.

"Isn't this too close?" she asked.

"No, not to start with," I said. "We will move back each time until we are at a hundred yards for the AR15. That's because it has iron sights. When I teach you to shot the Remington with the scope, we will get out to at least five hundred yards."

I showed her how to line up the iron sights, front post nestled into the blade sight groove. After she said she understood, I had her watch as I inserted a magazine into the rifle. I pulled back the charging handle and laid the rifle across the backpack. I told her to lay down behind the gun, snug it against her shoulder, and not put her finger on the trigger until after she had lined up the sights on the first target on the right.

She nestled the rifle against her shoulder as I had shown her and lined up the sights. Just as she was reaching her finger for the trigger, I yelled, "Stop."

Catherine flinched and asked, "What?"

I yelled loudly, "Boys come on out from back there." Two boys and a young girl stood up behind the bank we had the targets in front of and ran off towards the cabins laughing.

Catherine looked surprise and asked, "How did you know they were there? I didn't see them."

I smiled at her and said, "Catherine, all you were thinking about was shooting. When I first sat on the log and closed my eyes, I heard them whispering behind the bank. I didn't say anything because it wouldn't have taught you anything. Always be aware of everything around you. Don't just focus on one thing or thought."

She looked sheepish and said, "Sorry, but I was so excited."

I smiled and said, "Excitement is an emotion, just like fear, hate, love, and confusion. Whenever you feel any of these emotions, stop and listen to your surroundings. This will help you calm yourself and do the right thing."

I then told her to pick up the rifle and aim again with her finger off the trigger, then when she was ready, to shoot the first target on the left. She started aiming right and then realizing that I had changed targets swung the rifle to the left. She slowly put her finger on the trigger and squeezed. The rifle went 'click' and nothing happened. She looked at me confused and asked,

"What happened?"

I said, "First, it could be a hang fire and the primer could still make the gun go off, so keep pointing it at the target. Second, did you check to see if the rifle was loaded?"

"I saw you load it." She said.

"No," I said, "you saw me insert a magazine and pull back the charging handle. You didn't check to see if it was loaded."

She looked embarrassed and said, "You're an asshole, you know that? Can I shoot sometime today?"

I laughed and said, "I guess that's enough safety training for today. I'm sure you will remember all of it. Okay, here is a loaded magazine. Take the empty one out and insert this one and pull the charging handle yourself; so you're sure it's loaded."

I had her shoot for about an hour, checking the target after each shot. We moved back to fifty yards after twenty shots, because she was a natural. She actually shot better than I do. She hit the five inch circle every time and most times hit or nicked the one inch circles. When she shot the wild melon with the board behind it, she whooped when it exploded. When we went to look at it, she noticed the bullet hole in the board behind it. I had her shoot the sheet metal and saw her surprise when she heard it ricochet off into the lake. We shot ten shots from fifty yards and she hit every target.

I moved her back to a hundred yards where she had difficulty seeing the small targets behind the front post of the iron sights. I told her how a bullet drops as soon as it leaves the barrel and the sights were set so it would shoot three inches high at a hundred yards. She intuitively lined the target right on top of the front post and shot twenty more times. She hit every five inch circle. We stopped there, because she was getting tired from walking the hundred yards to the target after every shot. I planned it that way or she would have run me out of ammunition.

That evening I set up my reloading equipment and taught her how to replace the rounds she had shot. She didn't like it because it was tedious. She had to resize every piece of brass first, put the primer in, then measure the powder for each round, and then seat the bullet to the proper depth so the cartridge would fit into the chamber of the rifle.

She said, "I don't like doing this. Can't you do it?"

"Those are your fifty rounds," I said. "They should be good for about six more reloads before we have to replace the brass. If you want to keep shooting, you have to take care of those rounds, okay."

She looked at the rounds she had reloaded and her attitude changed. They were hers, not mine anymore. She placed them carefully into the shell bag I gave her and tucked them into her pack.

We shot every day, but only five or six rounds a day so we didn't use up all the powder and bullets. She didn't want to wear out the brass, so she kept track of how many times she reloaded each shell.

I trained her with the .308 and how to use the scope mil marks for different distances. I reloaded the rounds for this rifle because they required more care to be accurate at longer distances. I had her shoot the Sig and the Caspian out to about thirty feet.

She was hell on all the wild melons in the area. She recruited the boys to fetch them for her, and since she was the only teenage girl around they fought for her attention.

CHAPTER 7

I was sitting at the kitchen table with Bo and Marge one evening when Marge said, "The boys sure are taking an interest in Catherine. What do you have her doing to protect herself?"

I said that I was teaching her to shoot and would teach her how to fight when we got to our cabin.

Bo laughed and said, "Not that kind of protection."

"Oh!" I said and turned a little red. "Well, I guess I could have her shoot them in that case." We all laughed and then I said, "Seriously, I don't know anything about women's things. Marge, would you mind having some talks with her? Her mother died a couple years ago of a fever, and until then, I hadn't planned on teaching her what I am now."

Marge said, "I will Jack, that's why I brought the subject up. Besides that, we spend a lot of time together anyway. She has been helping me in the garden, and it seems that she likes growing things."

I laughed, "She likes eating things. I see her popping peas in her mouth while she's picking them."

Catherine spent the remainder of the two weeks with Marge; when she wasn't shooting that is. I helped Bo, John, and Ben finish building the smoke house and then net fish. I occasionally went hunting. I shot an elk and a large mule deer and added them to the small towns' larder. I used the shotgun and shot some partridge and grouse, and on one of these trips, I took Catherine along.

I had her shoot the shotgun at a melon to get a feel for the kick. I then explained how to sight down the barrel to the bead at the end, and how to lead the birds when they flew. Again she picked it up quickly. After missing the first bird because she stopped swinging when she pulled the trigger, she dropped the next two.

She giggled and said, "This is fun."

I said, "Yes it is; now you have to clean them."

I expected her to complain about this task, but she smiled and said, "I'll get the boys to do it for me."

"How are you going to pay them?" I asked.

"Oh they'll do it if I ask." She said.

I gave her a stern look and said, "If you ask someone to do something for you, you should always give them something in return. Just because they like you is not a reason to take advantage of them."

"Okay," she said, "I'll let them each shoot some of my cartridges."

"You can do that, but only if Bo agrees and I am with you when they shoot. Okay?" I said.

We came to end of the second week, and I told Bo that Catherine and I had to prepare to leave. It was the middle of June and I wanted to make sure we had a place set up before winter came.

The evening before we left, the small town threw a party. Bo and Ben cooked a small pig they had butchered, and the women made bread and cooked up a lot of vegetables from the garden. I spent the day with Catherine going through our gear and cleaning everything. As evening rolled around, everyone went to their places to clean up. I put on my best shirt and jeans, and was looking for Catherine to get her ready, but I couldn't find her.

The men and boys showed up clean, and I saw there really were boys underneath all that dirt. Marge was setting the table with one of the other ladies with sporadic help from the boys and men. I noticed Janice was missing too.

I was standing with my back to the lake when I noticed everyone look up past me and smile. I turned around and caught my breath. Janice was leading Catherine to the gathering and Catherine was wearing a bright blue sun dress. Her hair was pulled back in a ponytail. She was beautiful. I smiled at her and she lifted her chin and stared at me. "You look beautiful Catherine." I said. Then thinking fast I added, "You look just like your mother."

Catherine was the princess of the party. The boys pushed and shoved to get her things, while the men and women smiled at the chaos.

I asked Janice where the dress came from.

She said, "It was one of mine, but I never had a reason to wear it around here. I won't be in need of it, so we took it in and gave it to Catherine."

I don't like the idea of taking something for nothing and asked, "What can I pay you for it?"

Marge jumped in and said, "You hush now Jack, this is between us women and besides she worked hard for it. Janice made her re-sew it herself after we took it in."

I looked over at Catherine giggling with the boys and also getting some attention from the men. I said, "Well it looks like she did a good job. Thank you very much."

The party got going, and after dinner, Ben pulled out a twelve string guitar and everyone started singing. Catherine was dancing with the boys and I sat back and just listened. I hadn't felt this peaceful and happy in a long time. I closed my eyes and took in all the sounds. A while later, I heard Catherine sit down next to me and she asked, "What are you listening to?"

I turned to her and smiled. "I'm listening to happiness. No one is thinking about the past or worrying about the future. Everyone is just enjoying the present."

Then, Ben started a slow song, and Catherine reached for my hand and raised her eyebrow. I laughed and stood up taking her in my arms and slow danced to the end of the song. When it was over, I stepped back. Catherine reached forward and gave me a big hug and whispered in my ear. "I love you Jack."

"I love you too." I whispered back. I felt the love. It was

unconditional. It wasn't because she was a beautiful girl or because of anything she did, it was just because she existed. I can't explain it any other way.

Bo brought out some of his homemade beer and the party got real lively. I had one beer only as we had to leave early in the morning. The boys were each given one beer and they got a little loopy, dancing and giggling.

Bo sat down next to me and said, "I want to thank you for stopping by here and helping us out. You helped us get a lot of things done that probably would have had to wait 'til next year."

"You're welcome Bo, but thank you for having us. Catherine has been through some rough times and this helped her a lot. If you are ever up on the north shore make sure you look us up." I then told him where we were headed and how to find the cabin we were looking for.

Bo said, "We are planning on re-building a cabin cruiser and we may just take a trip up your way. We found an old thirty six foot fiberglass hull beached about a mile north of here."

I said, "Well that should shorten the trip, but how are you going to propel it? There isn't gas for motors anymore."

Bo laughed and said, "We got that figured out. The boys found a few old bicycles and we plan to hook them up to the prop shaft and take turns pedaling. As long as the lake is calm we should be able to make some headway."

I laughed and said, "I've heard of horse power, but I guess boy power will do too. I heard that down by Sandpoint, a man is tinkering with steam power again. You might want to plan a trading run down there."

Bo looked surprised and smiling said, "We'll do that. Then maybe we can find some more settlers to come up and help work the lake."

The party ended around midnight. The men carried the passed out boys and little ones to their beds and everyone filtered away.

Catherine and I went to bed and I fell asleep quickly. About an hour later, I felt Catherine slide into bed next to me.

She whispered, "Jack would you lay with me now?"

I didn't want to have my feelings from tonight change and said, "No, Catherine I love you, but I am too old. One of the boys will grow up and probably court you and I don't want 'that' to cause an issue. I will hold you only."

She sighed and said, "You will someday." I hugged her and kept my thoughts to myself.

CHAPTER 8

The next morning we were up early and to my surprise, everyone else got up. The men were a little red eyed, and the boys were moving pretty slow. I saddled Betty, and loaded the packs on Zack with a blanket in front of it for Catherine to sit on.

I don't like long goodbyes, but I knew this was going to take a little while. Catherine had made an impression on everyone there and they all wanted to hug her and say their goodbyes.

Little Bo waited until last, and I could see that he was holding something behind his back. He was already taller than Catherine even though he was two years younger. I could tell he was going to grow to be a big strapping man like his father. He smiled shyly at Catherine and then pulled a German Shepard puppy out from behind his back. "I want you to have him. He's the biggest of the litter and he liked you the best." He said with a red face.

I couldn't help notice the play on meanings here. Little Bo had followed Catherine around like one of the puppies that I had noticed the kids playing with during our stay, but didn't give it much thought at the time.

Catherine looked at me and asked, "Can I keep him Dad?"

"If you take care of him, clean up after him, and train him you can." I said. I thought to myself, *at least this will give her something to cuddle with besides me'*.

Marge had given Catherine a package of dry vegetables and vegetable seed, and Janice gave her a sewing kit and some cloth. The cloth was mostly dark green, almost the color of the evergreens.

Bo came up to me and picked me up in a big bear hug and said, "Jack it's been a pleasure having you two here. We are going to work on the cabin cruiser all winter and hopefully by next summer we can make a trip up your way."

With the goodbyes said, I went to help Catherine up onto Zack, but Little Bo beat me to it. I climbed up into Betty's saddle, waved at everyone and we headed to the west, past the old town of Coolin towards Nordman.

The puppy kept Catherine busy for the first day, squirming and yipping. I suggested she tie a line to him and have him follow Zack until he was too tired to act up. She did this and after a half hour he calmed down, panting, and yipped to be picked up. Catherine tied a blanket into a small hammock and put it around her neck. She put him into it and he fell asleep against her stomach.

I asked her, "What are you going to call him?"

Catherine said, "Well he smells like pee, so I am going to call him Billy."

It would take about a week to reach Nordman, taking our time. The old roads were choked with growth after twenty eight years. We traveled along elk and game trails that followed the old roads. We didn't see any signs of people or vandalism along the way. I took this as a good sign that our old cabin would still be okay. We stopped at a few houses and I was able to gather a few books to take with us for the winter.

It was early summer and as we were traveling, Catherine and I talked a lot. She wanted to know where I grew up, what my parents were like, and what the world was like before the 'Big Shit'.

One day, she asked me when my birthday was. I told her I was born on January 1st. I asked her when hers was and she said

August 26th.

I said teasingly, "So you're a Virgo, the virgin."

Catherine glared and said angrily, "What! I told you I'm not a virgin."

I laughed and said, "Easy there, I was referring to the Astrology sign for your birthdate. Back when I was your age, all the pretty girls thought that astrology would help them find the right boyfriend and they would live a happy life."

"Did it work?" She asked.

"I don't know?" I said. "The 'Big Shit' happened and screwed up everyone's life. So if Astrology predicted that, then I don't have much use for it."

"What's your Astrology sign?" She asked.

"Mine? Well, it's Capricorn." I answered.

"What's a Capricorn, some kind of vegetable?" She giggled.

"No, it is an ancient word for goat." I said.

She laughed and said, "It fits you, you old goat."

I smiled and laughed with her. She was quiet for a ways, and I could tell she was thinking hard about something. I said, "If you think too hard, you won't be able to reach your decision."

She looked at me with surprise and asked, "How did you know I was thinking about something?"

"Because when you think real hard, you get a crease between your eyebrows. What is it? Maybe I can help you decide." I said. I knew that just by listening, it would help her come to a decision.

"Well, you know so much. You can read and write and you know how to build and fix things." She said. "Will you teach me to read and write?"

I said, "Yes I will. I was hoping you would be interested and ask. We can gather some more books in Nordman at their old school, and after we get the cabin straightened away, we can start classes. We will have a lot of time this winter too."

At Nordman, we found the old school, and thankfully it had been left alone. Someone had taken care to close it up tight also. I got a window open, and we went in when the sun was shining in from the west. I found the math room and took a few books on arithmetic, geometry, and algebra. I didn't think she would have a need for calculus. I looked for the kindergarten room and there found some primer books on reading.

Catherine poked around and found the library. She was looking at the covers of each book, discarding the ones that didn't have pictures. She had a stack of books beside her and I looked at the covers. They all had pictures on them. The titles she had chosen were 'Tom Sawyer', 'Joan of Arc', 'The Adventures of Huckleberry Finn', and a bunch of 'Nancy Drew' mysteries.

I thought these would be fitting to start with, but asked her, "Why are you only taking books with pictures on the covers? There are a lot of books that are just as good with plain covers."

Catherine asked, "How can I know if I will like them, if they don't have pictures?"

"Every fiction book has a plot and characters that interact. You would be surprised what stories will grab your interest." I said.

As we looked around some more, I heard Catherine 'whoop'. I walked over to see what she had found. It was an old backpack, and in it were about a dozen comic books.

"Can I have these?" she asked. "This one has a man that looks like a bat, and this one has a man in blue with a big 'S' on his chest and a red cape. Look, this one has a man climbing walls like a spider."

I laughed and said, "Of course you can have them. I might enjoy reading them again myself."

She looked surprised at me and asked, "You've seen these before?"

I said, "I've not only seen those comic books before, I've seen all the movies they made based on these heroes."

Catherine looked at me and asked, "These guys were all heroes? What did they do?"

I said, "They fought bad men that tried to take advantage of the citizens of towns they lived in, or in the case of 'Superman', the guy with the big 'S' he fought bad guys all over the planet."

Saying that made me think of books I had forgotten to get. I looked for books on geography of the North America, and threw in a World Atlas. I also got a book on Astronomy.

Catherine saw the book on Astronomy and asked what it was. I said, "It's called Astronomy, and it's about the stars and constellations."

"Is that the book that the young girls used to use to find the right guy?" she asked.

I bent over and laughed. "No," I said, "Astronomy is about the stars and planets and how they move in the sky. You're confusing it with our short discussion about Astrology."

"Can we find a book on Astrology too?" she asked. "So I can find the right guy."

"You don't need a book on Astrology to find the right guy." I said. "You will feel it in your heart."

"I already know who the right guy is." She whispered to herself.

CHAPTER 9

We made camp by the school, and I asked Catherine if she had started training Billy? She said that she hadn't and didn't know where to start or even how to do it. I tossed her a picture book called 'How to Train Your Dog'. I thought that it would also help her to learn how to read.

Catherine paged through it and pointed to a couple of words asking me what they were. I looked at the corresponding picture and pointed to it. I asked, "What is the dog doing in the picture?"

She took the book over to Billy. He got up and started squirming around her feet. She showed him a picture in the book and he sniffed the book and then licked it. "No," she laughed, "Sit not lick." Billy looked up at her and I swear he smiled. He seemed to be in tune with her moods and responded to her laughter with a few yips.

It turned out Billy was a very smart puppy. Catherine had him sitting, staying, and lying down using the hand signals pictured in the book. She had a problem getting him to understand 'Quiet, don't bark'.

After about an hour, I said, "That should be enough for today. He seems to want to please you by doing what you tell him to. You should keep teaching him using the hand signals, so you don't have to tell him what to do out loud."

We ate dinner, and prepared to go to our beds. Catherine walked up to me and I was expecting her to ask me to lay with her again, but she simply asked, "Can I have a hug before I go to sleep?"

I said, "Of course you can." She melted into my arms and

pressed her small breasts against my chest and her hips against my groin and hugged me tight. She held it longer than was necessary. She finally let go, turned and gave me a sly smile over her shoulder as she got into her bedroll. Shaking my head, I thought, *'That little vixen will try anything'* and smiled to myself as I got into my bedroll.

I got up before sunrise, and restarted the fire. I went over to a wall behind the school and faced east towards the lake and waited for the sun to come up. I listened to the world wake up and cleared my mind. I was feeling very happy, and tried to clear my mind of all the reasons for this feeling. My thoughts kept coming back with one word. *'Catherine'.*

About a quarter hour later, I heard Catherine coming and then felt Billy jump up against my knees. Catherine sat down, and using her hand signals made Billy sit. She didn't say a word for a few minutes, so I glanced over at her and saw her sitting with her eyes closed and smiling. Billy had gotten bored and laid down to lick himself. After a short while with her shoulder touching mine softly, I asked, "Are you hungry?

Her eyes opened slowly and she smiled at me. "Yes, I could eat." She got up and swinging her hips slightly as she walked, she headed back to camp.

I thought to myself, *'She is never going to give up, is she?'* I followed her and Billy back to camp and made breakfast. I had noticed some wild chickens and a herd of goats around town as we arrived the day before, and told Catherine, "We should try to trap some of those wild chickens to take with us to the cabin. It would be nice to have fresh eggs for breakfast. After we get the cabin straightened away, I think I will come back and catch a few of those goats so we can have milk too."

Catherine asked, "How much farther is it to the cabin?"

I thought about it, and remembered the last time I was up here. It was about sixteen years ago. Jim and I had come up to see if the cabin was still there, and stayed for about three months. When we left, we covered all the furniture and boarded up the windows and doors. Thinking about Jim made me sad.

Catherine noticed the sad look on my face and asked, "What's wrong?"

I shook my head and said, "Oh it's nothing. I was just thinking about the last time I was up here. It's about fifteen miles from here, up towards Lionhead." I smiled at her and said, "Let's catch some chickens."

I found some old apple crates behind the old resort store and I had Catherine find some netting down by the lake. Catherine found about twenty feet of monofilament netting that was about five feet wide. It was a little rotted in areas, but still had some strength. I packed the crates with dry grass and secured the tops with rocks, and then we went hunting for chickens. I tried to toss the net over the chickens as they ran off, but they never let us get close enough. The chickens kept running into an old hedgerow and when we went to one side they would come out the other.

I had an idea, but asked Catherine what she thought we should do? She looked at the hedgerow and the trails the chickens had made through it. She sat down and closed her eyes and then smiled and said, "Why don't you sit here quietly with the net where these trails come out of the hedge, and Billy and I will go around and chase them to you."

I said, "That's an excellent idea. Where do you think I should sit, by these trails or those over there?"

She looked at the hedge and the trails. One trail was bigger than the other and looked to be used more by the chickens. She pointed to it and said, "That one. It looks like they use it more, and will probably take it."

"Ok," I said, "Let me get set up and give the chickens about ten minutes to calm down, then you and Billy can go around the other side and chase them to me."

I spread the netting out. I then propped it up with some forked sticks in a semi-circle around where the trails came out of the hedge and sat down to wait. I was prepared to grab the chickens that got caught in the net and put them into the apple crates. I closed my eyes and listened.

About ten minutes later, I heard Catherine yell and Billy started barking. They were running towards me and making all kinds of noise. I heard the chickens start cackling and then in a rush they came through the hedge. The net tangled them up, and I stood up and started taking them out of the net and putting them into the crates.

Catherine yelled through the hedge, "Did we get any?"

I laughed and said, "More than we need. We'll be eating chicken for dinner tonight." We had caught twenty chickens and I only had five crates. I could only fit three chickens into a crate, so we had five extra. I started sorting the hens from the roosters and putting them in separate crates. I kept the roosters separate because they would fight each other in the crates.

Catherine and Billy came around the hedgerow, and I saw Billy dragging a small chicken. "Billy caught his own dinner I see." Billy dropped his chicken and came over to the crates and started sniffing at them and yipping.

"No Billy! You have your own chicken." Catherine said in a stern voice. Billy backed away and went back to his chicken and started pulling the feathers off it. Catherine laughed because Billy had a feather beard after a couple minutes. Billy looked at her and his tail started thumping.

I said, "We will take thirteen hens and only two roosters. The rest we will clean and save for later."

"Why only two roosters?" she asked, "It looks like we have about five."

"We only need one rooster to start, but I'm taking two and we will keep them separate with the hens split up between them. That will give us more eggs and we will let some of them hatch so we can have a steady supply of chicken and eggs."

We spent the rest of the morning cleaning the birds and fig-uring out how we were going to load the crated chickens and get them the fifteen miles to the cabin. Catherine found an old 'Lit-tle Red Wagon' with wood slat sides that still had wheels on it. I found some old grease in tubes at the gas station and lubed the wheels and axles. Then we hitched it with rope behind Zack. I told Catherine that we would take turns riding Betty and walk-ing behind Zack to keep the wagon from tangling up.

We were all packed before noon and headed north out of town. I knew we wouldn't make it today as I had planned, but having the chickens was a bonus. We made it about halfway by that evening and camped in a small clearing beside the lake.

I set up camp while Catherine and Billy skipped along the beach picking up driftwood for our fire. I could still see the lit-tle girl in her and felt good that she was finding happiness in the present.

Catherine said she would cook dinner. I let her do it while I sorted through our gear and repacked Zack's load. I had noticed his packs leaning to the left as I was walking behind him with the wagon.

Catherine called to me about an hour later. "Dinner's ready."

I walked over to the fire and it smelled delicious. Catherine had baked the chicken in my Dutch oven with some dry vege-tables she had soaked in water. Marge had given us a supply of cauliflower, broccoli, peas, carrots, and green beans when we left Boville. All dried and stored in cloth bags so they wouldn't mold.

Catherine prepared a plate for me with dark meat and vege-tables, and took the breast meat for herself. I sat down on a log by the fire and tasted the chicken first. It was delicious. I could taste thyme, sage, rosemary and marjoram with just a hint of salt. "This is delicious." I said. "Where did you learn to cook like this? And where did you get the seasoning?"

Catherine's face lit up and she said, "Marge taught me how to cook and gave the seasoning and salt to me when we left. She said the way to a man's heart is through his stomach." She smiled shyly at me and said, "I'm happy you like it."

I gave her my biggest smile and said, "You keep cooking like this, and I am going to have to marry you."

She looked surprised and asked, "Will you marry me someday?"

I suddenly realized the trap I had stepped into and thought quickly. "It was just an expression Catherine. You know I love you, but I'm too old for you. We will find a nice young man for you someday."

Tears formed in Catherine's eyes and she stood up quickly and walked around to the other side of the fire and sat on a stump.

I asked, "Did I say something wrong?" I sat and watched her as tears fell from her lashes. I didn't know what to say, so I stayed quiet.

She ignored me and picked at her food. I let her stew, and after a while she put her plate down and called Billy over to finish her food off. After he finished, she scooped him up and climbed into her bedroll.

I cleaned up and checked the chickens and horses. Billy had squirmed away and came to see what I was doing. I shooed him away from the chickens and led him back to the fire. I climbed into my bedroll and Billy curled up next to Catherine. I could hear her sobbing, and it broke my heart, but what could I do?

CHAPTER 10

I got up early the next morning and found a few eggs in the chicken crates. I shredded the remainder of the chicken from dinner and scrambled it with the eggs. Catherine was still curled up in her bedroll and I nudged her and said, "Get up sleepy, breakfast is ready."

She looked up at me with red puffy eyes and said, "I'm not hungry." She rolled over to face away from me and covered her head with the bedroll.

Billy didn't care. He yipped at me and I gave him some eggs and chicken. I sat down to eat mine, but after a few bites, I wasn't hungry anymore. I gave the rest to Billy and he gobbled it down. *'How was I going to make this right between Catherine and me'*? I walked down to the beach and sat on a log, closed my eyes and cleared my mind of all thought. This was getting harder and harder for me to do with Catherine in my life. After a while, I heard Catherine coming up behind me. I stiffened a little when she wrapped her arms around my shoulders and laid her cheek against my back and hugged me. She said, "I'm sorry Jack."

I choked up and said, "No, it's my fault. I'm sorry. Let's just live each day as it comes and see what happens. Okay?"

She gave me a small smile and turned and walked back to camp. I could see the sway had gone out of her walk that had been there yesterday. Damn, how can a little girl make me feel like such an idiot?

We broke camp and I had Catherine ride Betty while I watched the wagon behind Zack. We didn't talk at all but made good time following the lakeshore and around mid-afternoon, I started recognizing the area. After about another mile, I called for Catherine to stop. She pulled Betty around and looked at me. I pointed up into the woods above the lake and said, "We're home."

Through the trees, we could see the cabin. There was a lot more growth around it, and I could see that the steps down to the beach had washed out. I told Catherine to wait while I un-hitched the chicken wagon and found a way to lead Zack up the slope. Billy ran ahead and showed me the easiest way up. When I reached the cabin, I yelled down. "Leave the chickens for now and bring Betty up the path we took."

Catherine led Betty up the slope following our tracks and when she reached the cabin, I was already pulling the boards off the door to get in.

Catherine said, "This is a cabin? It's huge."

The cabin was actually my parent's retirement home. It was two stories and had a large living room with a huge fireplace, a large kitchen/dining room with a walk in pantry, three bed-rooms, two bathrooms and a den that was my father's library. It also had a two car garage and a large utility shed in the back. I would have to figure out how we could use the bathrooms with the septic system, or I would have to dig a pit for an outhouse.

I opened the front door and saw that everything downstairs was still covered and there was no damage. It was really dark, so I pulled some more boards off the windows to get a better look.

Catherine walked in and looked around. She started un-covering the furniture and took the covers outside to shake out the dust. I went upstairs and saw that one of the back bedrooms had water damage from a leak in the roof. I would have to fix that immediately, because in July, the wet season started. All the glass in the windows was still good. It was triple pane. My dad had the house built to be very efficient for heating and cool-ing.

I went out to the shed and found the ladder Jim and I had used and climbed up on the roof and took the boards off of all the windows and found the spot in the roof I would have to fix. I then did the same on the ground floor. I went inside and through the kitchen and into the garage. I unlocked the garage doors and released the handle on the automatic door opener and raised one of the doors.

Catherine came out and asked what we were going to use all the room in the garage for. I said that I planned to make a stable out of the garage and a chicken coop out of the shed. I told her that all the animals needed to be inside during the winter.

It was getting late in the day, so I went down to the beach and carried the chicken crates up to the shed and let the chickens loose inside. I kept the roosters in the crates though. There would be plenty of bugs for them to eat until I could figure the feed problem out. I took Betty and Zack into the garage and took off the saddle and packs. Then I let them roam the area around the house to feed. While I was doing all this, Catherine had gathered a couple loads of firewood and took them inside to the fireplace. It was going to get dark in a couple hours, so I started a fire and asked Catherine to check the beds upstairs and to see if any of the blankets were still in good enough condition.

I went to the kitchen and found some candles my mother always kept around and set one in the kitchen, two in the living room, and one into a candle holder that I took up to Catherine. She had only made up the bed in the master bedroom, and looked at me shyly.

I said, "We can share a bed tonight, but only to sleep. We will make up one of the other rooms tomorrow." She looked disappointed, but I intended to stay firm about not having sex with her. She was too young.

We went downstairs and I got one of the chickens we had cleaned the day before and took it to the fireplace. She ran over and took it from me and said, "I'll cook again. You need to go down to the lake and bring up some water for the horses and chickens and then bring some for us."

I said, "We shouldn't have to do that after today. This house has a hand pump for water in the kitchen for when the power used to go out. It's attached to the well. I'll try to fix it tomorrow." I went out to the garage and got a couple buckets. Then I placed a half plastic fifty five gallon barrel in the garage for the horses. I took an old gallon ice cream bucket out to the shed for the chickens. It took me twenty trips to the lake to get enough water for everything, and my arms were killing me when I finished. I put Betty and Zack in the garage to show them the water and put a rail across the opening but left the door open.

When I went inside the cabin, I could smell dinner. Catherine was cooking in the fireplace with the Dutch oven again and she had found some tinfoil in the kitchen and cooked a couple potatoes in the coals. I plopped down on the sofa and laid my head back. I was tired.

I felt Catherine shaking my arm and she said, "Wake up sleepy. Dinner is ready." I hadn't realized that I had fallen asleep.

We had another marvelous dinner on the coffee table in front of the couch and I noticed Catherine had given me the dark meat again. I asked, "How did you know I preferred the dark meat when I eat chicken?"

Catherine said, "I watched what you picked when we had the feast before we left Boville."

"Well thank you, that was very thoughtful." I said. "What do you prefer though?"

She said, "It works out perfect for birds, because I like the white meat."

We smiled at each other and then took the dirty plates into the kitchen and cleaned them in a bucket of water I had set in the sink. Billy had been gone most of the evening and we heard him yip at the door. Catherine let him in and we gave him some leftovers and a bowl of water.

I told Catherine that I was exhausted and we had a lot of work to do over the next few weeks, so it was bedtime. Since we were inside, I stripped down to my underwear and climbed into the right side of the bed closest to the door. I put my pistol on the nightstand, and leaned the AR15 in the corner. Catherine didn't undress until I had blown the candle out. I felt her climb under the covers and snuggle up against me, and I realize she was naked. Just then, Billy yipped and I reached down and picked him up and he climbed between us. I felt the bed shake as Catherine rolled over on her back and shook her head and huffed. I whispered, "I told you."

Catherine said, "I know."

It didn't take long and I was out and sleeping like a log. Later that night, I felt Catherine move Billy and snuggle up against me. It didn't bother me and I fell right back to sleep.

CHAPTER 11

I must have been real tired, because I didn't wake up until I heard Billy bark downstairs and Catherine shush him. It was already light out. I got dressed and went downstairs.

Catherine had made breakfast. She found a few more eggs in the shed and heated up the cooked chicken, and she even fried up some leftover potatoes.

I smiled at her and she smiled back. I was happy to see that the disagreement we had the previous day was not going to be a problem. "It smells delicious. Thank you." I said, "When did you get up?"

"Billy woke me up about an hour ago to let him out to pee and it was so calm and quiet that I sat on the beach for a little and watched the sun come up." She smiled.

I could see that she was finding her happiness again and decided to leave it at that. We had a lot of work to do over the next few weeks, so I wouldn't get a chance for a couple mornings to sit and listen myself.

We ate our breakfast and while we were cleaning the dishes, I tried the hand pump in the kitchen. It was rusted tight, so I went into the garage and got a pipe wrench and found a box of plastic quarts of motor oil that hadn't been opened. I took the top off the hand pump and with some pliers pried the plunger mechanism out. I could see that the rubber O-ring parts had deteriorated and the hole the plunger went through in the top cover was rusty. I found an old bicycle inner tube in the garage that still had some flexibility and cut some pieces to fit the plunger. I used a wire brush to clean the rust off and wiped it all down with some oil. I didn't use a lot though, so it wouldn't taint the water that came up.

I then went out to the pump house and switched the well head from automatic to manual. Hopefully I would get enough suction to draw water. I levered the hand pump up and down about forty times and started to get a trickle of rusty water. After about twenty more pumps, the water started coming faster and after about ten minutes of pumping it started to clear. The lever was still a little tight, so I put a couple drops of oil on the joints and it started smoothing out.

Catherine had been cleaning the house and was in the pantry checking out what we had available to use. I called her out and said, "Try the pump."

Catherine pumped it a couple times to prime it and then water started pouring out. It was still a little rusty, but that would clear up. The only metal part was the hand pump and suction pipe. The underground piping was all plastic. She laughed and said, "Well I guess you won't wear yourself out hauling water anymore."

I laughed at that and said, "What do you mean me? You would have had to haul water too."

She just smiled and said, "Sure."

Now that I had that task completed, I went outside and up onto the roof to check on the leak. I pulled some of the cedar shingles off and found where it was leaking through. I went out to the shed and found some old tar paper and a bundle of shingles my dad had always kept around. While I was there, I found a roll of chicken wire. I called Catherine out to the shed and asked her, "Do you think you can figure a way to use this wire to separate the chickens to the back of the shed?" I handed her a hammer, a side cutter and a box of large metal staples.

Catherine looked at the situation, and started rearranging the piles of stuff stacked up in the shed. While she was doing this, I went back and repaired the roof. Billy was running around sniffing at everything, and I heard Betty snort. I had forgotten all about them. I went to the garage and removed the rail and let her and Zack out. They stayed close to the cabin and started feeding on the grass. I thought they should have a lot of the area cleaned down in a couple of weeks, and then we can start removing the brush and plant a garden.

I went back to the garage and mucked it out. I thought the concrete floor is going to be hard on their feet and I would have to find a way to soften it. I heard Catherine yelp and say, "Son of a bitch."

I walked back to the shed and saw that she had about half of the roll of wire stretched across the back of the shed and she was trying to hold it tight and hammer a staple at the same time. She hit her thumb with the hammer and yelped, "Ouch, you stubborn bastard." I laughed and she turned with her thumb in her mouth and glared at me.

I asked, "Would you like some help?"

"Yes that would be nice." She mumbled sarcastically around her thumb.

I went over and held the wire tight while she stapled it to the wall. She hit her fingers a couple more times and glared at me. I just looked away when it happened and pretended to be checking the stuff out in the shed. I noticed that most of the yard tools were still in good condition. There were also some handsaws, a couple of axes and a hatchet. There was also a long two man hand saw.

My dad had always competed in the lumberjack festival in Nordman and had the saw and some tree climbing spikes. I thought a lot of this was going to come in handy. I just wish I could use the chainsaws, but without fuel, they were worthless.

Billy came in and laid something down at Catherine's feet. I looked and saw that it was a mouse. "Well, it looks like we don't need to get a cat." I laughed.

Catherine said, "No Billy it's your kill, I don't want it. You can keep it." She ruffled his ears and smiled at him. Billy picked the mouse up and ran back outside.

I said to Catherine, "Now that we have the wire up, we need to clip the chicken's wings and cut some grass to throw into the pen." I caught one of the hens and with a garden shears I cut the primary flight feathers off of one wing.

Catherine asked, "Why don't you cut both wings?"

"I only cut one, so they feel out of balance when they try to fly. After a while, they stop trying. Okay, now that you know how to do it, you catch the rest and I'll cut some grass." I said.

I took the hand scythe out and went up the hill behind the shed to a small meadow. While I was cutting grass, I noticed that about a hundred fifty yards behind the cabin along the old road, there was and elk and deer trail. This was a good sign I thought. I hauled the cut grass back to the shed and saw that Catherine had chicken feathers all over her and she was cussing at a couple hens that were sitting up in the rafters. "Come down here you stubborn bitches." She yelled.

"Do you need some more help?" I asked. The rafters were about ten feet up.

She glared at the hens and said, "I've been chasing these two for a half hour, now I can't reach them."

I laughed and said, "Outsmarted by a creature with a brain the size of a pea. Why don't you go get the net we used to catch them?"

She smiled sheepishly and said, "Why didn't I think of that?"

We finally caught the last two errant hens and clipped them. I found an old sheet of plywood and placed it so that it split the chicken pen in half and then we got the roosters clipped and separated the hens in about half. I threw the grass into each side of the pen and noticed the chickens pecking the seed heads off of the cut grass. They also started hunting for bugs. I placed an old ice cream bucket with water in each pen. I told Catherine that we would make an outside pen tomorrow with the remainder of the wire and I would cut holes in the wall so they can go in and out. We would also make a gate to get into the pens to gather the eggs.

We had accomplished a lot in a short time and went back to the cabin to eat a cold lunch and relax a little. After lunch, I took an axe and started clearing some of the brush and small trees that had started growing in the old yard area. Billy kept getting in my way and I yelled to Catherine, "Can you control Billy while I clear this brush? I think we will put our garden here, but I don't want to accidently hit Billy with the axe."

Catherine let out a piercing whistle and Billy ran over to her. She signed for him to sit and then to stay. Catherine was cleaning another of the chickens we had caught the previous day and she threw the head, feet and guts for Billy to chew on. She said, "I'm getting tired of eating chicken. Are we going to get something else soon?"

I told her about the game trail behind the cabin and said we would plan a hunt tomorrow. I cleared out a twenty by thirty foot area, and brought Betty and Zack over to clean the grass down. After a couple days, I would have to turn the sod over and break it up so Catherine could plant some of her seeds. I yelled over to her as she was soaking some vegetables for dinner. "What did Marge give you to plant in the garden?"

Catherine thought for a second and said, "She gave me sweet corn, potatoes, peas, green beans, cauliflower, broccoli, asparagus, tomatoes, strawberries, mint, thyme, rosemary, cumin and some other herbs."

I said, "Strawberries, yum. In the fall we will have to gather blackberries from the woods also. I think my mom had some raspberry bushes over there too. I am going to have to split some rails to make a fence to keep the horse out too. When the chickens get used to their new home, we can let them loose in the garden to keep the bugs down."

It was getting late, and Catherine gathered some more firewood and went inside to cook dinner. I walked the property to see what trees I would have to cut down and which ones I could split into rails. I wish I had some barbwire, but I was able to find enough trees that were the right size to make the fence.

I decided that before dinner I would go down to the lake and see if I could catch any fish. I went to the garage and got an old Zebco fishing pole and found my old tackle box. There was a spool of fishing line that was still good after I cut the yellowed parts off that had weathered and I reeled it into the Zebco. I took a ten gallon bucket with me and went down to the shore. I tied a steel leader and swivel to the end of the line and looked through my old lures. I found one that was tiger stripped like a baby Northern and clipped it on. After a couple casts, I felt a hard hit. I let it go for a bit and felt a second hit. When I felt this, I jerked the pole back and set the hook. I whooped loudly as I felt the fish start to run. Billy came running down to the beach and started barking. As I fought the fish, Catherine came down and watched. After about ten minutes, I landed a nice ten pound Walleye. I smiled at Catherine and said, "Well we won't be eating chicken tomorrow." I put the Walleye in the bucket of water and carried it back up to the cabin. Catherine carried my tackle box and pole. Billy ran around us barking.

When we got to the cabin, I took the Walleye out back of the garage where my dad had built a fish cleaning station. I wiped it down and filleted the Walleye. I took the fish skin, guts and head into the shed and split it up amongst the chickens. They tore into it and fought for the best pieces.

Catherine said, "I didn't know you could feed that to chickens."

I told her that chickens were not vegetarians, and that they needed protein not just seeds. Catherine jolted and ran to the cabin, "I forgot about dinner." She yelled back.

I took the Walleye fillets into the kitchen and put them into a bucket of cold water. I heard Catherine in the living room say, "Oh good, I didn't ruin it. Dinner's ready." She yelled.

We ate another excellent dinner and after cleaning up, we sat on the couch. Catherine asked, "Would you read to me?"

I smiled and asked, "Yes what would you like to start with?"

She went over to her stack of books and came back with the "Adventures of Huckleberry Finn". I took the book and opened it to the first chapter. Catherine sat down and leaned against me with her head resting against my shoulder. I started reading, but hadn't gotten halfway through the first chapter when I heard her snoring softly. It had been a long day and we had accomplished a lot. I was tired too, so I put the book down and slowly picked her up and carried her upstairs. She put her arms around my neck and nuzzled my shoulder. I put her into bed and she looked at me sleepily and said, "I love you Jack."

"I love you too, sweetheart." I said. Billy jumped up on the bed as I climbed in to my side and Catherine said, "Oh Billy."

CHAPTER 12

We got up early the next morning and had a light breakfast of just eggs. I got the .308 out and cleaned it. I had Catherine watch me again so she would remember how.

Before we left, I put water in the horse's barrel and filled the chicken's buckets. I took the Walleye fillets out of the bucket of water and wrapped them in a wet towel so they wouldn't dry out or get mushy.

I asked Catherine, "Are you ready to go hunting?" She nodded, so I handed her the .308 and had her load it and made sure she put the safety on. I took the shotgun and we hiked back to the game trail.

When we got to the trail, I looked for fresh sign, and noticed deer tracks heading north around a line of trees. I pointed this out to Catherine, and she knelt down and looked closely at the tracks. I said it looks like a doe and a couple of yearlings. She asked me how I could tell, and I pointed to one larger set of tracks followed by two smaller sets. She asked, "But how can you tell there aren't more?"

I pointed to the larger tracks and said, "See here where a smaller track covers part of the larger one. That means the doe was leading and the smaller ones were following. Here is a smaller track partially covered by a different smaller track, so that tells me there are a least two smaller deer."

She looked closely and saw what I was pointing out. She asked, "How did you learn all this stuff?"

I said, "After our parents passed away and Jim had found me, we spent ten years traveling through the mountains and hunting. After a couple years of tracking animals, I became pretty good at reading their sign."

Catherine frowned when I mentioned Jim and said, "I hope we never see that bastard again."

I looked at her and said, "Catherine, he is the only brother I have and I still love him. He has to live with the choices he's made, we don't."

I heard her whisper to herself, "Other people have to live with his choices too." I pretended that I didn't hear and started following the tracks.

We tracked for about a quarter mile, when Billy came running up. I told Catherine that she would have to control him so he wouldn't scare any of the animals we were tracking. She signed for Billy to sit and bent down in front of him. She looked him in the eye and said, "Follow close and be quiet." I swear Billy nodded.

We had gone another eighth of a mile when I noticed a flicker at the edge of a meadow ahead of us. I pulled up my binoculars slowly and saw the white butt of a mule deer and its black-tipped tail flicking. I motioned for Catherine and Billy to stay still and slowly handed the binoculars to Catherine and pointed to where I wanted her to look.

She raised the binoculars slowly and looked where I was pointing. She smiled at me and nodded. Then she scanned around that spot and held up three fingers. I nodded and started to slowly crouch and duck walk over to a fallen tree beside the trail. Catherine mimicked me and Billy crouched to his belly and crawled after her.

When we got to the fallen tree, I took the binoculars back from Catherine and looked over the trunk. I placed my pack slowly on a spot that was bare of branches and motioned for Catherine to place the .308 on top of the pack. She eased the rifle up onto the pack and knelt behind it. She looked through the scope and searched for the deer. When I saw that she found them, I motioned for her to wait. I looked through the binoculars again and saw that the doe was in the middle and one yearling was to the right facing directly away from us. The other yearling was standing broadside to us on the left.

I motioned to Catherine to the left and using my fingers signed 'small'. She nodded and readjusted the rifle to the left. I whispered, "Whenever you're ready."

Catherine lined up the crosshairs behind the right shoulder of the smaller deer on the left and slowly released the safety. I placed my hand on top of Billy's back and held him still. Catherine glanced at me and I nodded. She placed her finger on the trigger and started to shake. I leaned forward placed my other hand lightly on the middle of her back and whispered in her ear, "Take a deep breath and clear your mind and don't think." She closed her eyes for a second, took a deep breath, slowly let it out and I felt her shaking slow down. She opened her eyes, and realigned the crosshairs and slowly pulled the trigger. The rifle surprised her when it when went off. I watched the deer run off.

"I missed!" she cried.

"No," I said because I had heard the 'wop' when the bullet hit, "you hit right where you were aiming."

"Why did it run off then?" she asked.

Since we had no need to be quiet anymore, I stood and said, "Animals are tough. They can sometimes run a ways even though that was a kill shot. Let's go look for blood."

We got to the spot the deer had been standing and Billy immediately found the blood trail. He started to follow it and I told Catherine to stop him. She whistled and he looked over his shoulder at her. She motioned for him to come back. I sat down against a tree and closed my eyes.

Catherine asked, "Aren't we going to follow it?"

I said, "I think it was a kill shot, but in case it's wounded, we should wait about a half hour before tracking it. It will lie down and bleed out that way, and we won't scare it farther away from the cabin."

Catherine sat next to me and held Billy. We both closed our eyes and listened. I could hear the sounds returning to the woods after the loud noise of the rifle. Then I heard a thrashing sound in the direction the deer had run. I glanced at Catherine and could see she heard it also. She kept her eyes closed and listened until the thrashing stopped then she opened her eyes and looked at me.

"Is it dead now?" she asked.

"We'll give it ten more minutes just in case." I said.

After we waited and started to follow the blood trail again, Billy shot ahead. Catherine started to whistle him back, but I said, "Let him go. He'll make our job easier." We went about a hundred yards and heard Billy in the brush ahead yipping. I pushed through and saw the deer lying on its side. Catherine started forward and I stopped her.

I said, "Never trust that the animal is dead. Approach it slowly and use a stick to poke it. If it's just wounded, it could get up and hurt you." This was a lesson I had learned the hard way when I was seventeen. I got some bruised ribs because of it. I didn't want Catherine to learn the hard way as I had.

Catherine looked around and found a long branch. She peeled some of the small twigs off of it and used it to poke at the deer. I knew it was dead, because Billy was sniffing all around it, but I wanted Catherine to do this to remember the lesson.

Catherine poked it a couple times and said, "I'm sure it's dead."

"Okay, let's drag it out of this brush to a clear spot and I will teach you how to gut it."

It was a yearling male. We dragged it out to a spot that had enough room to lay it out. I then got my gutting and skinning knives out of my pack. I showed her how to gut the deer and when I was finished, I had blood up to my elbows. I set the heart and liver aside, and let Billy sniff around the rest of the gut pile.

I turned to Catherine and asked, "Do you want to go back to the cabin and get Zack or do you want me to?"

She thought about it for a second, and I could tell she didn't want to sit in the woods alone while she waited for me, so she said, "I'll go get Zack."

I said, "Take Billy with you and bring a tarp and some rope with Zack."

She looked around and then back to me. I said, "Follow the blood trail back to where we sat down, and then follow the game trail back to the cabin."

Catherine and Billy headed out, and I sat down closed my eyes and waited. I stopped thinking and enjoyed the sounds of the forest. After about a half hour, I started thinking again. *'Catherine is such a pleasure to have around. I know she will keep trying to sleep with me and yes I would like to.'* I frowned and thought, *'Quit giving me those thoughts brain. It's not appropriate given our age difference.' 'But you want to don't you?' 'I said shut up. I'm not having this conversation even in my head.'*

Just then, I heard Billy running to me and opened my eyes as he leaped into my lap and started licking my face. Catherine wasn't far behind with Zack.

We put the tarp over Zack and lifted the deer up on his back. Gutted, the deer only weighed about a hundred pounds. Zack had done this many times before and stood still while I tied the deer down. We headed back to the cabin and on the way I noticed Billy stop and sniff and look into some bushes. I handed the shotgun to Catherine and pointed to the bushes with my chin. She motioned Billy to stay and flushed four Ruffed Grouse up. She led them and shot two in the air. Billy ran and got them and brought them back to her. I was amazed that a German Shepard was such a good retriever, but remembered that Catherine had been training him to fetch with a stick.

Catherine said, "Good Billy, thank you." She ruffled his ears and he licked her hand and wriggled around her feet. She tied the legs of the grouse together with a strap and hung them over Zack's neck.

When we got back to the cabin, I found a large tree branch that was about 16 feet up and horizontal. I threw a rope over it and tied one end through the backs of the knees of the deer's hind legs and then put Zack's pack harness on. I tied the other end of the rope to Zack and had him pull the carcass up until it was hanging right below the branch. This put the deer about eleven feet off the ground.

Catherine asked why I put it up so high. I told her that there were still bears in the area, and I was going to let the carcass cool over night before I skinned it and we butchered it. I tied the other end of the rope to another tree and said, "I need to clean up and get all this blood off me."

I went inside and got some clean clothes and soap that Marge had made and given to us. I went down to the lake, and stripped down. I heard Catherine and Billy up on the porch and knew she was watching me. The thoughts I had while sitting in the woods came back to me, and I thought. 'Down boy.' The cold lake water helped with that. I washed everywhere and thought about how we could use the fireplace to heat water and use the bathtubs in the house to wash up in. My mom had a cast iron kettle that held about ten gallons of water that could be held over the fire on a bar that was set into the stonework of the fireplace. I decided that tomorrow, I would check out the septic tank and make sure all the sinks, toilets, and tubs drained properly. I thought Catherine would love a warm bath.

When I got back up to the cabin, I could smell fish frying inside. I walked in and Catherine turned and smiled at me and then blushed. I nodded and said, "I know, I saw you watching but it doesn't change anything. Okay?"

"Come on Jack, it's just the two of us. No one else will know." She said.

"I will know and the answer is still no."

"You'll change your mind someday." She whispered to herself, but just loud enough for me to hear.

I ignored it and said, "That fish smells great."

Catherine said, "I'm frying it in cornmeal that Marge gave me."

I took my dirty clothes into the laundry room and threw them into the deep soaking sink. I poured a bucket of water on them and left them to soak. When I came back out, dinner was ready. We ate in silence. Catherine kept glancing at me and then looking away. I asked, "Would you like me to read to you again tonight?"

"Yes, but you will have to start over. I think I fell asleep last night."

We cleaned up and then sat on the couch with Catherine leaning against my shoulder again. She was a little whiff, and I said, "You need to take a bath tomorrow. You are starting to stink."

She punched me in the shoulder and said, "Just read please."

CHAPTER 13

I skinned the deer the next morning and we cut it up. We didn't have a refrigerator, but the house had a cold cellar. I hung the meat quarters down there and surveyed it for rodents. It looked clean and secure.

After that task was done, I found the septic tank top and dug it out. Once I removed the lid, I could see that it was only about half full. It held two thousand gallons, and should last us a while. I checked the leach line and could see that it was plugged, so I removed the cap from the cleanout and found my dad's plumbing snake. I twisted it down the line until it popped through at the septic tank. I pulled it back out and ended up with a pile of dirty crap and roots that I shoveled up and hauled off into the woods.

While I was doing this, Catherine cleaned out the chicken pen and put fresh cut grass into each side. Billy ran back and forth between us checking our work. I closed up the septic system again and went to help Catherine with the chicken pen. We took the remaining chicken wire outside. I dug some postholes and planted three posts. After I had them set securely, we wrapped the chicken wire around and stapled it down. I left one end loose and wired it shut to use as a gate. Once this was done and I used another old sheet of plywood to separate the two pens. I then cut holes in the shed wall. I kept the boards I cut to make doors that I could close them back up with in the winter.

The chickens slowly came out of the shed when we finished and started scratching around a couple of bushes we had left inside the area.

This task done, Catherine, Billy and I went in to have lunch. I asked Catherine while we ate if there was anything we needed to do. She got a pencil and paper for me and we made a list.

- Get the garden ready
- Fence the garden in
- Plant the garden
- Build a storage for hay for the horses in winter time
- Go back to Nordman and catch some goats
- Hunt and dry meat for winter
- Build a smoke house to smoke fish and meat
- Cut and store firewood
- Muck the garage and store the horse droppings for fertilizer
- Repair clothes
- Teach Catherine to read and write

Catherine looked at the list and had me read each one to her again as she followed along. She said, "That's quite a list, but I'm sure it's not everything."

I said, "No, I'm sure a lot more things will come up that need attention as we get these done. But, after lunch, I think we will take it easy and do some fishing. Betty and Zack still need to get the grass down in the garden area, so we will have to wait on the garden a few more days."

"Fishing?" she said, "I bet I can catch the biggest one."

"You're on."

We went out to the garage and I set up another pole for her and we went down to the beach. We cast a few times and then Catherine whooped, "I got one." She jerked the pole back and the lure came out of the water a landed behind us.

I laughed and said, "You can't catch them on the beach."

She looked confused and said, "But I felt it hit the lure."

I told her that predator fish like Walleye and Northern will strike a bait fish once to stun it and then come back around to gobble it up. She should stop reeling when she feels the first strike and wait to set the hook when she feels the second strike.

After a couple more casts, she caught a medium size Northern. She fought it for a few minutes and then landed it. I held it down with my foot and with a needle nose plier removed the lure from its mouth. I showed Catherine the teeth and said they would tear her fingers up in she tried to take the lure out by hand.

We fished for a couple hours and caught three Northern and four Walleye. I loved watching Catherine fish. She whooped every time she hooked one and laughed as she fought it to shore. She did end up catching the biggest one, a Walleye about seven pounds. It took her about fifteen minutes of running up and down the beach to land it. Billy chased after her barking and then pounced on the fish when she pulled it up on the beach. Billy jumped back as it flopped and then pounced again until I could get to it to remove the lure.

We had a great time laughing and joking about Billy the fishing dog. I went back up to the cabin and brought down a couple buckets and we took the fish behind the garage to clean them. It was midafternoon and I showed Catherine how to fillet them. I pointed out how the Northern still had bones in them, while the Walleyes didn't. I then had Catherine clean the grouse from the day before, and then we went inside to cook dinner.

Catherine cooked the grouse in the Dutch oven and fried the fish. She boiled some vegetables and I boiled some water in the big kettle. Catherine asked, "What's all that water for?"

I said, "You're going to take a bath tonight, Stinky."

"Oh." She asked. "Where? In the lake?"

I told her that the reason I fixed the septic was so we could use the bathtub in the house. We ate dinner and then I carried the hot water into the bathroom. I poured it into the tub and told her to add cold water until it felt the right temperature.

She got some clean clothes and went in to bathe. She was in there for at least an hour before she came back out.

I said, "I thought you fell asleep in there."

Catherine replied, "It felt so good I didn't want to get out. I haven't had a warm bath since we left Boville."

That evening, I took one of the primer reading books and

had Catherine sit next to me on the couch. When she sat down, I said, "You smell really good, almost flowery."

Catherine smiled at the compliment and said, "I found a jar of pink crystals that smelled real good and when I poured some in the water, they dissolved. That's what you smell."

"Oh," I said, "you found some of my mom's bath salts. Well, they make you smell real pretty, so they're yours."

I showed Catherine the alphabet and taught her the alphabet song. Once she could recognize the letters in both upper and lower case, I took a beginning reading book and had her sound out each word. After about an hour, she said, "I'm tired of reading 'See Dick run', 'See Dick jump', 'See Jane sit', can't we read something else?"

I said, "Okay, your choice."

She grabbed a Superman comic book and brought it over. I had her sound out each word and had to explain to her what 'ker''ip''tow''night' was. She started recognizing some of the same words as we read together and after we finished that comic, she ran to her pile to get another one. I told her that was enough for tonight and she looked disappointed. I said instead I wanted her to practice writing her name. She got some paper and a pencil from the den and I wrote her name at the top. I had her tell me what each letter was and to spell it out loud for me a few times. Then I had her write it ten times. She had difficulty writing it until I asked her to switch hands and try writing it again. She turned out to be left handed for writing, but did most other things right handed.

She said, "But you write with your right hand. How come I can't?"

I said, "I don't know why. Some people just find it easier with one hand than the other."

We finished up the lesson and went upstairs to bed. I didn't like it, but we always seemed to end up in bed together. Catherine snuggled up against me and God she smelled good. I had a hard time going to sleep.

CHAPTER 14

C atherine and I worked hard for the next couple weeks. I chopped wood every morning, and we got the garden dug out and turned over. I cut down the trees I had surveyed and split the logs to build the fence around the garden. Once I had the posts set, we put the fence up to the confusion of Betty and Zack. I cleared some more brush out and built a large pile on the beach. Betty and Zack worked on the new areas clearing the tall grass down for us. The area around the cabin started looking well taken care of.

We took the horse droppings we had piled beside the garage and mixed it in with the soil in the garden. I hoed out some rows while Catherine followed behind me and planted her seed. After the garden was planted, Catherine watered the rows every morning. She didn't have to do this a lot, because it started raining every afternoon for a couple hours. While it rained, we continued her reading and writing lessons. She learned fast, because she was motivated to be able to read to herself.

After the rain stopped every evening, we fished for about an hour and started smoking them in the little smokehouse I had built. We were starting to fill the cold cellar with smoked fish and some of the venison I had smoked.

Billy ran all over the area and checked in every couple of hours. I told Catherine that she should spend about a half hour a day training him. She started that while she was waiting for dinner to cook. Billy was an exceptionally smart dog, and loved Catherine's attention.

Every evening we read. Catherine would cruise through the primers and then read her comics. I read 'Tom Sawyer' to her steady interruptions to explain the meaning of words. I always told her to read the sentence before the word and the sentence after it and try to figure it out. She usually did, but I always helped her when she got stuck.

We turned the other two bedrooms into storage, because I couldn't get her to sleep in one of them. She climbed into bed with me every night and cuddled against me. After a while, I think she grew accustomed to the fact that I wouldn't have sex with her. I never grew accustomed to it though.

Every evening after a hard day's work, I would go for a swim to clean the sweat and dirt off of me. Catherine would join me frequently and we would end up racing and wrestling in the water. Catherine was an excellent swimmer and slippery as an eel. I have never been happier in my life.

As the garden started to sprout, we took turns shooting rabbits to save it. We ended up with rabbit stew about twice a week. Billy helped out a lot. He chased the rabbits away and caught a few. I had him pee on all the fence posts to deter them also. We still lost some of the sprouts.

It was about the middle of July and I told Catherine one morning that I planned to go back to Nordman and catch some goats. She immediately said she wanted to go with me. I said I would only be gone for a couple days and that we couldn't leave the garden unattended. I knew she was scared to be alone, but I told her that Billy would be staying with her. She cried, but I held firm and told her that she had to stay.

I waited a couple more days for her to get used to the idea, before I left. I saddled Betty and packed Zack with a couple days' supplies and the gear I thought I could use to catch the goats. I told Catherine to keep busy and the days would go by quickly. She still stood on the porch and pouted as I rode off.

It was only fifteen miles to Nordman, and following the beach most of the way, I made it by midafternoon. I set up camp and scouted out the goats. I figured out where they traveled and fed, and came up with a plan to rope a few of them. That evening I searched the school library and found a few of books I wanted to give to Catherine.

The next morning, I saddled Betty and rode slowly up to the herd of goats. They didn't spook because I was on Betty, and after a couple tries, I was able to rope a nanny. She had a kid, and it followed as I pulled her back to camp and hobbled it. I went back and was able to rope a couple more nannies that didn't have kids. Once I had them all hobbled back at camp, I went searching for a billy goat. I spotted a couple munching on some grass at the edge of town, and I circled around them so I would have room to chase them into the open. I went for the smaller one, approaching slowly on Betty. When I got close enough, I threw my rope and caught him around the horns. Instead of running away, he turned and charged us. Betty was a good horse and she sidestepped the charge, but the rope got tangled around a tree. I jumped off Betty and ran to tackle the billy. He saw me coming and charged. Luckily Betty backed up and pulled the rope tight around the tree and stopped the billy short. I tackled him and tied off his feet, but not without taking a few kicks in the leg.

I had four goats and a kid. Now I had to figure out how to get them back. When I carried the billy back to camp, I noticed that the nannies calmed down with him there. I thought about it and came up with the idea that if I blindfolded the billy, he would be easier to control. As soon as I put the blindfold on, he calmed down. It was too late in the day to head back, so I settled into camp for a second night.

The next morning, I tied the goats in a line with the billy in front and still blindfolded. I tied the rope to Zack's harness, and led them down the trail. The billy resisted to start with, but hearing Zack's hooves in front of him, he followed. The nannies followed him docilely and the kid followed its mother.

It took me a little longer to get back leading the goats; because they got tangled up a few times until we got down on the beach. When I got close to the cabin, Billy came running down the beach barking. The goats went crazy and started pulling on the rope. I heard Catherine whistle loudly and Billy stopped and turned back to her. She came running down to the beach and signaled him to come. He ran back to her and she scolded him. He looked contrite, and crouched in front of her. She motioned him to stay.

Catherine smiled up at me and said, "I thought you'd never get back."

I responded, "I said I would be gone a couple days. Look at the lovely goats I caught."

Catherine walked up to the goats and looked them over. The kid walked up to her and sniffed at her hand. She laughed and scratched its head. Then she asked me why the billy was blindfolded.

I said, "Because he's a mean bastard. He kicked the crap out me when I caught him."

Catherine laughed and said, "Then, that's what we will name him'; 'Mean Bastard'."

I asked Catherine to get Billy and take him up to the cabin while I moved the goats into the garage. She signaled for Billy to follow her and put him inside the cabin. I pulled the goats up to the garage and left them tied up while I figured out how to keep them inside. I knew that goats could climb and jump, so I had to figure something secure. I should have done this before I left. I finally figured the nannies would stay put and I would let Mean Bastard wander. I put some of the split logs across a quarter of the garage and moved the nannies inside. We threw a bunch of grass down and they settled in. After I took care of Betty and Zack, I untied Mean Bastard. I took his blindfold off and ran like hell up onto the porch when he started chasing me. Catherine stood on the porch and laughed. Mean Bastard gave up and started checking his new home out. He heard the nannies in the garage and went over and stood guard there.

I told Catherine to let Billy out to get him and Mean Bastard used to each other. Billy ran out and spotted the billy goat and headed towards him. Mean Bastard saw him coming and chased him up onto the porch. Billy stood on the porch and barked at Mean Bastard, until the goat walked back to the garage.

Catherine came up to me and hugged me tight. "I'm glad you're home." She said.

I hugged her back and said, "I am too. I missed you." I felt like a big part of me had been made whole again. *'What was happening to me?'* I thought.

I went inside and got some clean clothes and then went down to the lake for a swim to clean up. When I finished, I went back to the cabin and out ran Mean Bastard again. I decided that I would shorten the name to MB since I would be running from him all the time. I walked into the cabin and smelled dinner cooking. It smelled great after two nights camping. Catherine said, "I'm making a venison roast and potatoes."

"Smells wonderful." I said. "What did you do while I was gone?"

"I shot a deer that was trying to eat up our garden." She said.

"Really?" I said. "How did you hang him with the horses gone?"

"I didn't. I quartered it on the ground and hung it in the cold cellar." She said.

I was amazed, but realized I shouldn't be. Catherine was a very capable young girl and she paid attention to everything I taught her. "I'm proud of you." I said.

We enjoyed the rest of our evening together talking about what we did and laughing at my efforts to catch MB. When the talk slowed down, I stood and reached for her hand and led her to bed. She looked expectant, but I shook my head and said, "I love you Catherine but you know how I feel about that."

We slept holding each other for the first time, instead of me turning my back to her and her snuggling against me. I slept the best I had in a long time.

CHAPTER 15

The next morning, I took a little goats milk from the mother nanny and Catherine watched me. She went out the back to avoid MB and gathered some eggs. We were getting about ten a day now, and I told Catherine to leave some to be hatched. She marked those with a pencil so she would know which ones they were.

After breakfast, I went out on the porch and headed to the garden to see how it was growing. When I came around the corner of the cabin I ran face to face with MB. He chased me back onto the porch. I thought this has got to stop.

I went out the back and found an old branch that was about the length of a baseball bat and about as round. I took it back through the cabin and asked Catherine to follow me. We went out on the porch and I told Catherine to stay right behind me. We stepped off the porch and started towards MB. He turned and saw us coming and lowered his head and charged. I pushed Catherine to the side and when MB was a few steps away, I swung the branch and hit him across the forehead at the base of his horns. It stunned him and he dropped to his front knees. He shook his head, looked up at me, and mewed. I yelled "That's enough out of you MB."

He stood on wobbly legs and walked back to the garage. That was the last time he chased us, though he still liked to chase Billy. They started making it a game. MB would chase Billy around the cabin and slow down, then Billy would catch up to him and chase him around the cabin. They would do this a few times until they tired of the game.

MB worked out to be a blessing. He couldn't get through the fence into the garden, but he chased every rabbit away that tried to. One evening while Catherine and I were sitting on the porch, MB mounted one of the two single nannies and bred her. Catherine looked at me and lifted an eyebrow and smiled at me. I laughed and shook my head no. She just shrugged and kept smiling at me. *'Damn how this little girl made me feel uncomfortable at times'.*

We planned hunting a couple more times. I wanted to get an elk before the rut started and the bulls got rank. When we went, we found a small herd of single bulls, and I had Catherine shoot a young one. It was across a canyon and at least 400 yards away. She sighted on its shoulder and I saw her close her eyes, take a deep breath, open her eyes, let it out and squeeze the trigger. We heard the 'Wop' when the bullet hit, and the elk took a couple steps and dropped. The rest of the herd ran up and over the hill.

We gutted it and I had to quarter it to get it to fit on Zack. When we got back to the cabin, I noticed a canoe pulled up on the beach. I motioned for Catherine to stay put, but she shook her head 'no'. I tied Zack to a tree and pulled my Colt. I pointed to Billy and Catherine motioned him to heel.

We edged around the cabin and I saw two men sitting on the porch watching the lake. I yelled, "Hold it right there Tom Gray Wolf." The men jumped to their feet and turned towards us. I walked around to the steps and walked up to them staring at the taller of the two men. When I got a couple feet away, I slid the Colt back into the holster and gave Tom a big bear hug. Catherine held back and I noticed that the other man was actually a boy about 17 years old.

I told Catherine to come up and meet my old friend Tom. Catherine shook hands with Tom and he looked at her strange and then shook his head. Then Tom introduced the boy. "Jack, Catherine this is my son Jason."

Catherine looked at the boy and saw a handsome young man. He had long straight black hair like hers, dark piercing eyes and a quick easy smile. He shook my hand and then Catherine's. He held Catherine's for a few moments longer. Catherine smiled back at him.

Tom said, "I thought that was Betty roaming around the cabin when we got here. Where's Jim?"

Catherine scowled at the mention of Jim and Tom and Jason noticed it. "Did I say something wrong?" he asked.

"I'll tell you later." I said, "Jason, you were only four years old the last time I saw you."

Jason replied with an easy smile, "I don't remember you much, but dad talks about you all the time. He says he taught you everything you know."

"Hah," I said, "He wishes he knew everything I do. Well, now that we have a couple more strong backs, how about helping us unload the elk Catherine shot."

Both men looked at the young girl with surprise and then nodded agreement. It only took the four of us about fifteen minutes to store the elk in the cold cellar, but Catherine had to introduce each of them to Billy first. Billy sniffed their hands when they held them out and gave each of them a lick to show that he approved.

I put Zack up and wiped him down, and then went back to the porch where Tom was sitting alone. I sat beside him and asked where Catherine and Jason got off to.

Tom said, "Catherine said she was going to start dinner and Jason offered to help."

I laughed and said, "I'm sure he did. I saw the way he looked at her."

Tom got serious and asked, "It's okay isn't it. She's not yours is she?" Then he said, "There is something familiar about her though."

I smiled and said, "Actually it's great. I kind of adopted her and she needs someone closer to her age to associate with."

We heard laughter coming from inside the cabin and I relaxed. Tom looked at me and asked, "So where's Jim?"

I sighed and said, "Jim finally lost it. He and his men went south and I dread to think what they are up to. So, what are you doing down here? The last time I saw you, you were headed up to Creston to find some of your tribe."

"Well, I found a bunch of relatives and friends so we moved down to the east side of the lake here. Our village is across the lake and about five miles south." Tom said. "Jason and I were down at Nordman, and saw horse tracks leading this way and decided to check them out."

"Those were mine." I said. "I was down there a few days ago catching some goats."

"We know." Tom said. "That billy goat is a mean bastard. He chased us up onto the porch when we were scoping the place out."

I laughed and said, "That's actually his name, but we call him MB for short."

Just then Catherine yelled, "Dinners ready."

Tom and I went in and sat at the kitchen table that Jason had cleaned off and set for dinner. I looked between Catherine and Jason and asked Tom, "You two can stay a while can't you?"

Tom glanced at Jason and said, "We can probably stay a couple days, but we need to head back across the lake before too long or Angie will start to worry. We've been gone two days already."

I looked at Catherine as she was serving fried fish and roasted chicken with vegetables. I said, "It's nice to know we have some close neighbors. There is another settlement down east of Coolin called Boville. The founder Bo is from up in Canada and they are looking for places to trade."

Tom said, "Yeah, they passed through our place on the way down two springs ago, but we haven't seen them since."

The conversation stayed light through dinner, with Jason staring at Catherine and she would give him a little smile and go back to eating. Catherine had made some mint and blackberry tea and we each took a glass and went out onto the porch. MB eyed us and I yelled at him to go back to his nannies. He heard me and turned back to the garage.

Catherine asked Jason if he wanted to go fishing and he jumped up and said, "Sure, I'd love to."

After they had walked off, Tom looked at me and said, "I've

never seen the boy so smitten."

I thought I better say something, so I told Tom that she always slept with me. He raised his eyebrows and I hurriedly said, "But sleep is all we do. There is too much of an age difference between us and I saved her from being raped by Jim. So be careful talking about him in front of her."

Tom nodded and we listened to Catherine whoop and Jason laughing as they caught fish. After a while, I told Tom that I would straighten out the front bedroom for him and Jason. Tom came and helped me move stuff out that we had stored there and made the bed. We heard Catherine and Jason in the back of the garage cleaning their fish and laughing.

Later that evening, we sat in front of the fireplace and Tom and I talked while Catherine read some of her comic books to Jason. They sat shoulder to shoulder with their heads together and lost themselves in the stories.

When they finished, Tom asked Jason to come out onto the porch so he could talk to him. I knew Tom was going to explain the sleeping arrangements. Catherine and I heard Jason say, "That's disgusting."

Tom replied, "Jack is an honorable man and you will treat him with respect. Do I make myself clear?"

Jason sullenly replied, "Yes."

When they came back in, I noticed that Jason wouldn't look at me and only glanced at Catherine. He said goodnight and headed upstairs.

Tom said, "He'll get over it. Give him some time."

Catherine looked at me confused. Tom headed upstairs and I started straightening up the living room. Catherine helped and then we went upstairs. After we got into bed, Catherine whispered to me, "What was that all about?"

I told her that Jason liked her and didn't think it was appropriate for her to be sleeping in the same bed as an old man.

Catherine got angry and said, "It's none of his business. I kinda like him too, but I love you Jack."

I grunted and as I was falling asleep, I thought, *"It's going to be an awkward couple of days."*

CHAPTER 16

The next day, Catherine cooked a big breakfast for us and Tom and I went out to the shed afterwards so I could show him the stuff my dad had left. We had discussed trade the night before and Tom said that they were still scavenging things from abandoned homes and towns.

Jason followed us and halfway there, Tom turned to him and asked, "Aren't you going to hang out with Catherine today?"

"No." Jason said stubbornly.

I looked at Tom and said, "Can you give us a minute. The shed is open. Take a look around." I then turned to Jason and asked, "Can I speak to you for a minute?"

"What would you have to speak to me about?" he asked angrily.

"Catherine." I said matter of factly.

Tom smiled to himself and walked off to the shed. Jason looked at me and it was hard to tell with his tanned complexion, but I believe he turned a little darker. He stuttered, "Wha... wha... what about Catherine?"

I figured out at breakfast that the straight approach was the best. Always forward. I said, "I know you like Catherine, and she likes you. But you have to consider what has happened in her life and why she makes the choices she does. You need to consider her feelings and not get angry with her, or she will stop liking you."

"Sh... Sh... She would?" he asked.

"Yes." I said. "She is a very headstrong young girl and if you treat her wrong she will hold it against you."

I told him how she became an orphan. How I had stopped Jim from raping her. How she had ran away from Elmira and followed me and then heard the shots coming from town. How out of sympathy I had taken her along with me. Jason listened to me and I could see his attitude changing.

I said, "I love her like a daughter, and just because she is scared to sleep alone is not a reason for you to be angry with her or to even assume that something 'disgusting' is happening between us. So if you really like her, you will go to her and apologize and stop ignoring her. Okay?"

Jason looked sheepish and then looked me in the eye and said, "I'm sorry to you too. I shouldn't have thought those things."

I laughed and said, "Apology accepted. I was seventeen once myself, and I understand that we don't always read the situation correctly. Our brains make up stories that we think are the truth. I still have problems with that. Now go talk to Catherine."

Jason walked back to the cabin with a spring in his step and I went to the shed. Tom was watching through the open door and said as I approached, "You always go straight at 'em don't you Jack. Jason needed that, but not from me."

"You raised a fine young man there." I replied.

Tom and I worked out some trades for the excess gardening tools. I got the promise of 50 pounds of flour and 20 pounds of cornmeal to be delivered before winter. Catherine's garden wouldn't provide a lot this first year.

Jason and Catherine came running up and Jason asked, "Can we take the canoe out, dad? I want to show Catherine how to catch Lake Trout."

"Sure." Tom said, "But be careful. If the wind picks up, it will push you east and it will be hard getting back here."

"I know that, dad." Jason said as Catherine and he raced down to the beach.

"Kids!" Tom said. "They already know everything."

I just smiled, thinking, *"Catherine is the first kid I've been close to and it hasn't been easy."*

Tom helped me build a fleshing beam and we cleaned the elk

hide from the day before. I had kept the head so we could use the brains to tan the hide. Tom asked why I hadn't kept the hooves to make glue. I said I hadn't found a need for glue yet. Tom laughed and said, "Need or not, you can trade it."

"Yeah I guess so. It's been a while since I've been in the trading business." I said.

I asked Tom if there was anyone around that had any reloading supplies. Tom said that there was an old man up at Bonners Ferry that used to work at Black Hills Ammunition and had his sons travel to the plant in Rapid City and trade for some of the old tooling. Tom said he is making brass and bullets, and has developed some interesting mixtures of smokeless powder.

"You don't mean Craig do you?" I asked. "I've known him for years, but I thought he just did Gunsmithing."

"Yeah, that's him." Tom replied.

This got me excited and thought that I would have to plan a trip there in the spring before we put the garden in next year.

With guests, I hadn't planned on doing much around the cabin, and felt the present was best suited to catching up with an old friend. Tom and I went out to the front porch and sat watching the kids fishing a ways out on the lake.

I turned to Tom and asked, "Do you know what the date is today?"

Tom thought about it for a minute and said, "Well we left the village three days ago, and it was July 27th, so I guess it would be July 30st.

I said, "That's about what I thought. I have a request of you, Angie, and Jason."

"And what would that be?" Tom asked.

"Would it be possible for you to plan a trip back here on August 26th? It's Catherine's birthday and I would like to throw her a party."

"Do you just want the three of us, or should I invite a few more people?"

"A few more wouldn't be a problem." I said. "We would have to make up the back bedroom and have the kids sleep in the living room. Who do you have in mind?"

"Well, I was thinking about my brother Jeremy, his wife Elizabeth, and their daughter Rebecca." He said. "Rebecca is Catherine's age, and being Jason's cousin is no competition for her."

"That would be great." I said. We continued making our plans and I showed Tom the books I had gotten in Nordman to give her. Tom asked what she would like for presents, and I said she would always love a book, but that she needed clothes or cloth to make some clothes out of.

Tom said he would let Angie, Elizabeth and Rebecca decide what to give her, and on his trip back tomorrow, he would tell Jason the plans and let him decide what to give her.

I told him to try to plan on arriving around noon; weather permitting, and I would have Catherine away hunting until around one in the afternoon. We laughed and got into the planning as co-conspirators to surprise Catherine.

An hour later, Catherine and Jason came back with a couple ten to fifteen pound Lake Trout. They were laughing and joking about the fishing trip. Catherine almost tipped the canoe over trying to land the larger trout.

Tom turned to me and said, "Jack you would have made a great dad if you had settled down."

I laughed and said, "I couldn't find the right woman." Tom raised his eyebrows, but didn't say anything.

Jason and Catherine told us their fishing stories over dinner, laughing and teasing each other. After dinner, Tom said that he and Jason had to leave early in the morning to make it across the lake before the winds picked up. Jason started to ask if he could stay, but Tom just shook his head and went up to bed.

Catherine and Jason talked until late, and around midnight, I felt her crawl in bed next to me. She snuggled up against me and whispered, "Are you awake."

I rolled over and said, "I am now. What's up?"

"Can we go visit Jason's village?" She asked.

I said, "Yes we can."

"When? Can we go on my birthday?" she asked.

I thought real quick and said, "Yes, but that's about a month and a half away, and we have a lot to do around here before winter."

"Great." She said as she snuggled against me.

CHAPTER 17

T om and Jason left the next morning early, and Jason lingered with Catherine while I helped Tom load up. Tom whistled to Jason and said, "Come on we need to go while it's calm."

Jason looked over his shoulder and then quickly pecked Catherine on the cheek. He turned and ran down to us with a big smile on his face.

Catherine and I watched them paddle away and when they were a long ways out, Jason turned and waved. Catherine waved back, and then we turned back to the cabin. I said, "We have a lot to do if we are going to plan a trip for your birthday."

Catherine lit up and asked what we needed to get done. I said, "First we need to make some long term plans for the winter. We need to put up hay for the horses and goats. I need to chop enough firewood and we need to get the old canoe down from the rafters in the garage."

We settled into a routine for the next three and a half weeks. I chopped wood every morning, while Catherine tended the garden. After lunch, we went to the meadow back of the house and while I cut hay, Catherine gathered it into bundles and tied it with string. Catherine stopped me and asked, "How much hay are we going to need?"

I thought about it and said, "Well, they can probably forage until mid-October and then start in again at the end of April. So that's six and a half months. Figure thirty days per month, that's about a hundred ninety five days. We are going to need a bundle a day per horse, and two bundles a day for the goats. Then we

95

need at least 10% more just in case. So how much is that?"

I had been teaching Catherine math, and liked to present her with problems like this. Catherine was quick. She said, "Well that's four bundles a day for 195 days, so that's 4 times 200 minus 20, right?" I didn't answer. She went on, "So 800 minus 20 is 780, times 10% is 78. So we will need... 858 bundles."

I saw the surprise in her face at the size of the number and laughed, "That's right; it's a lot isn't it."

"Where we going to put it all?" she asked. "There isn't enough room in the shed for that much hay. The shed is twenty by sixteen and a quarter of that is for the chickens."

"I guess we will have to think on that." I said. "What worries me is this field isn't big enough to produce that many bundles." I looked around at the meadow. It was about three acres.

While I was thinking Catherine said, "It's too bad we don't have any other feed to give them."

"When we go trading next spring, I think I will try to get some oats. We can plan to plant some wild oats in this meadow. That will help with next..." I stopped talking because Catherine was smiling at me and winked. I thought about what I had just said and laughed. "Shut up, you know what I mean."

Catherine smiled and said, "I didn't say anything."

'Damn, damn, damn you girl, you always put those thoughts into my head. Why me?' I thought happily. I went back to cutting hay and Catherine giggled behind me. I could feel my face turn red, and thanked the exertion and sweat that covered it up.

We worked hard every day, and every evening, we went swimming to wash off the dust and itch of the hay. I always swam in my underwear, and Catherine would swim in shorts and an old t-shirt of mine. Today she had chosen a white t-shirt, and when she went under and swam up to me, she might as well not have a top on at all. I could see her small breasts and erect pink nipples right through the shirt. I quickly swam out a ways and after I was sure I had control of myself, I started floating on my back and trying to clear my mind. *'God, I hope Jason takes her off my hands or to be more accurate, off my mind. She needs to focus her attention on someone more her age.'*

After about ten minutes, I swam back and Catherine looked at me shyly and asked, "What's wrong? Did I do something?"

I looked her right in the eye and said, "You know damn well what you did, and from now on wear a dark colored t-shirt when you swim."

Catherine looked down at herself and looked up at me and said, "Oh that." Then she stood up in the water in front of me, stood there for a minute then turned and strutted up to the beach.

'She's impossible.' I thought.

August 25th came up fast with all the work we were getting done. That evening, I told Catherine that we needed to go hunting the next day to put some more meat up for winter. She got excited and asked what we were going to hunt for. I told her we should try to get a mule deer, but an elk or small moose would do. I told her to go to bed and I would clean up and be up in a minute.

After she had gone upstairs, I went into my father's den and got out the books I had gathered on my last trip to Nordman. 'The Wizard of Oz', 'Alice in Wonderland', and a few Dr. Suess books. I wrapped them in a flowery kitchen towel and tied it shut. Then I hid it under my dad's desk.

I went upstairs and found her asleep. I fell asleep fast and we got up before dawn the next morning. It was her birthday and she didn't even know it.

I loaded Zack with his harness, a day pack and a blanket for Catherine to sit on. I thought *'I need to get her a saddle.'* I saddled Betty and Catherine came out with a pack. She saw my questioning look and said, "Lunch."

We rode the game trail until around ten o'clock before we saw some fresh tracks. I had Catherine get down and tell me what she saw. She looked at the tracks, and counted the differences and said, "I think there are five of them. Looks like three adults and a couple young ones. It's definitely mule deer, not elk or moose."

I asked how fresh, and she checked how dry they were by feeling the bottom of one track. It still felt hard and moist she said, so they couldn't be more than a half hour old. I nodded and asked what her plan was. She looked at the direction they went and from our previous trips out here, said we should tie off the horses and hike to the northeast until we got to a small ridge about a quarter mile away. From there we could glass the valley beyond and try to catch up with them. She said it didn't look like they were in a hurry.

I nodded okay, and got off Betty and tied her to a tree with some grass growing near it. Catherine did the same with Zack, and I took the day pack off him and shrugged it on. As we walked towards the ridge, we ate some of the food Catherine had brought.

When we got to the ridge, we crawled to the top and lay still for a moment listening. There were the usual sounds, and we both sat quietly for about fifteen minutes. Catherine had the .308 resting on the day pack, and was the first to notice a difference in the sounds. She pointed to a small group of Ruffed Grouse about a hundred yards away that came out the bushes suddenly. I gave her the binoculars and she focused on the bushes behind them. She held up five fingers and whispered, "Two does, a young buck, and two fawns."

"Take the buck." I whispered back. "We don't know which doe is feeding the fawns."

Catherine nodded and waited until the buck had walked clear of the bushes. She lined up the scope on him and as she watched, she noticed the buck and does perk up. Suddenly, they bolted away from the open and pogoed up the other side of the valley. Catherine said, "Damn him." She stood up and whistled real loud, and Billy came running out of the brush. He hadn't left with us in the morning, which was not unusual, but he must have followed later and then tracked the deer.

Billy ran up to us, tail wagging and big dog smile on his face. "Billy," Catherine said angrily, "you ruined everything. Now we won't catch up to those deer and today is wasted. Bad dog!"

"Don't be so hard on him; he is just being a dog."

"But he ruined our hunt." She said angrily. "That was the only fresh sign we saw all morning. Today is ruined."

I looked at her and said, "Everything can't always go perfectly. We should head back and try again some other day. If we make sure we take Billy with us, he won't ruin it."

Catherine fumed all the way back to the cabin, and as I had planned it was around one o'clock when we got back. Catherine noticed smoke coming out of the chimney and said, "I thought I put the fire out before we left. I better go check it." I knew she had.

"I'll come along and then come back and settle the horses." I said.

Billy was at the door whining and scratching to get in and Catherine said, "You wait. You already ruined today."

Catherine opened the door and jumped back into my arms when a bunch of people yelled, "Happy Birthday!"

CHAPTER 18

Catherine stood against me with shock on her face, until Jason and Tom came forward and said, "Happy Birthday, Catherine." Then they each gave her a hug. They started introducing the other people present, when I saw Angie standing by the kitchen with a strange look on her face.

I walked over and gave her a big bear hug and said, "Angie, you get prettier every time I see you."

"Oh you big brute, put me down. You know I'm a married woman." She said smiling.

"Well, if it doesn't work out with Tom, you know where to find me." I said.

I put her down and heard an "ahem" from behind me. I turned and saw Catherine looking at me, so I turned and said, "Catherine, I would like you to meet Angie."

Catherine looked at Angie, and her jaw dropped open. Angie smiled at her, but stood still where she was. Catherine stuttered, "Y... Y... You... look exactly like pictures I've seen of my mother."

I looked between them and thought, *'Why didn't I notice it before, Catherine has a lighter complexion, a ponytail, and she was much younger, but she could be a twin sister of Angie.'*

Angie looked at Catherine and turned and went to sit on the sofa. She said, "I see what you mean Tom. Catherine, would you sit next to me please? I have some questions I would like to ask you."

Catherine walked around the couch and sat next to Angie still in shock. Everyone else went quiet and stood where they were.

Angie asked, "What do you remember about your mother

and father, Catherine?"

Catherine said, "I don't remember them at all. I was an baby when they were killed, and my dad's sister raised me. I was named after my mother."

Angie asked, "And was your father's name David?"

"Yes, how did you know?" Catherine asked.

"Catherine, a little over sixteen years ago, my identical twin sister married a man named David Barstow up in Creston. We were all living there at the time. David and my twin sister Catherine headed south that year and we never heard from them again." Angie said.

Catherine replied slowly, "That was my mother's name." and then as if a light went on, "So...so...so... that makes you my aunt."

Jason yelled, "Nooooo!" and ran out the door.

Tom started after him, but Angie said, "Give the boy some time, Tom. We all have a lot to process and we have a birthday to celebrate." She reached over and gave Catherine a big hug. "Happy Birthday, little Catherine."

Everyone sat around while Catherine asked Angie questions about her mother. About an hour had gone by and Jason had not come back. I went to Tom and asked, "Do you mind if I go find Jason and have a talk with him?"

Tom said, "Jack, I would appreciate that. When I talk to him, he listens to me, but doesn't seem to hear me. In this case, I don't even know what to say to him."

I went outside and looked around. I saw Jason sitting on the beach with his arms across his knees, his forehead resting on his arms and wet eyes staring at the ground. I walked down and sat next to him and looked out over the lake. We didn't talk for at least ten minutes.

Suddenly, Jason burst out, "Why does she have to be my cousin? I love her. Why is this happening to me? What did I do wrong to deserve this? Can't we just go back to the way it was?"

I gave Jason a little smile and said, "That's a lot of questions, which one do you want to start with?"

Jason got angry and said, "This isn't funny."

I looked him in the eye and said, "I know it isn't funny and I'm not trying to be. Seriously, which question would you like to start with?"

Jason calmed down a little at my direct approach and asked, "Why is this happening to me?"

I looked at him and shook my head a little. "Do you think this is just happening to you? What about Catherine, who thought she was alone in the world without a family? What about your mother who didn't know for years what happened to her twin sister? I know this is a blow to your heart, and you think it's bad. But it is also good. Catherine has family. You're part of it, and Angie has closure."

Jason just shrugged and I saw that he was still quite a ways from accepting it. "Why do you think you did something wrong to deserve this?" I asked.

"Everything was perfect." Jason said, "Then the world pulls this crap on me. It has to be out to get me for some reason. If this is how it is, I won't ever fall in love again."

"Jason was everything perfect? Did Catherine say she loved you? Or is this the picture you created in your mind of a perfect world?" I said. "The world didn't do anything but keep turning day after day. It doesn't care what takes place on it. It just exists. It was your thoughts that created that picture."

"Well..." Jason started thinking about what I had said. "Catherine always said she liked me, but that she loved you. Since you were a lot older and not interested in her, I thought I had a shot."

'Not interested? Ha!' I thought. *'Shut up brain and pay attention to the conversation. What you think or want isn't relevant.'* I said, "How can an inanimate object like the world be out to get you? Our thoughts make up pictures and stories of how we want the world to be for us. These are just illusions. How often does any of it ever happen the way we envision it?"

"I guess not often." Jason said. "But why can't we go back to the way it was?

I shook my head and said, "I have wished that many times in

my life. What if the 'Big Shit' hadn't happened? What if my parents hadn't died? But, I've come to realize that is all in the past. It already happened and I can't change it. I can only live in the present and deal with whatever the current situation is. The past is gone and the future isn't written yet. Can you live with that?"

Jason looked at me sadly and said, "I guess I'll have to, but I'm never going to fall in love again."

"There you go trying to predict the future." I said. That brought a small smile to Jason's face, and then he covered it with his hand.

Jason asked, "How did you get so wise?"

I replied, "I'm not wise, I've just made a lot of mistakes and realized that I have to live in the present to be happy. No remorse for the past and no illusions about the future. Speaking of present and happy; a young girl was surprised on her birthday with more than I even thought would happen. Did you get her a present and will you try to make this a happy occasion for her?"

"Yes." Jason said.

"Okay, let's go back to the party." I said.

CHAPTER 19

Jason and I walked back towards the cabin and I noticed that I had forgotten all about Betty and Zack. I asked Jason, "Would you help me put up the horses first?"

Jason was looking for any reason to not go back into the cabin and agreed quickly. We took the horses around to the garage and took the saddle and pack off of them and wiped them down. While we were doing this, Angie came out.

She walked over to Jason and gave him a hug. She said, "Your father told me his suspicions, but we didn't want to tell you until we were sure. I'm sorry it was such a shock to you."

"Mom, Jack and I talked and even though I hate it, I will be alright." Jason said.

Angie looked at me and smiled. "Jack you always have a way to bring calm to those around you. Thank you."

I just smiled at her and nodded my head a little. Then I said, "Well Jason, we might as well go in. We're finished here. Remember, always forward."

Jason looked a little scared as we went into the cabin, but Catherine immediately came up to him and gave him a long hug. He hugged her back and tears started forming in his eyes.

Catherine wiped a tear away from her own eye, and said, "I'm sorry things didn't work out the way you thought they would, but I love that you are my cousin."

Jason said, even though it was difficult, "I am too." Then he added quickly, "By the way, we have some great presents for you."

This comment got the party started. Jason hung back while

everyone started getting everything ready. Angie, Elizabeth, and Rebecca unpacked a bunch of food, and to my surprise they had even made a birthday cake.

Tom, Jeremy, Jason and I went up and sorted out the bedrooms, and when we came back down, Angie had an early dinner started in the fireplace. Catherine tried to help, but since she was the birthday girl, she wasn't allowed. Instead, she went upstairs to our bedroom and changed into the blue dress that Janice had given her.

She looked beautiful, so I sat next to her on the sofa, and she punched me in the shoulder. "You said my birthday was in two weeks. When is it?"

I smiled and said, "Oh it was just a little fib. Tom and I planned this when they were here before. Your birthday is actually today."

She gave me a big hug and then kissed me full on the lips. "Thank you, this is a wonderful surprise."

I noticed Angie watching and blushed a little. She just smiled and went back to cooking. We had dinner at the kitchen table and then had the birthday celebration. Catherine cut the cake and passed it around. We all thanked Elizabeth and Rebecca for making it. It was delicious. I can't remember the last time I had anything sweet to eat.

"Well, I think it's time for presents." I said. I went into the den to get the present I had wrapped for Catherine and had to crawl under the desk to get it from where I hid it. While I was down there, I noticed a sliding panel behind the drawers. I thought, *'I'm going to have to check that out later. No telling what dad had hidden.'*

I took the present out and saw Catherine sitting in the middle of the sofa with Angie on one side and Jason on the other. She had the biggest smile I had ever seen on her face. Jason handed her his gift. It was about five feet long and bundled in some old camouflage cloth. She opened it carefully. It was a recurve bow and twelve arrows with target and broad head removable tips.

He said, "I know you can shoot a gun, so I thought I would teach you how to shoot a bow and arrow."

Catherine hugged him again and said, "I love it Jason, and you will teach me won't you?"

Jason nodded and said, "Yes, I promise."

Elizabeth, Rebecca, and Jeremy had gotten her some newly made clothes that I was sure would fit her better than the boys clothes she had.

Elizabeth said, "We guessed at your sizes, but Tom pointed out a girl in our village that was about the same as you. I hope they fit you."

Catherine said, "I love them. Thank you very much."

Tom gave her a tackle box full of fishing lures. He said, "I know how much fun you have fishing, so I thought you could use some more lures. These are made by a craftsman in our village. I hope you like them."

Catherine laughed and said, "Thank you Uncle Tom. I'm sure I will get a lot of use out of them."

It was my turn, and I handed her my present. I said, "When I went and caught the goats, I thought you might like these."

She opened it and squealed, all the books had plenty of pictures to go along with the stories; especially the Dr. Seuss books.

"Oh thank you Jack. These are great." She said.

Angie waited until last and handed Catherine a medium sized rectangular package. It looked like another book to me. Catherine ripped the paper off it and I saw that it was a picture album. She opened it and paged through it a ways and then surprised asked, "Are these pictures of my mother?"

Angie said, "Yes, and there are pictures of your father and grandparents in there too."

Catherine teared up and hugged Angie hard. "Oh thank you, thank you, this is the best." She went back to looking through the pictures slowly and asking Angie when and where they were taken.

We all sat and listened and I thought to myself, *This couldn't have turned out better. Well at least for Catherine.'* I had Tom and

Jason help me set up some board games in the kitchen, and we played Monopoly, Yatzee, and cards until late in the night.

I had to rethink the sleeping arrangements, so I had Rebecca sleep with Catherine, and Jason and I set up bedrolls in the living room. Tom, Angie, Jeremy, and Elizabeth took the other two bedrooms.

When it was 'lights out', I lay there thinking how happy I felt that I could make Catherine happy. After about a half hour, Jason asked me if I was asleep.

I said, "No, why do you ask?"

Jason asked, "How come you never got married? Didn't you ever fall in love?"

I thought for a minute and said, "I guess I never settled down in one place long enough to fall in love. I was always moving around and fighting marauders with my brother."

"But there has been women in your life hasn't there?" he asked.

"Yes." I said. "There was always a widow or two in the towns we worked in that wanted me to stay, but I didn't have strong feelings for them, so I moved on." I knew where this conversation was headed.

"You seem to have settled down now though." He said. "You love Catherine don't you?"

'Okay,' I thought, 'I know where he's headed, and his ego is still bruised so be careful.' "Yes, I love Catherine very much, and she loves me more than she should for a girl her age. Even though I discourage her at every turn, she still tries to tempt me. But, you should have a sense of my morals by now, and should understand that I am too old for her. I was hoping you would be able to take her off my hands someday, but I'm sorry that won't happen. So I guess you and I will have to find her a suitable man."

Jason sighed and said, "I guess we will. Good night."

CHAPTER 20

The next day, I asked Angie and Tom how long they could stay. They said they hadn't made any plans, and would like to see what happens. Angie said she wanted to get to know Catherine. Tom said that the men could help me get things organized for winter.

We built a lean-to onto the side of the garage to hold firewood and bundles of grass. We had to stack the firewood to the outside to keep the horses and goats from eating all the grass up. With the help of Tom, Jason, and Jeremy, we were able to put up another four hundred bundles of grass for winter. This gave us around seven hundred bundles, so when they left, that would only leave a couple hundred for Catherine and I to finish. We also cut and split about ten cords of wood and cleared more brush away from the cabin. The brush pile on the beach was getting much larger.

Every evening, Angie and Catherine would sit on the porch and talk. Catherine always brought the picture album and asked questions about her mother and father. Angie would listen to the questions and provide answers if she had them. One evening, I overheard Catherine ask, "How old was my mother when she married my dad?"

Angie said, "She was 17."

Catherine looked at me and then asked "How old was my father?"

Angie thought and said, "I think he was around 40, he was much older than my sister."

Catherine looked at me again and winked. I just gave my head a little shake 'no'. Catherine mouthed 'We'll see.'

As a week passed, Tom said that they had to start planning to head back. We had gone hunting and shot a moose and two elk and they were taking a bunch of the meat back with them. Jason had shot one of the elk with his bow and arrow, and Catherine was impressed. They spent a couple afternoons together teaching Catherine how to shoot a bow.

While they were practicing, Catherine asked Jason, "How do you get so close to the animal without it seeing or hearing you?"

Jason said, "I practiced a lot sneaking up on rabbits and squirrels until I got my first deer. Deer are smarter and can seem to sense when something is watching them. You have to be downwind of them and watch where you place your feet. You can't move until they lower their head to feed or look away from you. It takes a lot of practice and patience."

"I want to learn to do it." Catherine said.

Jason said "Okay, there are plenty of rabbits around let's try to sneak within ten feet of them."

They practiced all afternoon. While they were doing that, Angie came up to me and asked if I would take a walk on the beach with her. We went down to the beach and walked a ways in silence. I was enjoying the company and the quiet noise of the lake lapping the shore, birds flitting in the bushes and chirping at each other. We found a log to sit on and sat quietly for a while.

Angie finally said, "You know Catherine is in love with you, don't you Jack?"

I said, "Yes I know, and I try to discourage her."

"Jack, don't you know that you can't discourage her. She talks about how much she loves you all the time. When she asked me how my sister and her father dealt with the age difference, I only told her that they loved each other." She said. "Do you love her Jack?"

I was quiet for a long time, and Angie waited quietly. Finally, I said, "Yes I love her very much. But she is too young to marry and I'm way too old for her anyway."

"You can think up all the excuses you want Jack but that

isn't going to change how you feel about each other." She said.

"I know but I still feel it's wrong." I said.

"Wait a few years and see what happens. You have us and we are just across the lake so if she falls in love with a younger boy then you can suffer alone. Right now, though she is suffering because she doesn't want to lose you."

"I've spent most of my life alone, I guess I can withstand it, but you need to help me find her a younger man." I said.

Angie said, "I will do no such thing. If she finds it on her own, it will be real. If we try to force it on her, she will become more determined."

I whispered to myself, 'Women'.

Angie said, "I heard that, and you men think you can fix anything, but 'women' as you put it just want you to be there."

I laughed and said, "Angie, you sure know how to ruin a nice quiet walk on the beach."

She laughed and said, "You're welcome."

"But I didn't say 'thank you'." I said.

"You're welcome for the advice that I'm sure you won't take." She said.

We spent the next day preparing and packing up the meat they planned to take back. After we had everything prepared, we spent the evening having a second party. It turned out that Elizabeth and Rebecca could sing and with Jeremy on a six string guitar, they entertained us with songs. I found an old set of yard darts and we played until it got too dark to see. Jason and Catherine were a team and they annihilated the rest of us. Jason started showing off by flipping the darts in the air and sticking them in the center of the circle.

After a light dinner, we all sat around a fire pit on the beach and sang songs and laughed at Tom and Jeremy's jokes. Catherine sat next to me and leaned her head against my shoulder. She looked at Angie and said, "I'm going to miss you when you leave."

Angie said, "Oh pish. You can come over anytime you want. It's only three hours by canoe. I plan to come back often to see my niece."

Catherine perked up and asked me, "When can we go visit?"

"Well we planned a visit in a couple weeks anyway, so we can stick to it."

The next morning everyone got up early so our guests could head out while the lake was calm. We packed the canoes and starting saying our goodbyes on the beach.

Angie hugged Catherine and said, "Sweetheart, if you need anything, remember we are only three hours away." Catherine teared up and hugged her back. Then Angie gave me a hug and whispered in my ear, "You do the right thing, Jack, even if you think it's the wrong thing."

I looked at her and said, "I can't."

Everyone else looked at us and wondered what we were talking about. Everyone gave Catherine a hug and said 'see you soon'. Jason came up to me and stuck out his hand and said, "Thank you Jack."

I hugged him instead and whispered to him, "You're a good man Jason, just try not to predict the future and enjoy what happens now."

He laughed and said, "I'll try."

Again everyone looked questioningly at the strange conversations taking place. They loaded up and started across the lake. Catherine and I sat on our fishing log and watched them until they were out of sight.

Catherine stood and hugged me and said, "Thank you Jack. That was the best birthday I have ever had."

"You're welcome sweetheart. I'm glad you enjoyed it."

CHAPTER 21

Catherine and I spent the next couple weeks finding and cutting more grass for the winter. We put up another 200 bundles and felt we should have enough to last. We would fish every evening and then go inside and read. Catherine would lean her head against my shoulder and follow along as I read out loud to her. I never tired of this, but after a while, I had her read out loud to me to give her more practice.

Our lives couldn't be better, and I started wondering why I resisted accepting Catherine's love for me. As these thoughts started coming to me, I would go down to the beach to sit and listen and clear my mind. I came to realize that thinking thoughts like these would make me unhappy, and that would show up in our relationship. So, I accepted that I loved Catherine. I couldn't think of any reasons why I loved her, just that I did.

That evening before we sat down to read, I looked at Catherine and said, "Catherine, I love you more than I've ever loved another person, and I don't know why."

Catherine smiled at me and said, "I have been waiting for you to realize that."

I felt a little embarrassed and said, "It doesn't change how I feel about sleeping with you though. If you will bear with me, we can wait and see if you find someone younger."

Catherine looked at me sadly and said, "There will never be anyone else Jack."

"Catherine, you shouldn't think that way. You are still very young and have a long life ahead of you. If something was to happen to me, you would still have to go on."

Catherine laughed and said, "I've heard you talking to Jason about not trying to predict the future and just be happy in the present. Why can't you take your own advice?"

"Catherine, I am the happiest I have ever been, with you in my life. I guess I am better at giving advice than taking it." I smiled. Then trying to change the subject I said, "Do you still want to read?"

Catherine looked at me and sighed, "I think I would rather sit on the porch and look at the stars."

"Do you want to be alone?" I asked.

"Of course not, Jack. Whenever we are together, I want you right next to me." She said.

We sat together on the porch swing. I held her close with my arm around her shoulder and she leaned her head against my chest. We sat like that for about an hour I think. I couldn't tell, because time stopped for me. I wanted to stay like this forever.

I heard her snoring softly and eased out and picked her up. I carried her up to bed and lay her down. Catherine reached up and hugged me around the neck and whispered, "Lay with me tonight Jack."

Even though I wanted to, I said, "Not tonight. Let's wait and see what happens. I am not trying to predict the future; I just need time to get used to the idea. Okay?"

Catherine huffed and said, "You know you want to."

"I know I frustrate you Catherine, but I still need to live with myself and I wouldn't be a good lover to you with these thoughts running through my head. Please try to understand." I pleaded.

"Okay." She said sadly, "I do understand, but you need to get over it. I will be here for you no matter when you decide you can.

She rolled over and closed her eyes. I realized the conversation was over and lay down beside her and tried to go to sleep. I chased thoughts around in my head for hours. *'How can I love someone so much and deny her what she wants? Why does my age matter? Why does her age matter? What happens if we do have sex and then she falls in love with someone else? What would I do then'?*

Needless to say, I found no answers.

I woke up the next morning and realized that it was already late. I went downstairs and Catherine had breakfast waiting. She came up to me and put her arms around my neck and kissed me passionately on the mouth. I didn't resist.

She said, "If you won't lay with me, I would appreciate at least some contact with you. So kiss me every morning and every night before we go to sleep."

"Okay." I said and realized that all my barriers were starting to fall. I needed some distraction, so I went on, "We should plan our trip to see Angie and the rest, before the fall weather starts up."

Catherine perked up and asked, "When can we go?"

I said, "We can leave tomorrow and spend today getting everything around here buttoned up. If we are going to take the canoe, we need to get the horses, goats and chickens settled in for a couple days. I don't think we should let them run free while we are gone. There are still bears, wolves, and coyotes in the area that could cause problems with us gone."

We spent the day making a makeshift corral around the front of the garage and set aside some bundles of grass to put out in the morning. I filled all the water barrels to the top and put the chickens inside the shed that evening.

We went to bed early, and I kissed Catherine and held her as she went to sleep. I felt her warmth against my skin and felt the happiness overwhelm me. I fell asleep and had dreams of having sex with Catherine. I woke up in the morning and realized that I had an erection.

Catherine was awake and looking at me. She asked, "What were you dreaming about? You kept saying my name."

I blushed deeply and said, "I don't remember." I waited until Catherine went into the bathroom to brush her teeth and quickly got out of bed and put my jeans on. *'Dammit, what was happening to me'?*

❖ ❖ ❖

We ate a light breakfast and checked on the animals and then packed the canoe for a two day trip. Billy rode in the middle. The lake was calm and we made it across in about a half hour. We headed south, and it took us another two and a half hours before we came in sight of the village. Some kids were playing on the beach and saw us. They started running back to the houses yelling and we saw some of the men come down to the beach. I could see Jason in the group and relaxed a little. It was always an anxious time approaching a village during the 'rough times'.

When we got close, Jason 'hallooed' and Catherine waved back. We came ashore and Jason and another young man helped pull the canoe up on the beach. We got out and Jason started the introductions. "This is my cousin Catherine and her guardian Jack."

A group of the young men eyed Catherine appreciatively and I suddenly felt jealous. *'Geez Jack, this is what you wanted. For her to find a young man; why are you getting so jealous? It's up to her who she loves.'*

As we were being introduced, Angie and Tom walked down and Catherine ran up to them. Angie and Catherine hugged for a long moment, while I shook hands with Tom.

Tom said, "We were wondering if you were going to make it over before the fall weather started. It's great to see you." Then Tom got a big hug from Catherine. He got a huge smile on his face and said, "Welcome Catherine, you remind me so much of Angie when she was your age." Then looking at Angie, he said, "But you are more beautiful now, dear."

Angie smiled and said, "Good save, honey."

We unpacked the canoe, and everyone helped carry our stuff up to Tom and Angie's. Angie made up a bedroom for us and we settled in for lunch and visiting. I talked about being prepared for the winter with Tom and Jason, while Angie and Catherine sat on the porch and talked.

After lunch, Tom and Jason showed us around the village and introduced some of the residents. Tom said that there were eighty one people living there with three newborns on the way in the next five months. Jason and Catherine took off to see the fish house and I noticed a number of young men following behind. Catherine asked if I would keep Billy with me. He was eyeing the other dogs in the village and growled a few times, but he was still a puppy.

Tom took me to Jenkin's Trading Post and I traded some smoked venison for some cloth for Catherine, a bunch of candles, and some more flour and cornmeal for the winter. Tom, Billy and I headed back to their house and sat with Angie on the porch talking.

We heard a commotion down by the fish house and I saw Catherine running towards the house with Jason walking angrily behind her. When she reached the porch, I could see she was crying. I stood and she ran into my arms. I hugged her and asked, "What's wrong Catherine."

Catherine said, "I want to go home right now. I hate it here."

"Catherine what's wrong?" I asked again. She just hugged me tighter and kept crying.

Jason walked up and I could see he had a cut lip and a large red mark on his cheek that I was sure was going to turn into a black eye. "What happened, Jason?" Tom asked.

Jason said hurriedly, "George and some of the boys were hitting on Catherine and I told them to stop because she was uncomfortable. George asked why she doesn't like men, and Catherine said she was in love with Jack. George called you an old pervert and Catherine slapped him. Then he called her a slut and pushed her down. I hit him and the fight started."

I said, "I hope you look better than he does."

Jason smiled and touched his cut lip and said, "All of them will remember not to fight with me. I think I broke George's nose and George's brother may have some bruised ribs."

Angie ran into the house and came out with her medical bag. I remembered that her mother had been a doctor and had trained Angie in trauma care after the 'Big Shit'. Angie and Tom headed out to find George and his brother, while I tried to console Catherine. Jason went inside and got a wet wash cloth to hold against his cheek and cut lip.

Catherine said, "I don't like it here, I want to go home."

I said, "It's too late to leave today, but we can leave in the morning if you really want to. Let's wait and talk to Angie and Tom before we decide."

As we were talking, a couple large men came walking up and asked where Jason was. Jason came out of the house and I could see fear in his eyes. Jason asked, "What can I do for you Mr. Murphy."

Mr. Murphy stepped forward and reached to grab Jason. I stepped in front of him and blocked his way. Murphy said, "Get out of my way. I'm going to teach this injun a lesson."

I said, "Not today. Let's let everything calm down and talk this through."

Murphy swung at me. I stepped forward into it and blocked the punch. I continued moving forward and pushed him back into his friend. I said, "That will be enough. You need to calm down Mr. Murphy. This isn't going to solve anything."

Murphy lunged forward and tried to tackle me around the waist. I side stepped and pushed him down on the ground. He got up and rushed at me again.

There was a loud gunshot right behind me and we both stopped. I turned to see Catherine pointing her Sig at Mr. Murphy. She was rock steady and just stared at him. Finally she said, "Leave now, or I swear I will shoot you."

Murphy and his friend finally noticed the crowd gathering and Tom and Jeremy running up to the house. He turned and grabbed his friend and sauntered off into the village.

CHAPTER 22

Tom, Jeremy, and a few of the other men from the village watched Murphy and his friend walk off. I looked at Tom and he shrugged.

"The Murphy's and their friend Bob Smith have been a problem in our village since they arrived this spring. They came without any women and have been causing trouble with most of the teenage girls and some of the married women. There has been more than one fight and some serious injuries. The town council will have to deal with this, and since it involves Jason, Jeremy and I can't sit on the hearing." Tom said.

I looked at Catherine as she stared angrily at Murphy and his friend walking off. I walked over and put my arm around her shoulder and took the gun out of her hand. She leaned into me and started shaking. I hugged her and said, "Everything will be alright. The town has ways of handling situations like this."

Catherine looked at me and said, "There is only one way to deal with people like that."

I let the comment go and asked Tom what would happen next?

Tom said, "The town council will have a hearing tonight to discuss what happened and make a ruling."

"Will they call witnesses?" I asked.

"Yes, they will call everyone present at the fight to get their version of what took place and then what happened here?" He said.

"What do you mean by 'what happened here'?" I asked.

"Catherine discharged a firearm in the town limits and threatened another person. That is a very serious situation." Tom said.

I looked at Tom in disbelief and he shrugged. "Not my decision Jack. We put those rules in place after some of the other altercations the Murphy's have been in."

Catherine grabbed my arm and said, "Let's leave now. I don't want to stay here any longer. If this town can't get rid of its bad men, then I don't want anything to do with it."

Angie had come up at the end of the conversation and heard Catherine's statement. I saw the shock and anger on Angie's face and she turned to the crowd that had gathered and said. "I told you months ago that this was going to happen with the Murphy's but none of you listened. We have guests in our village for the first time and this happens. I'm ashamed."

Someone in the back of the crowd yelled, "Yeah but she's your niece. Of course you would take her side."

Angie flared up and said, "This is not about sides. It's about right and wrong, good and bad. We have survived the 'rough times' by working together and taking care of each other. If I had taken sides, I would not have tended to the Murphy boys injuries."

Some people in the crowd mumbled agreement and finally a group of elderly men stepped forward and their leader said. "The council will decide what should be done."

The crowd broke up and headed back to their work or homes.

I looked at Tom and Angie and asked, "What now?"

Catherine interrupted angrily, "We're leaving. I don't care if it's late or not."

I hugged her and she started shaking again. I said, "No, we have to see this through. We can't get past the 'rough times' if we don't try to recreate some form of law."

I heard her whisper to herself, "There is only one law bad men understand."

I could tell she was thinking of Jim again and held her tighter. I said, "I will not let anything happen to you." She hugged me back and slowly stopped shaking.

◆ ◆ ◆

That evening the people gathered around the town center, and the council set up a table and chairs. There were five of them, with Tom and Jeremy abstaining. We arrived and stood to the right of the council. On the left, the Murphy's stood with their friend Bob. I could see that all of the town's people kept a distance from them.

The town council leader, Gerard Perot, stood and said, "We are here to address the altercation that took place this morning by the fish house and then the ensuing confrontation at Tom Gray Wolf's home."

Mr. Murphy yelled, "That damn Injun boy attacked my sons for no reason at all, and then that little bitch pulled a gun on me." He pointed at Catherine.

The leader raised his hand and said, "You will get your say Mr. Murphy, but we are looking for facts that caused the situation to happen, not accusations."

Jason was the first witness and told his story. The council called some of the town's young boys to give their statements, and all of them verified Jason's version.

George got up next and said that he was only teasing and then Catherine had slapped him and he just reacted. He hadn't meant for it to happen, but then Jason attacked him and his brother.

They called Catherine up next and asked her what happened. Catherine looked at the council and the crowd gathered, squared her shoulders and said, "I have nothing to say to this council or this town. I will leave and never come back."

The leader looked shocked, and then angrily said, "That still leaves the issue of you discharging a firearm in the town limits and threatening Mr. Murphy."

Murphy smirked and nudged his son George.

Catherine looked at the leader and then the crowd of people. "You all may believe you are safe and secure in your little village, but I lost my parents and my home to bad men just like the Murphy's. There is only one way to deal with them. You can do what you want with me, because you will never have to see me again. But you will not find the peace you are looking for unless you are willing to do what is necessary. Yes, these are 'rough times', but it's not us that make them rough. It's others that feel they can treat people any way they want to and never suffer the consequences. I leave you to your peace." She turned and walked back to me.

Murphy looked angrily at Catherine as she walked back to me and then turned and whispered to his friend Bob.

The crowd murmured in confusion as the town council talked amongst themselves. After about a half hour of arguing, the council leader stood and held up his hands. The crowd edged forward and quieted down. The leader spoke. "We have decided that since no one was seriously hurt at the fish house, that altercation will be dismissed."

I noticed Murphy smile and nudge his son George again.

The leader continued, "Since the young lady would not speak in her defense to the issue of threatening Mr. Murphy and has agreed to leave the village, we consider that issue resolved."

The crowd rumbled angrily and there were shouts from the back. "She was right. We should listen to her."

The leader held up his hands again and the crowd quieted down. "As far as the Murphy's are concerned, this is the last time we will accept them in front of the council. If there is even one more incident, they will be banished from the village."

The crowd yelled angrily, the council turned and left. I took Catherine's hand and we walked back to Tom and Angie's.

Catherine leaned against me and said, "We should have left this afternoon."

"Catherine, they are trying to do the right thing. If they turned everyone away that came to the village, there would be no growth. People deserve a chance." I said.

"Not the Murphy's." she said. "You know I'm right about them. You fought men like them more than half your life."

"You're probably right, but I was talking about the council's decision." I said. "It's difficult holding a group of people together and decisions like this are neither good nor bad. They are both. Good for the group in the long run, but bad for some individuals in the present."

"Jack, I love you, but you're wrong. This will be bad for the group in the long run." She said.

Angie, Tom and Jason caught up with us after stopping to talk with some other people. Angie hugged Catherine and said, "I am so sorry this happened to you here and I am very proud that you said what you did and didn't apologize. So many people are afraid of the Murphy's and whenever they bring these problems to the council, the council backs down."

Catherine looked at Angie, smiled and said, "I believe in only one solution to problems like the Murphy's and should have taken it this morning."

Angie looked shocked, but Tom and Jason smiled with approval. Angie said, "You can't mean that, Catherine."

"Angie, you are a healer and I appreciate that, but there are some people that will never fit into your society and just like healing an infection or sickness, the bad parts need to be removed." Catherine said.

"You're not alone in that belief Catherine." Tom said. "There are a lot of us in the village that believe the same thing."

We continued walking to their house and when we got to our room, I asked, "Catherine, when did you become so wise and grown up?"

Catherine looked at me and said. "I lost my parents to raiders when I was an baby. We were attacked dozens of times after that. Many times from groups that came to live in Elmira. That is until you came. After you left, your brother did the same thing the Murphy's are doing. This village will suffer because of their tolerance. That was my life until I met you, and I won't be a part of it again. If I can, I will not hesitate in the future. That's how I became so wise and grown up as you say."

I smiled at her and held her until we both fell asleep.

CHAPTER 23

T he next morning, I got up and left Catherine to sleep. She was worn out from the stress of the previous night. I found Tom sitting on the porch with some tea and sat down next to him.

"Tom," I asked, "what can you tell me about the Murphy's?"

Tom was quiet for a moment and then said, "They arrived here around the end of April. They came in from the south and said they passed through Elmira earlier that month."

I stopped him there and said, "Jim and I were in Elmira for the last year and they never passed through there in April. What else do you know about them?"

"The four of them showed up with their horses and a couple pack mules. They set up camp by the feeder creek south of here and said they were planning on panning for gold. They put up a wall tent and no one has seen them panning for gold yet. That's been five months. They trade at Jenkin's Trading Post with silver and gold coins, and every once in a while they go hunting. Most of the time, they sit around doing nothing or walking around town causing trouble." Tom said.

"They probably came down from the north and circled to the south before entering town." I said. "It's been my experience that men traveling alone and stopping at small towns are usually running or hiding from something. I would have known if they came up from Elmira."

Tom looked at me hard and said, "I wish I had your experience fighting raiders and bad men. Most of us didn't question their arrival because they brought hard currency into town. But, since they have caused so much trouble many of us are questioning their motives for staying here."

"What kind of trouble have they caused?" I asked.

"Well, they have been accused of raping a young girl, but before it came in front of the council, she recanted her story. I believe it was out of fear that she did. Angie examined her and she had been molested. Other times they have been in drunken fights and some things have been stolen from homes since they arrived. There has never been any proof to implicate them, but all this started happening since they arrived." Tom said.

As we were talking, Angie and Catherine came out of the house. Catherine had her pack with her and threw mine to me.

"We're leaving Jack." Was all she said.

I nodded, and turned to Tom and Angie and said, "Keep an eye on the Murphy's. I think they are up to no good and someone will get hurt. Don't let anyone go around them alone."

Angie and Tom gave Catherine a hug goodbye, and then Angie came over to me. "She's a strong young woman Jack. Take good care of her." She whispered.

Jason was down by our canoe and I could see that he was developing a black eye. Catherine walked up to the canoe and threw her pack in and then walked up to Jason.

"Thank you for standing up for me yesterday Jason." Catherine said.

Jason smiled and winced from his cut lip and said, "Always. I don't like the Murphy's and it felt good to give them a little of their own back." They hugged and Catherine got into the canoe. Billy jumped in the middle on top of the packs.

Jason shook my hand and said, "Thanks Jack for stopping Mr. Murphy yesterday."

"You're welcome Jason", I said. "I've dealt with men like Murphy most of my adult life. Just promise me you will stay away from them. I'm sure they will try something again."

"I will." He said and then helped me push the canoe out into the lake. I jumped in and Catherine and I started paddling north up the lake. I noticed George and Andrew Murphy watching us from the fish house.

Catherine was quiet for a long time and I didn't want to interrupt her thoughts. We got into a rhythm and covered a couple miles before she stopped paddling and turned to look at me.

"What Catherine?" I asked.

Catherine looked determined and asked, "Can you teach me how to fight like you did with Mr. Murphy?"

"Yes." I said. "But it won't be the same for you as it is for me. I weigh a lot more and can use that against an opponent. I would have to teach you how to be quicker and how to break free if someone grabs ahold of you."

"I want to be able to stop someone from surprising me and pushing me down like George Murphy did." She said.

"Okay, we can work on it when we get back to the cabin. Let me think about it for a while to come up with ways someone your size can defend against a larger opponent."

"I don't want to just defend," she said. "I want to be able to attack if I have to."

"Okay, I'll think of something." I said.

We continued in silence for another few miles while I thought about what to teach her. As we turned west to cross the lake to the cabin, Catherine broke the silence again.

"What makes people turn bad?" she asked.

"That's a difficult question to answer," I said, "because everyone is different in their circumstances, what they think of themselves, and what they think of other people. No one is born 'bad'. As we grow up, the way we are raised has some influence on what we become. As we gain knowledge, we believe that what we think is the truth and that the world should follow some logical pattern. The world does follow a certain design, but when things don't go the way we may want them to, we may blame it on the world or other people as the problem. Once a person starts blaming something or someone for what happens to them, they change their actions and attitude. Instead of placing blame, we should accept that things have changed and change our actions to return to the path we wish to follow. We really don't have control over what happens around us. Do you remember always asking me as we traveled north what was going to happen the next day or week and I would always say 'I don't know and we'll see?' Well that is because the only control we actually have is at the present moment. Everything else is in the past and already happened and we can't change it, or it's in the future and we don't know what it will be yet. People become bad when they think continuously about the past that wasn't the way the wished it to be and then they decide to take what they want from others to make up for what they feel they lost or what they feel they are owed. A bad person can do 'good' and a good person can do 'bad'. So now that I say all of this, I guess that there isn't any real good answer to the question 'What makes a person turn bad?' I guess it could be because they haven't found a way to be happy."

"I'm happy when I'm with you Jack." Catherine said.

"I'm happiest when I'm with you also, Catherine." I said. "You can see by what each of us just said that the only time we are happy is in the present. We have happy memories, but we are happiest right now, when we are together."

"Yes, I see that." She said. "So let's forget about the Murphy's and just live our lives together."

"Great idea, we are almost home and even though I can't predict the future, I believe we will still have a lot of work to do to get ready for winter." I said.

"Ugh, don't remind me." Catherine said. "Since we weren't planning on being back today, let's take the rest of the day off and just lay around."

"Okay, after we make sure all the animals are good." I said.

◆ ◆ ◆

126

We arrived back at the cabin just before noon, and hauled our packs and the canoe up into the yard. Billy ran ahead and was greeted by the goats and horses. I checked their feed and water and decided to throw them another bundle of grass each, even though we had come back a day early. I checked on the chickens and let them out to roost in a small tree by the shed. Catherine went into the cabin and checked for any critters that may have found a way in. Everything looked secure, so she got some food out of the cold cellar and started making lunch. We ate a cold lunch with some hot tea. We hadn't said a word since we arrived and I finally broke the silence.

"Catherine, I thought of some things that I can teach you to protect yourself. Would you like to try them instead of just lay-ing around?" I asked.

She perked up and said. "Yes, that would be great."

We went out into the yard after cleaning up the kitchen, and I said, "I will explain the scenario first and then what you should do to respond to it, okay?"

"Can we try something like when George Murphy pushed me down first? She asked.

"Okay." I said. "Show me how he was standing and where you were."

Catherine positioned me facing directly towards her and then stood facing me with her feet together.

I said, "First never stand with your feet together during a confrontation. Always have them at least your shoulder width apart and your strong leg a half a step back. For you, that will be your right leg."

She stepped apart and back a half step with her right leg.

I asked, "Which hand did he push you with?"

"His right hand." She said.

"Okay, that means he's right handed." I said. "When I reach out towards you with my right hand, I want you to step in with your right foot towards my left shoulder and stay facing dir-ectly at me. We'll do it slowly at first."

I stepped forward and reached out my right hand towards

her and she stepped forward. I said, "Now I want you to reach up your right hand and push my left shoulder away from you."

Catherine pushed my left shoulder with her right hand and it turned me away from her and made my left foot follow, causing me to have to step back away from her to regain my balance.

"Did you see how I had to step away to regain my balance?" I asked. "Now when you have to do this move, make sure you do it like you want to hurt me. I want you to push as hard as you can."

"Okay." She said firmly.

"Let's try it again and this time a little faster." I said.

We got back into our starting positions and I asked her if she was ready. She nodded, so I reached out my right hand to push her and she stepped forward quickly and pushed my left shoulder hard. I stumbled backwards to regain my balance.

"Very good." I said. "We will practice that every day until you don't even have to think about it. Now another similar scenario is where the person grabs you by the shirt with their right hand before you can step in." I reached out and grabbed her shirt with a straight right arm. "Now, I want you to take your left hand and put it against the outside of my elbow and push it up and in."

Catherine put her left hand on my right elbow and pushed up and in. It forced my arm to lock straight and I had to let go of her shirt. She smiled and said, "That was too easy."

I said, "When you do this in real life, you will actually hit the outside of my right elbow as hard as you can and it can possibly break my arm. We won't practice at full force, but you need to be thinking 'Hit it hard' every time you do it." We practiced this move a couple times and then I asked her what she would do if someone grabbed her from behind?

She thought for a minute and said, "It would depend on how and where they grabbed me, I guess."

"Very good, they could grab you in a bear hug, or they could grab you by the neck with one hand." I said. I was glad to see she was thinking of different scenarios now.

"What do I do if they put me in a bear hug?" she asked.

I moved around behind her and put a bear hug around her shoulders pinning her arms to her side. I said, "Now as soon as you feel someone grabbing you like this, you have to move fast, or because of your size, they could pick you up. You need to make sure you keep your feet on the ground at all times." I picked her up and she squirmed, but couldn't break free.

"What do I do?" she asked.

I let her down and said, "As soon as you feel me reaching around you, and before I pick you up, I want you to lean forward and duck your head down to your chest."

I reached around her again and just as I locked my grip on her, she leaned forward and ducked her head. This forced me to lean forward at the same time. I said, "Now you have me with my face right behind your head. With your head ducked down against your chest, you can whip your head back and break my nose with the back of your head." She started moving and I let her go quickly and stepped back.

"Why did you let go?" she asked.

"I didn't want you to break my nose." I said.

"Chicken." She laughed.

"Yes I am." I said. "We can practice with me grabbing you from behind and you bending forward and ducking your head to throw me forward, but not the backwards head butt, okay?" We practiced this move a few times, and then I said, "Now if I was to grab you by the back of the neck with my right hand, I want you to turn quickly to your left and in towards me."

I grabbed her and she turned quickly to her left and was facing me. I said, "At the end of your turn you need to bring your right knee up and hit me in the crotch."

She laughed and said, "You mean in the balls?"

I smiled and said, "Yes, for a man it would be in the balls, but a woman could grab you the same way, and it would still hurt her to get a knee in the crotch. After you give them a knee in the crotch, they will let go and bend over forward. When they let go, step back and grab their head on either side and bring your knee right back up into their nose."

We practiced this slowly a few times, exaggerating the moves. After going back through all of the moves a few more times, I said, "That's enough for today. Let's follow your plan and lay around the rest of the day."

CHAPTER 24

W e spent the next two weeks practicing her defensive moves and working around the cabin. By now, it was the end of September and it was getting chilly at night. We took all the produce in from the garden and started drying the vegetables and spices.

We would cuddle in front of the fireplace every night and whenever Catherine started rubbing my leg or openly suggesting we have sex, I would stop her. She was frustrated with me, but she quit getting hurt by my constantly putting her off. She would just smile at me and say, "You will give in someday."

One evening I said, "We should make a couple more hunting trips before it snows."

"What should we go for?" She asked.

"It would be nice to get a young moose, but we should also try for some grouse and smoke them." I said.

We planned a hunt a couple days later and left that following morning, heading northwest along the mountains. We got a dozen grouse on the way, but didn't see any sign of moose. We came to the mouth of a canyon with a well-used game trail leading to the north. There was fresh sign of elk and deer using it so we headed up the trail.

We were about a mile in and the trail was getting narrow and heading up the side of the canyon. It was very quiet and I started getting an uneasy feeling.

"Catherine, I think something has spooked the animals in this canyon. I don't hear the usual sounds." I said.

Catherine smiled and said, "I noticed that about twenty minutes ago. What do you think it is?"

"I'm not sure, it could be wolves or a bear, but I haven't

noticed Billy getting interested in scents in the wind. The trail turns around a rock outcrop about three hundred yards ahead if I remember correctly and on the other side is a small meadow. We can turn the horses around there and head back down. There is no sense continuing ahead if the game is spooked." I said.

As we sat and talked, we heard men laughing up ahead around a bend in the trail. It was too narrow to turn the horses around, and I didn't like the idea of turning our backs to the men approaching. I quickly got down off of Betty and motioned for Catherine to get down from Zack. I pulled the .308 out of its scabbard and handed it to Catherine. I handed her a loaded magazine and whispered to her. "Climb up the side of this ridge here and get down behind a log at least forty yards up. Make sure you have a clear view of me and the trail in front and behind me. Take Billy with you."

We had been together so long now, that Catherine didn't hesitate. I tied the horses to a tree by the side of the trail and walked forward about twenty feet and sat down against a tree trunk. Catherine was so quiet; I barely heard here climb the side of the canyon. I heard Billy though. When all sound stopped, I watched the trail ahead. I could hear horses walking down the trail and thought I could make out four different voices. After about five minutes, a horse and rider came around the bend in the trail about a hundred fifty yards ahead. The rider stopped immediately when he saw me and turned and said something to the riders behind him. The rider sat and watched me for about fifteen minutes.

Catherine climbed the side of the canyon quickly and noise-lessly. Billy rushed up ahead and made scrambling noises. When she was about forty yards up, she found a tree that had blown over in a storm and picked a place about halfway along its length that was level and free of branches. She motioned Billy over and made him lay down beside her while she set the rifle up on the tree with her day pack as a rest.

While she waited, she scanned the area in front of and behind Jack. He just sat down against a tree and closed his eyes. A short while later; she heard noises coming up from below Jack in the Canyon bottom. She had a clear view of the bottom, and saw a man sneaking along and angling up behind Jack, Betty and Zack. She waited until he was set behind Jack, and aimed the .308 at his chest.

I heard noises in the canyon below me and knew someone was sneaking around behind me. I just hoped Catherine was watching behind me. Soon enough, the rider started forward and two riders following him came into view. They walked their horses slowly forward until they were about fifteen feet from me. The lead rider was on a beautiful chestnut mare, and the riders following him were on an Appaloosa mare and a black stallion. They eyed me closely and finally the leader got down from his horse. They were an ugly bunch. The leader had long greasy hair and rotten teeth, and the two younger men behind him looked similar enough to him that they could be related.

"Whatcha doing out here all alone Mister?" he asked.

"Hunting and traveling north to Calgary." I said.

"You live around here?" he asked.

"No, I'm just headed north to Calgary for the winter." I repeated.

The two men behind him were in line, so the rear man didn't have a clear view of me, but the second man could see me clearly over the leader's horse.

"Nice pistol you have there." The leader said.

"Yes it is." I said.

"I think you should give it to me." He said.

I looked at him hard and said, "You can have part of it."

He turned slightly towards the other two riders and laughing said, "You hear that boys, he said I can have part of it. Which part?"

As he turned away, I saw the small pistol drop from his sleeve into his right hand. I pulled my Python and shot him in the chest. At the same instant, I heard the boom of the .308 and heard a meaty 'thwop' behind me. I didn't hesitate; I rushed forward to put the leader's horse between me and the second rider. The leader fell back against the horse and it pushed against the second rider's horse. I reached the leader's horse a split second later, just as the second rider got his horse under control and pulled his pistol. I ducked down behind the leader's horse just as he shot at me. Then his head blew up, and I heard the second boom of the .308.

The blast of the pistol from the second rider was right next to the head of the leader's horse, and it reared back and stepped on my left foot. I felt the bones break, and fell back to the side of the trail. I could see the rear rider trying to back his horse up and turn around, but the trail was too narrow. I heard the third boom of the .308 and that rider fell from his saddle.

Catherine could hear the conversation between Jack and the leader of the group. She listened, but kept her aim on the man behind Jack. She kept both eyes open as she looked through the scope so she could see what Jack was doing also. When he pulled his pistol and shot the leader, she eased the trigger on the rifle and shot the man behind Jack in the center of the chest. She chambered another round quickly.

She saw Jack rush forward and watched as the second rider pulled his pistol and shot at Jack. Jack fell backward behind the leader's horse. 'Nooo...' She didn't hesitate, bringing the rifle to bear on the head of the second rider and pulled the trigger. His head exploded. She reloaded without thinking. The last rider was trying to back away, and she eased the scope around to his chest and fired a third shot. She watched as he fell from his horse.

'No', she thought, *'Jack can't be dead.'*

I yelled, "Catherine wait, don't come down yet. We don't know if that is all of them."

Catherine yelled, "I thought he shot you when you fell back."

"No, the horse knocked me down." I yelled not wanting to worry her. The pain in my foot was getting worse.

We waited for another ten minutes and as the adrenaline wore off, the pain in my foot reached a point where I was about to pass out.

"Catherine come on down now." I yelled.

I heard Catherine and Billy sliding down the side of the canyon and a minute later she was standing in front of me.

"What's wrong? Are you hit?" she asked.

"No," I gasped, "the horse stepped on my foot and I think it's broken. Go down the trail with Billy and get the fourth man's horse and then come back here."

She looked determined to stay, so I smiled at her and said, "I'll be okay for a few minutes until you get back."

Catherine headed up the trail with Billy in the lead and before they had gone fifty yards, I passed out.

Catherine went down the trail with Billy and kept the rifle ready. When she reached the bend in the trail, Billy had already gone around. She heard him yipping, but it was a sound he made when he was happy.

Catherine came around the bend in the trail; she saw the fourth man's horse tied to a tree. At the base of the tree, three young girls were also tied up. She rushed forward and asked, "Who are you?" Then she realized they all had gags over their mouths. She cut them loose and said, "All those bad men are dead, but Jack is hurt. Bring the horse and follow me back down the trail." She turned and rushed back to Jack.

◆ ◆ ◆

I was in a stampede and my left foot was stuck in a hole. Horses were racing by me and I was sure I was going to get trampled...

"Jack, wake up, Jack!" I heard Catherine pleading.

I opened my eyes and saw Catherine and three dirty faces looking at me. Two of the faces had at least one black eye and cut lips. One was redheaded and one was blonde. The third was a tiny little brown haired, brown eyed girl. Or boy, I couldn't tell through all the dirt.

"Who are you?" I slurred.

"I found them tied to a tree with the fourth guy's horse. What do you want us to do?" Catherine asked anxiously.

I tried to focus my thoughts and saw Angie's face in my mind. "You need to get me to Angie."

I felt someone pulling my moccasin off and the pain made me pass out again. Then I felt someone pulling me up into a sitting position. I had no measure of time.

Catherine said, "Jack you need to wake up so we can get you up onto a horse."

I shook my head to clear it and tried to ignore the pain in my foot. Catherine and two of the others got behind me and under my arms and lifted me to my feet. The little girl, or was it a boy was watching with huge brown eyes and was holding onto Billy's neck. I put my weight on my right foot and they steered my horse Betty beside me. Pushing from behind, I was able to pull myself up onto the saddle. My left foot was wrapped in a cloth and I could see blood soaking through. *'This is not good'.* I thought. I leaned forward and wrapped my arms around Betty's neck and muttered to Catherine, "Tie me to her back so I don't fall off."

Catherine got a rope and wrapped it around Betty and tied me tightly to her saddle. I lost consciousness again.

I opened my eyes and saw a torch bobbing ahead of me. It was dark. I heard horses shuffling behind me and saw three people I didn't know riding them. Catherine was walking ahead and carrying the torch. I passed out again.

I felt arms pulling me down off of Betty. It was light out. *'Where was I?'* Catherine and two other people helped me up the stairs of the porch, into the cabin and lay me onto the couch. *'I'm at my cabin'.* I opened my eyes and saw Catherine looking at me with tears in her eyes.

"You need to get Angie." I whispered.

"I can't leave you Jack," she cried, "and I can't paddle the canoe by myself."

I grunted and passed out again.

When I opened my eyes again, I was looking at Angie. She lifted my head and said "Drink this Jack. It will make you sleep while I fix your foot."

When I finally woke up, Catherine and Angie were sitting across from me and Tom, Jason and some other men I didn't know were standing behind them.

"I'm thirsty." I rasped.

Catherine jumped up and got a glass of water. She held it for me as I drank in sips.

"Are you hungry?" Catherine asked.

"No, just thirsty." I mumbled.

Angie stepped in and held another glass to my lips and said, "You need to drink this and sleep some more so your foot can heal."

I sipped it and it tasted horrible. Catherine gave me sips of water to wash it down. I closed my eyes and slept.

CHAPTER 25

I *was at the bottom of a deep dark mine shaft, and I could hear a monotone humming. Was it some type of machine? I could see light above me. I started climbing out.*

I slowly opened my eyes and tried to focus. I turned my head towards the humming sound and focused on it. Slowly my vision returned, and I could see a small child sitting next to Billy on the floor petting and hugging him. The child was the source of the humming. The child had straight brown hair, round ears that stuck out on the sides of her head through the hair, a pointed little nose, and a small chin. I rasped, "Hi."

The child looked at me with huge brown eyes and let out an 'Eeep' and ran from the room. Billy followed after the child. A moment later, Angie and Catherine came into the living room and smiled at me.

"You scared Mouse." She said.

"Who? What?" I rasped. "Water please."

Angie held a glass of water to my lips as I scooched up. The movement sent shooting pain up my left leg forcing a groan out. After a few sips, I cleared my throat.

"How long have I been out?" I asked.

"Only about twelve hours." Angie said.

"What day is it?" I asked.

"You want to know how long since you got hurt?" Angie asked.

"Yes." I said. "How long did it take for you to go get Angie, Catherine?"

"Catherine smiled and said, "I couldn't leave you, and none of the girls could handle a canoe. I couldn't go alone, so we improvised."

"Okay, … girls?" I asked.

"You know the brush pile we had been adding to since we arrived here. Well, Lizzy and I lit it on fire and threw green pine branches on it so it sent up a lot of smoke. About three hours later, Angie, Tom and Jason showed up with nine other men." She said.

"Well thank you and good thinking." I said. "Could I get something to eat? I'm starving. You can tell me the rest of the story after I eat something."

Angie nodded to someone behind the couch and a slim red haired freckle faced girl came around with a plate of food. She was very pretty despite the black eye and cut lip. She looked familiar. Like someone I had dreamt meeting.

"This is Lizzy, Jack." Angie said. "She is one of the girls you saved."

She saw the confusion on my face and said, "Eat and we will talk after."

I took the plate from Lizzy and smiled at her. She blushed a deep red and it showed all the freckles on her face.

"Thank you, Lizzy." I said.

"N… N… No thank you, Mr. Jack for saving me, Pam, and Mouse." She stammered.

"Just Jack is fine, Lizzy." I smiled at her again and she blushed even redder. "I guess you can catch me up on what I missed after I eat." *'Who are Pam and Mouse? Well I can guess who Mouse is, but what a weird name. Pam I have no clue.'* I thought.

I ate, but was full after I had about a quarter of the meal. It was just a meat sandwich with some potatoes fried on the side. While I ate, Lizzy and Catherine went back into the kitchen whispering to each other.

After I finished and handed the plate to Angie, I asked. "How bad is it?"

Angie had a serious look, and said, "You are really lucky you didn't lose the foot. If Catherine hadn't sent up the smoke when she did early yesterday morning, I probably would have had to remove it. You had most of the bones broken and a few toes broken also. I was able to reset the bones and stop the bleeding where they poked through the skin. Now we have to wait for the swelling to go down so I can check the set and then we need to put a cast on it."

"How long?" I asked.

"Always straight to the point, huh Jack?" Angie said. "Probably about ten weeks before the cast comes off."

"Ten weeks?" I said. "I can't lie around that long. Winter's coming and there is still a lot to do around here."

"You won't be lying around for ten weeks. You will have to move around to exercise, and Jason said he would make you some crutches." Angie said.

"That's not what I meant and you know it. I can't do the hunting and feeding the animals if I can't get around good." I argued.

"You're not alone, Jack. You have help from Catherine and we will help as much and as often as we can." Angie said.

"Where are Tom and Jason?" I asked.

"They took a few of the men with them and followed your trail to see to the dead men and try to find out where they came from. There wasn't much on the horses Catherine returned with, so they must have had some things cached close by. Jason will find it if it's there." Angie said.

"Why did so many men come with you?" I asked.

"It's a long story, and I think we should wait until the men that left get back to tell it." "In the meantime, I think it is time you met the girls." She nodded to someone in the kitchen and a few moments later, Lizzy, a pudgy young blonde and the little child came around the couch into the living room.

"Jack, you've met Lizzy," Catherine said. "This is Pam and Mouse."

Mouse let out an 'Eeep' and ran over to Billy and sat down hugging him. Billy looked as happy as a dog could look.

Catherine smiled at her and as I sat up, Pam came over to me and hugged me hesitantly.

"Thank you, Mr. Jack for saving us." Pam said with tears in her eyes.

"You're welcome; Pam, but I can't take the credit. Catherine did most of it and just Jack please." I said a little embarrassed.

I looked over at Mouse and decided it was an appropriate nickname. She just stared at me with those huge brown eyes.

Angie shooed the girls back into the kitchen and sat down opposite me. She had a concerned look on her face, so I said. "What?"

"Those girls have all been molested and the older two have been beaten badly. I've given them a thorough exam and they are a little undernourished, but hopefully, neither Pam nor Lizzy are pregnant. Mouse hasn't reached puberty yet so she isn't." Angie said. "We still haven't asked them their story yet."

I felt the rage well up inside me. "I should have shot those bastards as soon as I saw them. I have seen and killed enough bad men to know the likes of them. I won't hesitate next time. I couldn't imagine Catherine going through that."

"We'll get their story after they have had a chance to settle in. For now though, I think you should rest some more and we'll talk after dinner. Tom, Jason and the men should be back by dark, and we have a large meal to prepare." Angie said.

I just nodded, deep in my own thoughts. *'Why do I always give men like that the benefit of the doubt? What they did to those poor girls is unforgivable. I know, I know. I'm not a murderer, and things turned out okay. Except for my foot that is.'*

CHAPTER 26

I woke up just after dark to the sounds in the kitchen. As I listened and tried to clear my head, Tom, Jason, and a couple men from the village came in the front door. They had a grim look on their faces.

Tom sat down beside me after I sat up and asked, "How are you feeling Jack?"

I smiled faintly and said, "I've been better, but never worse."

Catherine, Lizzie, and Angie came in from the kitchen and handed around plates of food to all the men. Lizzie handed Jason a plate and he smiled at her and said thank you. She blushed and looked down then smiled up at him. Jason blushed and glanced at his mother. She just smiled at him and handed me a plate. We ate in silence and I could tell something was bothering Tom.

After we finished, I looked at Tom and said, "Okay, out with it. You have something on your mind."

Tom looked at Jason and the other men and shrugged. "Catherine was right Jack. About a week ago, the Murphy's killed Mike Jenkins and robbed the Trading Post. Their trail headed north and we followed it until we lost it in a canyon. When we got back to the village, we saw the smoke coming from here and thought the worst. Mr. Murphy kept bragging about taking care of the do-gooders across the lake. We were relieved to find you guys alright."

I looked down at my foot, and Tom quickly said, "Well, mostly so."

"So, you thought they came around the lake and hit us, right?"

"Yes," Tom said, "We should have sent someone across right

away to warn you, but the village was in a panic. We followed their trail for 3 days before we lost it. Then we headed back."

"What about the men Catherine and I shot?" I asked.

Tom got a strange look on his face and turned and asked Angie, "Would you take Lizzie and Catherine into the kitchen."

Catherine got a stubborn look on her face and looked at me. I said, "I will let you know everything after we are done talking. You must be upset having killed three men two days ago."

Catherine replied angrily, "I didn't kill men two days ago, I killed animals."

"Okay," I said, "you can stay and listen but let them finish so we get the whole story."

Tom looked at Jason and said, "Show it to him."

Jason pulled a folded piece of paper out of his pocket and handed it to me. I gave him a questioning look and he said, "We found their cache about a hundred fifty yards up the trail in a small meadow. This was in it."

I unfolded the paper and my eyes went wide. It was a hand drawn picture and physical description of me with a $1000 reward for anyone that killed me. At the bottom it said "Bring the girl with him to me in Lewiston unharmed: Signed Jim Anders." I dropped the paper and everything started swirling around me.

Angie and Catherine rushed forward. Angie yelled for Lizzie to bring a wet towel and she placed it on my forehead. Catherine picked up the paper and stared at it.

"I'm sorry Jack." Tom said.

Jason and the men shuffled around and whispered "Sorry."

Catherine looked angry and said, "That bastard. I'll kill him."

Angie hugged her and said, "We have other things to worry about right now."

"No," Catherine yelled, "I'm going to go to Lewiston and kill the bastard."

I was too shocked to say anything. I looked at Tom and Angie and asked, "Could I have some time alone for a bit?"

Tom and Angie moved everyone out into the kitchen, but

Catherine sat down beside me. I had never seen her so angry. She stared at the paper. I reached over to put my arm around her and winced from the pain in my foot. She leaned against me and laid her head on my chest. I slowly took the paper from her hand and placed it on the coffee table.

"What are we going to do Jack?" Catherine asked.

"I don't know. I still can't predict the future and I don't plan on doing anything until I can walk again."

"Oh," she said, "I'm so angry I forgot. I'm sorry. Even though I hate Jim I know he's your brother."

"Jim has lost it by the looks of it." I said. "I'm sorry he is not the same as he was when we were kids, but it looks like I don't have a brother anymore. And I wish you weren't involved."

Tom and Jason came back into the living room and sat down a little while later. Tom looked at me hard and said, "Looks like we have a raider problem again. I'm going to need some advice from you on how to prepare for it."

I looked at Tom and Jason and could feel the fear they felt. I said, "Tom, if you and your men could draw a plan of your village for me, I will design some fortifications for you. You will have to start training everyone, including the women to shoot."

Angie walked in and said, "Not me, I won't shoot anyone."

Catherine sat up and looked hard at her aunt. "Angie before I saw those men about to kill Jack, I didn't plan on killing anyone either. You will do whatever you have to and protect those that you love. Even kill."

Angie looked down and said, "I know you're right, but until that happens, I will save anyone that's injured."

"Then I'll make sure their dead so you don't have to save them." Catherine said angrily.

Angie looked at Catherine shocked.

Catherine smiled and said, "I won't apologize for that. When I said earlier that it wasn't men that I killed, just animals,

I should apologize to the animals because they act according to their nature. Those men are unnatural and shouldn't be allowed to live and hurt others."

I noticed the other men filtering in to listen and saw them nodding agreement with what Catherine was saying.

I quickly spoke up. "Angie I agree with you. We need a moral compass or neighbors will start killing neighbors over the smallest slight. We can't let this get out of hand. We will make preparations to stop raids, but we can't let fear run wild."

I saw that everyone was thinking about that, but Catherine still looked adamant. I looked at Tom and said, "Could you do me a favor?"

Tom said, "Sure, what do you need?"

"Could you send someone down to Boville and warn them. I think that the Murphy's headed north to throw you off the trail, but turned south where you lost them. It should take them a couple weeks of rough traveling to get to Boville and they have been on the move for a week. If you sent a canoe down the lake you should be able to beat them by a few days." I said.

Four of the men immediately volunteered to leave the first thing in the morning and travel hard to reach Boville. Tom gave them instructions to tell Bo everything that had taken place in the north part of the lake. Angie and Jason packed supplies for the trip with Lizzie and Pam's help.

I was exhausted and nodded off with Catherine holding me.

The next morning before sunrise the men left and paddled hard to the south. They stayed on the west side of the lake to stay in the calmer water.

After breakfast, Angie examined my foot and said that she would put a cast on it in a couple days. It was still swollen and red from the trauma with stitches all along the top. As she was examining me, I said, "Angie please don't change who you are. I agree with what you said last night and we need people like you to prevent more chaos from happening."

"Thank you Jack." She said gratefully. "How is it that you always see all sides of an issue?"

"I've seen this happen too many times before right after the "Big Shit". Neighbors killing neighbors. If we don't stand up for good, evil will always replace it." I said.

Angie just smiled and said, "You are always a good and forgiving man Jack."

I felt the back of the couch move and looked up into Mouse's big brown eyes. She let out an "Eeep" and ran back into the kitchen.

"That little one has been through the most. We don't know her name because she was taken by those men before Lizzie and Pam. She should be able to talk, but she was abused to the point of withdrawal." Angie said.

"Angie, could you gather the girls so I can talk to them?" I asked.

Angie called the girls into the living room and they looked scared. I smiled at them to ease their fear and asked them to sit down. Catherine sat next to me, with Lizzy on the other side of her. Pam took a chair, and Mouse sat with Billy on the floor.

"Lizzy, Pam, Mouse, I want to thank you for saving my life." Was all I said.

Lizzy and Pam looked shocked. Mouse just gave me a little smile. Lizzy said, "Mr. Jack..."

"Just Jack please." I interrupted.

Lizzy started again a little shyly. "J... Jack, I mean. You saved us."

"Lizzy, Pam, Mouse, if I had known you were there, I wouldn't have met with those men to talk. But because of what they did, it was fortunate that things turned out as they did. If it had just been Catherine and I, she would have had a difficult time getting me back here without your help and according to Angie; I may have lost the foot. So thank you." I said.

"Now I need to know how this happened to you and find a way to get you back to your families." I said.

Lizzy told the story for them with Pam interrupting every once in a while with her version. It turns out that those men were the Jacobs clan. I only saw three of them, but the man I shot was their leader, Joshua Jacobs. The man behind me was his brother Jacob, and the two younger men on the horses were James and Jonathon. What is it with the J's? Anyway they had come east from Spokane and already had Mouse when they came across Pam's family farm on the Idaho border. They killed Pam's father and brother, then raped her mother who fought them fiercely. They killed Pam's mother and found Pam in the root cellar and took her with them. They took turns raping her and always kept her and Mouse tied up. After about a week, they came across another farm and left Pam and Mouse with Jonathon while they went down and caught Lizzy walking along the trail and took her prisoner. They then turned south towards Priest Lake looking for a man that had a $1000 bounty on him. Pam and Lizzy were raped and beaten daily on the trip by one or the other of the Jacobs'. They tended to ignore Mouse during this time. When they came across me on the trail, Joshua recognized me from the picture, but wanted to torture me to find Catherine. The rest of the story was mine and Catherine's.

I looked at them and sighed. "I am very sorry for what they did to you girls, and they got what they deserved. Can you tell me how to contact any of your relatives to get you back to them?"

The girls looked at each other and I could see they had a connection from their ordeal. Lizzy and Pam nodded to each other and Mouse let out a quiet 'eeep'.

Lizzy, always the spokesperson for the group said, "We don't have any relatives that are alive." Then hurriedly she asked, "Can't we stay with you and Catherine?"

As they pleaded with me, Jason and Tom came in from outside. Tom looked at Angie and said, "We can take you back to our village and find you families to live with."

Mouse jumped up and ran over to me and hugged me and said in a whisper, "No, please."

Everyone was shocked, me most of all. No one had ever heard her speak. She held onto me tightly and started her humming sound. I hugged her.

Lizzy stood up and said, "We don't want to leave, can't we stay with you, puhleeze."

I was torn. These girls have been hurt so much, but I didn't have enough supplies to feed and clothe three more girls.

Angie could see my indecision and said, "We can work it out so you can stay as long as Jack is okay with it."

All four girls, Catherine included looked at me pleadingly. Mouse tightened her grip on me and looked up at me with those huge brown eyes.

"I guess we will work something out." I said. They all smiled and Mouse climbed up into my lap and hugged my neck. It almost brought me to tears.

"Enough for now! Tom and I have some things we need to discuss." I exclaimed.

CHAPTER 27

"Tom, were you able to draw up plans of your village for me?" I asked.

"Yes." He said while pulling a large piece of paper that was rolled up from behind the couch. It was an old poster I had in the back bedroom from a rock band called Aerosmith. They had drawn the village on the back of it. He handed it to me and sat down next to me. We unrolled it in our laps and I could see the outline of the lake shore and details of all the buildings drawn on it. There were ten pine trees drawn at the top.

I asked, "What are these pine trees for?"

Tom laughed and said, "That's the name of our village; 'Ten Pines'. I guess you wouldn't know that since you only spent one night there."

I studied the drawing and asked questions on how many paces it was between buildings. There were twelve houses in a semi-circle around the village center, anchored around the Trading Post. There were another ten houses, twelve barns and the fish house outside these spread out haphazardly. There were lines indicating the trails in and out of the village to the North, South, and East. There was a feeder stream to the North and one to the South. I asked Tom how many paces the streams were across and how deep they were. As Tom gave me his estimates, I placed the drawing on the coffee table and used a pencil and wrote notes at each point I asked about. I drew lines between the twelve houses and the Trading Post on the back sides of each building.

"This is your final defensible area." I said indicating the village center. "Build walls along the backs of these buildings. I would suggest they be made of five to six inch round pine logs about twelve feet long and buried at least three feet into the ground. This will stop horses, but not men. Build platforms on the inside so a man or woman can stand on them and shoot out, and duck down when they need to reload."

"What about the buildings outside the circle?" Tom asked. "The people that live there aren't going to like leaving them unprotected, me included. This is our house here." He pointed to one of the houses drawn outside the circle I had drawn. It was closer to the lake.

"Well Tom, it's the middle of October now and the ground is going to start freezing. Dig the ditch for the logs as quickly as you can and set as many logs as you can before it starts to snow in mid-November. Raiders hole up for the winter and won't be coming around until it thaws in April. As far as the buildings outside the circle, you will have to be prepared to lose them if attacked by a large enough group." I said. "These ones closest to the village center but still outside the circle should be fortified with heavy shutters with shooting holes in them. They will provide fields of fire here, here, and here." I pointed and drew triangular lines from the sides and back of the houses. "That only leaves four houses and the barns and fish house outside the protected area. These six houses closest to the circle should have a path from them to the inner circle that can be covered by shooters inside the circle with a crawl space to get under the wall. I would suggest making lift gates here and here." I drew them on the map. "It will inconvenience those living outside the wall, because they will have to walk around to them, but they should get used to it."

Tom looked at what I had drawn and shrugged. He said, "It's going to take a lot of work to build this but I think everyone will be up to it after we tell them about the Jacobs coming after you. I think you and the girls should move over to the village also."

I shook my head and said, "We will be safe here at least until spring. I don't want to uproot everyone and split them up by moving in with others in your village. You seem to be pretty crowded as it is over there."

Tom nodded and said, "We are, and we were planning on expanding next spring."

Since I didn't get any argument from Tom, I continued, "You will need to clear all the trees and brush at least a hundred paces from these six outer houses. You can't leave anything for Raiders to hide behind. What about this ridge to the East of the village? How high do you think it is?"

Tom thought about it and then asked a couple of the younger men in the group how high they thought it was. It seems it was the favorite place for the younger members of the village to hang out to get away from their parents. One of the boys, Sammy said, "It's probably at least a hundred feet up."

I asked, "How far is it from the village?"

Sammy thought and said, "About five hundred yards at least."

I took another piece of paper and drew a line with a ruler two inches up. This would scale to fifty feet per inch. Then I drew a line thirty inches long attached to the base of the line. Tom and the other men looked confused, but then I drew a line from the top of the short two inch line to the end of the thirty inch line to get the angle. It was a very shallow right triangle. At the pointed end of the triangle, I drew a line a quarter inch tall straight up. Catherine and Lizzy had been leaning against the back of the couch watching, and Catherine giggled. I smiled back at her, knowing that we had been studying geometry to teach her how to estimate a bullets drop over long distances. I said, "Catherine would you like to explain to these men what this means."

"Sure." She smiled and said. "The two inch line is the height to the top of the ridge. The thirty inch line is the distance from the ridge to the wall you are going to build. The quarter inch line is the height of the wall. It's not really to scale, because if you put twelve foot logs three feet into the ground, it will only be about nine feet tall. So it should only be three sixteenths of an inch Jack. Anyone shooting from the ridge with iron sights will have a very hard time seeing a target, especially if it keeps moving. If they have a scoped rifle, which is rare, and they aim their crosshairs at a target at the top of the wall, the bullet drop will make the bullet hit lower on the wall. The angle is just over three degrees, so the distance will not be affected by much, but depending on the bullet weight and accuracy of the rifle, the bullet could drop anywhere from ten to twenty five inches."

Lizzy and all the men looked at her with surprise. Catherine just smiled and said, "I have hit targets as far out as six hundred yards. Not dead center, mind you, but I hit them."

I was always amazed at how quickly Catherine figured math problems in her head. I smiled at her and said, "I think you should put a watch tower on that ridge and man it during the months that the Raiders are active. You should also put hides back of the ridge for the watchers to retreat to in case a lot of shooters decide to use the ridge to shoot into the village. If you have men who are stealthy, they could also take out some of these shooters with arrows so it doesn't sound like a gunfight to the Raiders attacking the village directly." I looked at Jason, and he and a couple of the other young men nodded.

"That's all I have right now Tom. I will come over in the spring and check on your progress and make some other suggestions. I wish I had spent a little more time there, but this drawing should get you started." I said.

Tom asked, "Jack, are you sure you are going to be safe here until spring?"

"Yes." I said. "We didn't have raids in any of the towns we protected from mid-November until late April. They are typically lazy men and don't travel during winter if they don't have to."

"Well that's still a month away, and others besides the Jacobs could be looking for you and Catherine. You'll be laid up for a couple months, so if you don't mind, I am going to leave a couple men here until then. The lake will start freezing up around then and they can head back and help with the building." Tom said.

Jason looked at Lizzy and blurted out, "I'll stay." Lizzy blushed.

Angie had been listening from the kitchen and came in and said, "I have to stay for at least another week, so you can stay until then Jason, then you will have to take me back across the lake."

Jason looked like he was going to argue and then thought better of it. "Okay, Mom, then I can head back with some more supplies for Jack and the girls."

"That would be nice Jason." I said. "Thank you."

Tom rolled up the drawing and said, "Well I think I will head back in the morning. I will see who else should stay and let you know. It's late, and I think everyone should get some rest."

Everyone moved off, the several men that came with Tom went out to the tents they had in the yard, and Catherine and Angie sat down with me. Angie examined my foot again and said that she would have to find some white pine bark tomorrow to make the stuff for a cast.

Catherine said, "Jack, you stink. I am going to boil some water and wash you off."

I lifted my arm and sniffed, "Whew, you're right. That would be nice."

As Catherine put wood in the fireplace and went to the kitchen to get water for the boiling pot, Mouse climbed up next to me and stared at me with her huge brown eyes.

"Come here." I smiled and she crawled into my lap and put her arms around my neck. She started her monotone humming and Billy came over and climbed onto the couch next to me. Before Catherine had the water hot, both Mouse and Billy had fallen asleep.

Angie carried Mouse off to bed, and Catherine came over to me with a pan of hot water and some towels. She smiled at me and said, "Take your clothes off."

I took off my shirt and struggled to get my jeans off. Catherine eased the pants leg over my swollen foot and helped to remove my jeans. She nodded at my underwear and said, "Those too."

"Nope, just hand me the towels and the soap and water and I will take care of it." I said.

She dipped a hand towel into the hot water and rubbed it with some soap. I reached for it, but she held it back and told me to lean forward while she washed my back. She washed my neck and back, rinsing the towel frequently and applying more soap. When my back was finished, she reached around me and started washing my chest. When she got down to my belly, I grabbed her hand and said, "I can get that."

Catherine got a pout on her face, but let go of the towel. While I cleaned my underarms and belly, she dried my back. Then she came around and took the towel from me again and rinsed it and started washing my legs. She started at my good foot and washed up to my knee, and then she washed my ankle and calf on my bad leg. She rinsed the towel again and started washing my thighs. When she reached my inner thigh, I started to get an erection. She smiled and winked at me, so I stopped her again and finished my legs while she dried my lower legs. When she finished, I took the drying towel from her and finished my thighs. Then I laid the towel over my groin. It didn't hide that I had an erection, but it made me feel better.

We were finished and she brought me a clean shirt and pants. I put the shirt on and she stopped me when I tried to get the pants on. She took out a pocket knife and cut the threads in the seam of the left pant leg to the knee. When I moved the towel, she grinned at me again and looked at the bulge in my underwear.

"Your underwear stinks too. Let me help you change them for some clean ones." She said.

I put the towel back over me and slid my underwear down to my knees. I kept the towel over me and asked her to pull the dirty underwear off and put the clean pair on up to my knees.

She looked disappointed, but did as I asked. I pulled them on under the towel and then she helped me get the pants on.

When she finished, I asked her to help me to the bathroom. I hadn't eaten much in the last couple of days, but I was feeling the urgency now. She helped me stand, and Angie came back in and helped her get me to the bathroom. I leaned on the counter and then sat on the toilet. Catherine stood in the doorway waiting to help.

"I can get it from here." I said.

"It's not a problem." She answered.

"It is for me. I would like a little privacy." I responded.

She got a disappointed look on her face again and huffed as she closed the door. I could see Angie smiling at me behind her. I got my pants down and did my business, and then got redressed. I yelled for them to help me back to the couch.

Catherine yelled back, "Wait a minute while we change the cover on the couch with a clean sheet."

A few minutes later, Angie and Catherine helped me back to the couch. I said thanks and good night to Angie and lay down. Catherine tried to lie down beside me, but I moved so there wasn't room.

"You should sleep in our bed." I said.

"I don't want to sleep alone." She whined. "Pam, Lizzy and Mouse are in the back bedroom, and Tom and Angie are in the front bedroom."

"I'm sorry, but there isn't enough room on the couch for both of us to sleep." I said. I was thinking more of the closeness and with her beside me, I wouldn't get any sleep.

Catherine huffed again and said, "Good night," as she stomped up the stairs to the Master bedroom.

CHAPTER 28

The next morning, I was woken by thunder outside. Angie and the girls were in the kitchen making breakfast, and Tom and his men were out on the porch talking. Pam came out of the kitchen and handed me a cup of tea.

"Thank you Pam." I said. When I sipped it, it tasted like Chamomile tea, but it had a bitter after taste. "What is in this?" I asked her.

Pam looked down and said, "Angie put something in it that will help to reduce the swelling in your foot. I could put some honey in it if you like."

I handed it back to her and said, "That would be great. Thank you."

Tom came in and sat on the couch with me and said, "Well it looks like I won't be leaving today. This rain storm and wind has the lake to choppy to cross."

"How do you think the men you sent to Boville are faring?" I asked.

"I'm sure they made it to Nordman by last night, possibly Coolin, but they will have to hole up until this storm passes. It should only be one or two more days to Boville from there." He said.

Pam came back out with my tea and a cup for Tom. Mine tasted a little better. The rest of the men came in and filtered into the kitchen for breakfast. I noticed Jason walk over and start talking to Lizzy

I looked at Tom and said, "Well I think Jason is over Catherine."

Tom looked over his shoulder and smiled. Then he said, "He

will have to be careful, she has been through a lot and may not want the attention of a man right away."

Jason said something to her and she giggled and blushed. I said, "I think she feels safe here and I trust Jason to be careful. Since these girls are my responsibility now, I will have a talk with him later."

Tom laughed at that. Angie and Catherine brought breakfast out to Tom and me and asked what was so funny. Tom said, "Oh nothing." Then they went back into the kitchen. As we ate, Tom told me that he was going to take two of the canoes and five of the men back with him. He was going to leave Angie, Jason, and a couple of the men with two canoes.

I sat thinking for a minute and then asked, "Tom, did the girls bring back all of the Jacobs' horses? I seem to remember them riding them behind me when they brought me back here, but it seemed like I dreamt it."

Tom said, "Yes they did and they are some nice horses. We made a rope corral back by the meadow and hobbled them there."

I looked at Tom and asked, "Could you change your plans a little? Could you have a couple of your men take the horses around the lake to the North and back to your village? I don't have enough feed for six horses through the winter."

Catherine came back in and overheard our conversation. "I want to keep the black stallion Jack." She said hurriedly.

"I don't know." I said.

"Please, I am tired of sitting in front of the packs on Zack, and it's not fair to him to carry all the packs and me also." She pleaded.

She had a point, but it would still cause a problem with the feed. I asked Tom, "Does the Trading Post still have bags of oats?"

"Yes, the Murphy's only took the hard currency and some of the ammunition along with traveling supplies, food and such. They didn't take anything for their horses and mules."

I thought about it and said, "I will figure something out to trade for some oats, and Jason can bring me five fifty pound bags back with some other food supplies."

"The village council was talking about taking over the Trading Post from Milly Jenkins, and wants to get really picky about what they will trade for. Some of the council members were invested with Mr. Jenkins. The Trading Post was also pretty much our Bank and with all the currency gone they want to tighten up on the trade." Tom said.

A thought came to me at that comment and it had to do with Catherine's birthday party. I looked behind the couch and saw Mouse sitting on the floor hugging Billy. Billy was licking her face. I cleared my throat and said, "Mouse would you do something for me?" She looked up at me with those big brown eyes and then jumped up and ran over to the back of the couch. "Eeep!" She nodded.

"Mouse, could you go into that room there? It's my father's den. There is a big desk by the window. Crawl under the desk and you will see a hidden panel. Open the panel and see what's inside. Okay?" I asked her.

She looked confused, but Catherine got up and said, "Mouse, I will help you." She took Mouses' hand and they went into the den.

Tom gave me a questioning look and I just shrugged. "I don't know what they will find, but knowing my dad, he hid something of value in there. Something he didn't want a sixteen year old kid to know about."

We heard Catherine talking to Mouse and rummaging around and then Mouse started making little grunting sounds. There was a dull thump on the floor and then another and another. Then I heard Catherine grunt. She came into the living room carrying a canvas bag, followed by Mouse dragging a canvas bag along the floor. The bags looked heavy. Catherine came around the couch and set her bag on the coffee table. Mouse dragged hers around the couch, but couldn't lift it onto the table. Catherine said, "There's one more bag, I'll get it." Mouse shook her head 'eeeped' and ran ahead of her and dragged it back to the living room.

I looked at the bag on the table and saw that the top was wired shut. I asked Catherine to go into the garage and get me a plier from the toolbox. She brought one back and I leaned forward and worked the wire off the bag. I lifted the bag. It felt like about twenty pounds. I looked inside and smiled. "I love you dad." I whooped.

Everyone in the kitchen came into the living room as I dumped the bag on the coffee table. It was filled with pre-1964 silver half dollars, quarters and dimes. Everyone gasped. I pushed them to the side and asked Catherine and Mouse to put them back into the bag. Tom lifted the second bag onto the table and I worked the wire off of it. I looked inside and whooped again. I poured it onto the table. It was filled with one ounce silver dollars in plastic shields to keep the silver from tarnishing. They were almost pure silver. They said 99.96% silver. There were at least three hundred of them. Tom lifted the last bag up and I worked the wire off the opening.

I looked inside and said, "Oh my God." Everyone looked at me expectantly, so I dumped it onto the table. There were at least two hundred fifty gold pieces in it. It had everything from one tenth ounce pieces to one ounce gold pieces. It was the most hard currency I had seen in my life, and I was sure it was the most anyone else in the room had ever seen.

Jason said, "Jack, you're rich. What are you going to do with all of that?"

I thought about that for a second and then said, "I'll keep some of it and send most of it to your village Trading Post to replace what the Murphy's took."

Tom stopped me and said, "Jack, you don't have to do that. It's your money. You should keep it."

I said, "I don't want the responsibility of watching over this much money. Plus I need to pay you and your men for their time here and also Angie for doctoring me."

All the men were smiling at their instant good fortune, when Angie said, "Pish, you don't need to pay us for this. We would have done it anyway."

"Regardless." I said. "Your village won't survive without hard currency. People will move away without it. Besides, I need supplies to get us through the winter and can pay for them now. And I can pay to have them brought here, since I can't go get them."

Everyone started talking at once; the men talking to each other and Angie and Tom to me. Angie didn't want to take the money. I told her that word would get out that I had this money and it would make me a target for any 'get rich quick thief' in the area. I would have a difficult time protecting it. I also didn't want to put the girls into that situation. I told Tom that if they took the money on deposit and held it for me that I would pay the village five percent on every transaction. Tom said he didn't know if he could trust the council to hold that much money. He thought they might inflate prices to get more of it from me. We talked at length about how to handle the money, and came to the agreement that Ten Pines would hold it on trust at fixed prices. The prices would be set at the current rate and inflate only if supply of an item diminished. Catherine became our secretary and made a list of all the items and supplies we would need for the winter and what the current price of those items was. Most of the men and Angie and Tom helped her with the list and current prices.

I had Mouse and Pam put the coins back into the bags and set them by the fireplace in full view of everyone. Mouse held one of the one tenth ounce gold pieces out in her hand and looked at me with those big brown eyes.

I asked her, "Do you want that?"

"Eeep!" She nodded and gave a small smile.

I said, "Well, you did do most of the work getting them, so you can keep it."

She jumped up off the floor and ran over to Billy and showed it to him. He tried to eat it, but she snatched it back from him and held it in her palm and stared at it humming. Everyone smiled at her.

◆ ◆ ◆

That evening the storm let up and it started to clear. Everyone seemed in a good mood, and after dinner, I had Catherine and Jason count all the coins and make a list of them. It turned out that there were two hundred silver half dollars, four hundred silver quarters, six hundred silver dimes, two hundred ninety eight one ounce silver dollars, forty nine one tenth ounce gold pieces, fifty quarter ounce gold pieces, fifty half ounce gold pieces, and one hundred one ounce gold pieces. They brought the list to me, and I showed it to Tom and Angie.

Tom said, "Wow, that's a lot."

I said, "I will keep ten percent of it and send the rest back with you and your men."

Catherine and Jason heard this and asked me which coins I want to keep. I said, "Let's make it easy. Keep twenty half dollars, forty quarters, sixty dimes, thirty silver dollars, five of each smaller gold piece and ten one ounce gold piece."

They went back to the bags and counted out each type of coin. Then I had Catherine make out a receipt for the remaining coins for the village council to sign off on. Tom and Angie initialed a receipt that I kept with me. Tom said Jason would bring the village council receipt back with him when he brought supplies back. I had the men come around, gave them each a silver dollar and thanked them for helping us in our time of need and taking time out of their work to be here. I gave four extras to Tom for the men that went to Boville. I knew that each of them would fight for the chance to bring us supplies during the winter. That left me with twenty one silver dollars. Angie, Tom, and Jason refused to take any. I had a feeling that Jason was planning on moving in with us for the winter, or at least until I was back on my feet.

Tom and Angie went to bed early but most of the men sat on the porch and talked quietly. Jason, Catherine, Lizzy and Pam sat in the kitchen and played Monopoly.

Mouse sat next to me and hummed. I looked down at her and thought she was such a lonely little girl. She looked up at me and I asked her if she would like me to read to her. Her eyes lit up and she nodded quickly. I yelled for Catherine to bring me some of her books. I handed them to Mouse and told her to pick one. She looked at them and picked 'The Cat in the Hat' by Dr. Seuss. I took the book from her and she leaned against me so she could see the pictures. Billy climbed up on the couch and laid his head in her lap. I read slowly as she looked at the pictures. I would glance down at her every once in a while and she had a big smile on her face. After I finished 'The Cat in the Hat', she yawned and snuggled up closer to me. I put my arm around her as she hummed herself to sleep. A short while later, the game in the kitchen broke up and Lizzy carried Mouse up to bed. Catherine kissed me goodnight and went upstairs with Pam. I lay down and smiled and sent up a thank you to my dad.

CHAPTER 29

Tom got up early and sent some of his men to get the horses. Tom and Angie helped me out onto the porch. They brought them around to the porch and put the black stallion in the garage with Betty and Zack. Betty immediately bit him and pushed him into a corner. The stallion was young, only about five and Betty was twelve. He knew immediately that she was the new herd dam and didn't put up much of a fight. Zack just stood by and ignored them. I noticed that there were still four horses left. I didn't recognize two of them.

"Where did the fifth horse come from?" I asked.

Jason said, "When we found their cache, their pack horse was hobbled nearby. Catherine was in such a hurry to get you back here that she wasn't aware of it, and Lizzy and Pam didn't mention it."

Angie, Lizzy and Pam brought out supplies for the trip and the men loaded them onto the pack horse. I looked at the saddles and told Catherine to pick one that fit her. She looked them over and picked one that was smaller than the others. It looked like a fifteen inch, while mine was a sixteen inch. I was sure it would be a good fit for her. The men saddled two of the other horses, the Appaloosa, and the chestnut mare. Tom had gone back into the house for a few minutes and when he came back out, he handed me a piece of paper. It was a receipt for the horses, saddles and gear.

"If I can find buyers for these," he said, "I'll put the money on account with the trading post, unless you would like to trade them for some other animals."

"Like what?" I asked.

"Well, we have a couple new litters of piglets and lambs in town."

"I'll think about it and let Jason know when he brings Angie back."

Tom and his men headed down to the beach to load up the canoes they were taking and the two men assigned to take the horses said their goodbyes and headed north. Tom came back with a couple men and introduced them to me again. I had been delirious when I first met them.

Tom said, "I'm leaving William and Pierre here to watch the place until Jason and Angie come back. I don't think there will be any more trouble, but we can't be sure. They can do some hunting with Jason and Catherine while they are here. It will be around the end of October when they head back and that will leave about three weeks for Jason to bring supplies back and get back to Ten Pines before the lake freezes up."

I saw Jason listening and roll his eyes. I had a feeling that he didn't plan on going back until winter was over. I kept it to myself.

"I appreciate it Tom. I'm sure everyone at Ten Pines is wondering what happened here. Are you ready to go?" I asked.

Tom said yes, and gave me a gentle hug around the shoulders. He hugged and kissed Angie and shook Jason's hand. All the men leaving came up and shook my hand and I thanked them for their help. They all said good bye to the girls. The girls blushed and said thanks. Mouse sat with Billy and just looked at everyone, humming.

After everyone left, Angie and Catherine helped me back inside and Angie un-wrapped the bandages on my foot. It was still swollen and red, but it didn't look infected. Angie sent Pam into the kitchen to get some antiseptic she had made from honey and some herbs. She washed my foot with it and re-wrapped a clean bandage on. I felt uncomfortable with the attention and asked Angie what she thought it was going to be like when it was healed?

Angie got her medical bag and took out a small hammer

with a blunt pointed end. She asked me if I could wiggle my toes for her. I tried and was able to move all but my little toe, but it was painful. She took the bandage back off and rubbed the blunt end of the hammer along the bottom of my foot.

She asked, "Can you feel that?"

I gasped, "Yeess," as my toes curled down and the pain shot up my leg.

"Good," she smiled, "it doesn't look like you have nerve damage and you should get full use of it when it has healed. Now Pam and I are going to go find some white pine bark to make the plaster for your cast. I think I will give it another three days before I put it on though. I want the swelling down as much as possible."

I said, "Take one of the men with you while you are out."

They left with William, and Jason sat down next to me. Lizzy and Catherine were in the garage with the horses, and Mouse was on the porch with Billy and Pierre. I knew Jason had something to say, so I waited.

Finally, Jason asked, "Jack, do you think I should stay here for the winter?"

I smiled at him and said, "So I guess your prediction that you would never fall in love again was wrong."

Jason blushed through his dark complexion and said, "Well, I guess you were right about not trying to predict the future. I like Lizzy."

"I know." I said.

"It's that obvious?" he asked.

"Do you know if she feels the same way?" I asked.

"We get along great, and she is definitely not my cousin." He said.

"No, I'm sure of that." I said. Lizzy had reddish hair and freckles that stood out when she blushed. She was about Jason's age, slim and 5'6" tall. "I have to warn you to take it slow with her. She has been violently abused and may have a difficult time with affection from a man. But, if you are patient with her, she may return your interest."

"Then I can stay?" Jason asked.

"That's not up to me Jason. If your mother and father think it's okay then yes. Your help around here would be great." I said.

"Oh, they'll say it's okay." He said.

"There you go predicting the future again. Just be here in the present and we'll see what happens." I said.

Jason smiled and got up and said, "I'm going to go see what Lizzy and Catherine are doing."

I sat thinking for a while after Jason left for the garage. *'What was going on in my life? Now I'm running a house for abused women and orphans. I have never lived with women as long as I had with Catherine, and now I have two more and a child. How am I going to raise them to love the world again? What do I know about raising girls in the first place? Well, I haven't done so badly with Catherine, even though she wants me to sleep with her. That would be a bad example to set with Lizzy, Pam, and Mouse in the house now, after the abuse they had just been saved from.'* My thoughts swirled around these questions and I couldn't find any answers. *'Of course you can't find any answers. You're trying to predict the future. Just be the person you are and everything else will take care of itself.'*

I started nodding off, when I felt Mouse climb up onto the couch with me. I looked down at her and smiled. She stared at me and then got down and brought some books back. I guess that I was going to read to her. It was a good start. If she could get comfortable around me, she may get comfortable around other men someday. We sat together, with Mouse leaning against me while I read "Green Eggs and Ham", and "Horton hears a Who". It worried me that she chose books that were pure fantasy, but then again she was still a child. I watched her as I read and could see that she was starting to smile more. Angie and Pam came in as I finished the last book, and Mouse lost interest and followed them into the kitchen to see what they were doing. I finally nodded off.

I woke up with someone lightly shaking my shoulder. It was Pam. She looked embarrassed and asked hurriedly, "Are you hungry Jack? Angie asked me to wake you 'cause you need to keep your strength up."

"How long have I been sleeping?" I asked.

"For about an hour and its lunch time." She said shyly.

"Well, I guess I could eat then. Could you bring me some tea also, Pam?" I asked.

"Yes." She said and hurried back into the kitchen.

Pam came back with the tea, and Angie came out with a plate of food for me. I asked her if we could talk privately for a while. Angie got herself a plate and cup of tea and sat down in the chair opposite me.

"What do you want to talk about Jack?" she asked.

I remembered the thoughts I had before I read to Mouse, and finally said, "I don't know anything about raising girls."

Angie smiled and said, "No one does until they do."

"That's not much help Angie." I said.

"Jack you always worry too much about others and what they think. You are a good man and just being yourself would be a good influence on these girls. Yes they have been through a terrible ordeal of abuse and rape, but I can see that they respect you already. They can see that you are different than the men that took them and they also trust what Catherine thinks of you." She said.

"But I'm going to be laid up for at least ten weeks you said, and then it is going to be winter and we'll be inside almost all the time. What am I going to do then?" I pleaded.

"Be kind to them and teach them what you know." Angie said. "Help them learn and trust people again."

"You know I will Angie, but what about me? I don't know anything about women's things." I said.

"Jack, I've never known you to be a coward or shirk your responsibility, so all I can tell you is to learn to enjoy having them around." She said smiling. "Be there for them when they are happy, sad, angry or scared."

"That's not the women's things I'm talking about and you know it. I'm talking about the physical differences. What do I do about that?" I asked irritated.

"I will take care of their physical needs before I leave, and Catherine told me that Marge down in Boville showed her how to take care of herself. You're probably not even aware of when she is having her period are you?" Angie asked.

I turned red with embarrassment and said, "No."

"Those issues will take care of themselves. Lizzy and Pam already know how to take care of their own hygiene from their own mothers. I will check them periodically and keep an eye on Mouse as she grows. You worry about teaching them about the world and keeping them safe." Angie said.

"Angie I have to admit that it scares the hell out of me."

CHAPTER 30

Two days later just east of Boville.

T he Murphy's had made good time after they lost their pursuit by the men from Ten Pines. They had headed north for a couple days and hid in a canyon while Mr. Murphy continued on with the horses and lost the trackers by wading along a river for a mile or so. He caught up with Bob and his sons the next day, and they headed south. It had been tough to follow the old roads, which were choked with young growth. By following game trails they had meandered along for more than a week. Now they were a couple miles east of Boville. They were short on supplies.

Murphy looked at his son George and said, "Ride into their settlement and tell them that your mother is out here and really sick. They haven't seen you before and if you act desperate they will believe you. Get as many of the men as possible to follow you out here and we'll bushwhack them. Then we can head back into Boville and take what we need."

George smiled and said, "Not a problem." He rode out towards Boville.

Big Bo was in the smokehouse putting a new layer of soaked hickory chips onto the coals to smoke the fish, venison, and pork they had hanging. As the smoke thickened, he opened the door and stepped out. He immediately saw a rider coming from the east. He walked out to meet him and noticed that it was a boy about eighteen years old.

George looked at Bo and thought, '*that's the biggest man I have*

169

ever seen'. He stopped his horse and with a desperate look on his face said, "I need your help mister. My mom is a ways east of here and she is really sick. Can you bring some help?"

The boy looked suspicious in a way, but Bo was always willing to help others in need. He thought about how much help Jack and Catherine had been earlier that year. He finally asked, "Where you coming from son and where's your father?"

The boy ignored the question and said, "I really need some help, can you come right away, before it gets dark?"

As they talked, there was yelling down by the lake. Bo turned and saw two canoes approaching shore in a hurry. Strange he thought *'a bunch of visitors on the same day'.*

George looked up as Bo turned and George recognized four men from Ten Pines. He quickly turned his horse and galloped off to the east. Bo yelled after him, "Hey, I thought you needed my help."

Families started coming out of the cabins to see what all the noise was. Bo shrugged and walked down to the lake as the canoes came to shore. The four men jumped out and ran up to Bo. Bo recognized Eric the group's leader from Ten Pines from a few years earlier.

"We sure are getting a bunch of visitors all of a sudden." Bo said.

"It looks like we got here just in time." Eric said. "That was George Murphy you were just talking to. The Murphy's killed Mr. Jenkins and robbed the Trading Post in Ten Pines about ten days back. What did he want?"

"He said his mother was sick and asked for help to go get her." Bo said as the rest of the village gathered around.

"He doesn't have a mother." Eric said. "It looks like he was trying to lure you into an ambush."

Marge butted in and said, "What's going on Bo?"

Bo explained what happened to the rest of the members of the village. Marge interrupted again and said, "Let's move this inside and we can get the whole story."

Eric told a couple of his men to get their guns and watch

the tree line to the east while he talked to the members of Boville. When they were settled inside with hot tea and Marge had sent food and tea to the men outside, Eric told them how the Murphy's had showed up in April and how they had caused trouble from day one. He told them about the confrontation between Catherine, Jason, and George, and how Mr. Murphy had tried to beat Jason. He said Jack had stopped him and Catherine had threatened to shoot him if he didn't leave. Then the village council had let the Murphy's off.

Marge said, "Poor Catherine. Was anyone hurt?"

Eric said, "No, but Catherine told the village council off and said that if they didn't do something, the Murphy's would just cause more trouble. A few weeks later, the Murphy's killed Mr. Jenkins and robbed the Trading Post. It proves she was right."

"Well, we're glad you showed up when you did." Bo said. "I was just getting ready to take Ben and Marge out to get his mother."

"That's not all that happened." Eric said. "A group of four men, the Jacobs, tried to kill Jack and Catherine five days ago. It was Jack and Tom that sent us down here to warn you."

"Oh my God," Marge exclaimed. "Was anyone hurt?"

"Jack got a broken foot when a horse stepped on him, but he killed their leader first, and Catherine shot the other three dead. And that's not all. The Jacobs had taken three young girls hostage and repeatedly raped them." Eric continued. "Lizzy is seventeen, Pam is fifteen, and Mouse we don't know, but she is very young, nine or ten."

"What is happening to the world?" Marge said angrily. "I thought the days of raiders and bad men were finally over."

"It doesn't look like it." Eric said. "We will stay for a couple days if you don't mind and make sure the Murphy's don't come back."

"Please do." Marge said. "We can put each of you up in one of the cabins."

"I plan on posting a guard around the clock until we are sure they are gone. Any help you can give us to watch is appreciated." Eric said.

"What does Jack plan to do with the girls?" Janice asked.

"I think they are going to stay at Jack's cabin for the time being. Tom left some men there to keep watch while Jack's foot heals." Eric explained.

"Well if God had a say in it, they couldn't have been saved by a better person." Marge smiled. "Bo, we need to plan our trip up there in the spring to see if he needs any help."

George galloped down the trail and just before he got to their camp, Murphy stepped out and stopped him. "What's the hurry son?" He asked. "Where are the people from Boville?"

George jumped down from his horse and said in a rush, "Just as I was talking their leader into coming, by the way he is the biggest man I have ever seen, four men from Ten Pines showed up in canoes. So I high-tailed it out of there. I think we should break camp and get out of here before they come looking for us. I wouldn't want to tangle with that big dude."

"Shit." Murphy said angrily. "Now what are we going to do for supplies? Can we sneak in at night and steal some food?"

"I'm sure the men from Ten Pines recognized me." George said.

"So now they are telling their story to the people of Boville." Murphy said. "You're right son, let's pack up and head down towards Lewiston. We should be able to find something along the way."

Murphy, Bob, and his two sons quickly broke camp and headed southwest. They hoped the weather would hold for the next month.

That same time in Lewiston...

Brian walked down the street with his head down thinking.

172

'Why didn't I leave when Jack did, or for that matter when the other five men deserted on the way here. Jim has lost it. We shouldn't have killed those people in Elmira, and the people that resisted Jim on the way here. Now I have at least forty more deaths on my conscience even though I haven't killed anyone. I joined Jack and Jim nine years ago when they started the Raider Protection Association because my parents and brother had been killed by raiders when I was eighteen. I had been out hunting and came back to our cabin burned down and had to bury my family. I thought I was going to do some good joining with the RPA, but with Jack gone, we've done nothing but hurt people. Jim is obsessed with finding Jack and the girl he believes Jack took with him. The wanted posters he had made and handed out are getting all kinds of desperate men excited. I hope Jack watches his back or at least finds someplace with friends. Jack always made friends easily. Damn why didn't I leave when he did?'

Brian continued walking and finally reached the house that Jim had taken by killing the previous owner that refused to move out. He walked up the steps and knocked before going in. Jim had a tendency to have some young girl inside with him, even if they didn't want to be there. Jim yelled, "Come in Brian."

He opened the door and walked into the living room. Jim was sitting on the couch and there was a naked girl curled up at one end sniffling. Brian looked at Jim and thought, *'damn he is getting fat. I bet he has put on forty pounds since we left Elmira.'*

"Well, have you heard from the Jacobs?" Jim asked.

"Not yet." Brian said. "They were headed up to Spokane and then around to the north end of Priest Lake where you said your parents had a cabin. If they didn't find him there, they were going to head to Bonners Ferry to look around. If he wasn't there, they were going to head on up to Calgary. If they have to go that far, I don't think we will hear from them until spring."

"If those perverts touch that girl before they bring her to me, I'm going to cut their dicks off." Jim said angrily. The girl on the couch whimpered.

'You should talk, you're the pervert.' Brian thought. "I doubt we will hear from them anytime soon." He said.

"If they aren't back before spring, we are going to head up to Bonners Ferry with half our men. I'm going to leave the rest here to protect my interests." Jim said.

"Okay," Brian said. "Is that all?"

"Yeah, keep me informed if you hear anything. Now get out." Jim said angrily.

Brian left and as he was walking, he thought, *'Jim has sixty men now, with more joining each month. If he goes to Bonners Ferry in the spring, that's where I am going to get out of this mess. Maybe I will find Jack and warn him. Oh well, that's five or six months away. I guess I'll just lay low until then.'*

CHAPTER 31

Over the next two days, Angie prepared the fixings to make my cast and continued to monitor the swelling in my foot. It had diminished enough by the second day, so she mixed the plaster and wrapped my foot and leg up to the mid-calf with disinfectant soaked cloth.

"That's a little loose isn't it?" I asked her.

"When the plaster and cloth dries, it will tighten against your skin." Angie said. "Over the next ten weeks, your muscles in your foot and leg will shrink from disuse and it will get looser."

Angie propped my foot and leg up on a towel on the coffee table and started applying the plaster. She put a layer on and wrapped it with more cloth and did this for three layers. Once it was all in place, she had William and Pierre help move me to a chair in front of the fireplace. She propped my leg so it extended out to some of the heat emanating from the fire.

"You will have to keep your foot still until the plaster dries enough. It should take a couple hours." She said.

"What if my foot gets too hot?" I asked.

"Then we will move you back a little." She said.

"What do you want me to do until then?" I asked.

Mouse who had been watching the whole process quickly ran over to her books and brought one over to me. She climbed up into my lap and looked at me with those big brown eyes.

"I think you're going to be reading for the next couple hours Jack." Angie said with a smile.

"Okay Mouse, but get the big green book for me." I said.

Mouse looked disappointed, but went and got the book and climbed back up in my lap. I opened the book and showed her a picture of a boy painting a fence. I said, "This is called Tom Sawyer, Mouse."

Mouse looked at the few pictures as I read, and quickly became engrossed in the story. Angie came in from the kitchen periodically and checked the hardness of the cast. I enjoyed reading to Mouse so much that I barely realized when the two hours was up. Angie said she wanted to give it another hour, so I kept reading to Mouse. When Angie felt the plaster was hard enough, she asked me to try to move my foot. It was tight and I couldn't move my foot or ankle.

"Jason, you can bring them in now." Angie yelled.

Jason came into the living room with a couple of homemade crutches. They were made from stout branches with a fork at one end. He had padded these with towels. I put the book down and had Mouse climb down when he handed them to me.

"I made them a little long so you will have to stand up and try them so I can cut them to length." Jason said.

I held my cast off the floor and levered myself up with the help of the crutches. I placed them under my arms and stood straight. They were about four inches too long. I sat back down and Jason took them out to the garage and cut them down. When he brought them back, I tried them again and walked around the living room with them. It felt good to be mobile again. I went into the kitchen and around the kitchen table and then back into the living room. I turned from the living room and went into the bathroom. I needed to use it because Mouse had been sitting on my bladder for over two hours. *'Ahh, freedom again,'* I thought.

When I came back out, Catherine and the girls were back. I asked, "Where have you girls been?"

Catherine smiled and said, "We went out riding. Lizzy rode Betty, and I rode Black."

"Is that the name you gave your horse?" I asked.

"Yeah, it seemed fitting. He is a little feisty, but after a little while he got used to me." She said.

"What about you Pam? Didn't you go riding? Zach is a very

176

stable horse." I asked.

Pam blushed with embarrassment and said shyly, "I'm not very good on a horse. I was taking care of the goats."

"I hope MB isn't giving you any trouble." I said.

Everyone laughed. I looked at them confused and asked, "Okay what did I miss?"

Jason said, "Pam has MB eating out of her hand. He even lets her brush him."

Pam said shyly, "I had goats on our farm."

"Well good." I said. "I think if I'm going to be useless for ten weeks, we need to assign some duties around here."

Pam quickly said, "I'll take care of the goats. I've been milking the nanny every day, and one of the other nannies is pregnant."

Lizzy and Catherine said at the same time, "We'll take care of the horses."

"That means mucking out the horse poop every day also." I said.

Mouse looked at me expectantly, so I said, "Mouse, I would like you to take care of the chickens. Can you do that?" She nodded with serious look on her face.

Catherine said, "Mouse, I will help you to begin with and show you what needs to be done okay." Mouse gave a little smile and nodded again.

I looked at Angie and asked, "When will you be heading back?"

Angie replied, "I think I will wait a couple days to make sure your cast holds, and then we can head back."

It was the third week of October, and it was starting to get cold at night. I said that I thought it was too late in the season for any more raiders to show up, so William and Pierre should head back with her and Jason.

Jason looked at Lizzy and quickly jumped in and said, "Yeah, but I will be heading right back here with your supplies."

"I hope the weather holds until then so you can get back home." Angie said.

◆ ◆ ◆

Angie, Jason and the men left as planned a couple days later. I went out and sat on the porch and watched them load up and head out. I didn't want to try to make it down to the beach until I was used to the crutches. Mouse sat with me, while Catherine, Lizzy and Pam went down to the beach to see them off. They sat on our fishing log and waved goodbye until they were out of sight.

Lizzy got unexpectedly quiet while they watched the canoes leave. Catherine noticed and asked her what was wrong.

Lizzy started to tear up and asked, "Can you and Pam keep a secret?"

Catherine smiled and asked, "Is it that you like Jason?"

Lizzy turned red and said, "No, that's not it."

"But you do like him don't you?" Catherine teased.

"Yes, he is really nice." Lizzy said. "But I want to tell you something else. I lied when I said I didn't have any family."

"Why?" Catherine and Pam asked at the same time.

"Because, I don't want to go back to them." She said. She then told Catherine and Pam her story and how she had ended up captured by the Jacobs.

Catherine and Pam were shocked at what they heard. Catherine said, "You have to tell Jack the truth."

Lizzy cried and said, "No, he'll hate me and won't let me stay."

"No he won't." Catherine said. "Jack doesn't hate anyone and he won't make you leave."

"I'm scared." Lizzy said.

"You still have to tell him." Catherine said looking back at Jack and Mouse sitting on the porch. "Come on, now is as good a time as any."

The girls walked back to the cabin. Pam went into the garage to check the goats, and Catherine and Lizzy went up onto the porch. Jack noticed Lizzy holding back and misread the situation.

"Lizzy, Jason will be back in a couple days." I said.

Catherine grabbed Mouse by the hand and said, "Come on Mouse we need to go check the chickens." Mouse followed her around the house.

Lizzy stood on the porch looking down and wringing her hands. She was beet red and her freckles stood out.

"What's the matter Lizzy?" I asked.

Lizzy started sobbing and tears ran down her cheeks. "Please don't hate me." She said.

"I don't and I won't. Tell me what's wrong." I said. "Come here and sit down."

Lizzy sat in a chair a ways away from Jack and started crying again. "I lied Jack." She said crying harder.

I could tell it was serious in her mind, so I kept quiet until she was ready to talk. After a few minutes she took a few shuddering breathes and said, "The Jacobs didn't kill my family. They are still at our farm in Washington. I... I..."

"Take your time and tell me what's bothering you." I said.

She wiped the tears out of her eyes and said, "I... I... I was married before."

She saw the shock on my face, so I quickly squelched it and said, "Tell me from the beginning."

She sat wringing her hands in her lap and finally said, "My father hated me because I was a girl. He said girls were useless on a farm. He whipped me for the slightest reason. My two younger brothers got everything they wanted. My mother never stood up to him, and when I turned sixteen, he married me off to another farmer that lost his wife to a fever. He traded me for a mule. I thought that I was finally free from his abuse when I went to live with Charles, but Charles was worse. He beat me and forced himself on me every night. I didn't get pregnant, so he beat me more. I suffered through thinking that it couldn't get any worse. Then Charles started accusing me of sleeping with some of the young men in our town, even though I hadn't. He started tying me up whenever he left the farm for any reason.

After I turned seventeen, he left for town one day to trade for some supplies, and I got myself untied. I ran away. I was about ten miles east of the farm when the Jacobs caught me. That was three weeks ago."

I thought 'this girl has been damaged by men even more than I thought'. I said, "I'm sorry this happened to you. I don't hate you. You never have to worry about anything bad happening to you around me. Not all men are like that. You have seen the worst of them, but over the last week, you have also seen the best of them. The men from Ten Pines are all good men that help others whenever they can."

"But you said if we have family, you were going to return us to them." She sputtered.

"You don't have to worry about that." I said. "You can stay here as long as you like."

"You won't tell Jason will you?" She started crying again. "I like him and he won't want me if he knows."

"No I won't tell Jason, you will." I said firmly. "You can't keep this from him. Honesty is the only way for two people to form a bond."

"But he will hate me." She said crying.

"I've had a lot of talks with Jason, and I'll tell you the same thing I told him." I said. "You can't predict the future, and you need to let go of your past and just be here and now. Jason won't hate you. He may not like it, but he will see past it to who you are. So be honest with him."

"Will you be there when I tell him?" Lizzy asked.

"No, but I will talk to him after you tell him." I said.

"Thank you, Jack." She let out a big shuddering sigh and said, "I feel better now that I told you."

"I will always be here for you if you need to talk. Just always be honest with me okay." I said.

"Yes sir." She said with a small smile. "And thank you for understanding."

CHAPTER 32

Three days earlier, Tom and the men with him made good time crossing the lake and when they came into sight of Ten Pines, Tom slowed his canoe and talked with the men.

"I would appreciate it if you guys didn't mention Jack's money to anyone until after I have had a chance to meet with the town council. I don't know how it is going to go, and if I have to send the money back, I don't want to get the town's peoples' hopes up." Tom said. "I especially don't know how Gerard is going to react to it."

Gerard was the head of the town council and one of the members invested in the Trading Post. The men agreed to keep it quiet until after the meeting.

They continued on and some of the children playing on the beach ran to tell the town's people of their return. A crowd gathered as they beached their canoes and people started asking questions. "Was it the Murphy's that started the fire? Was anyone hurt? Where are Angie and the rest of the men?"

Gerard Perot showed up and pushed his way through the crowd. "Did you get our money back?" He asked with no concern for anything else.

Tom raised his hands and said, "Hold on everyone. It wasn't the Murphy's. Jack got hurt and Catherine started a brush pile on fire to get our attention."

The crowd started asking questions again. "What happened? How was he hurt?' Gerard said loudly, "Then you didn't get my..., I mean our money back. Why did you stay over there for a week then?"

"I will tell you everything at a town meeting tonight. I suggest we set up tables and benches in the big barn so everyone can fit and get out of the cold." Tom said. "That's all I'm going to say now, so go back to what you were doing."

Tom went home to check up on it, and started a fire in the fireplace. While he was preparing some tea, Jeremy and Elizabeth came in.

Tom asked, "Would you like some tea?"

Jeremy said, "Yes, thank you. We need to talk though."

"About what?" Tom asked.

"While you were gone, Gerard and a couple of other council members wanted to institute an emergency act through the council." Jeremy said. "I held them off until you returned."

"What do you mean an 'emergency act'? Tom asked.

"Gerard wants the council to take over the Trading Post, with him in charge and institute immediate price hikes." Jeremy replied. "He wants to increase prices on trade goods in store by twenty five percent and reduce the value of items brought in for trade by ten percent."

"That greedy bastard!" Tom said hotly. "He wants the people to suffer so he can get his investment back. How does Milly Jenkins feel about it?"

"Milly is still upset at the murder of her husband Mike, but doesn't want to turn the Trading Post over to Gerard. He is only offering her fifty percent of its value." Elizabeth said.

"Elizabeth, do you think you could go get Milly and her son Matthew and bring them here?" Tom asked. "I think I have a solution to this problem."

"What solution?" Jeremy asked.

"Just get Milly and Matthew and I will explain it all when they are here." Tom said with a smile.

Elizabeth left to get Milly and Matthew while Tom told Jeremy what happened across the lake as they waited. Jeremy had a lot of questions, but Tom remained cryptic about his solution.

A half hour later, Elizabeth came in followed by Milly and Matthew. Tom and Jeremy stood and hugged Milly and then shook hands with Matthew.

Tom started out saying, "Milly I haven't had a chance to express my condolences for Mike's death, and I'm sorry I wasn't able to catch the bastards that did it."

"Thank you Tom. It's been difficult preparing for the funeral and running the Trading Post. What with that pest Gerard stopping by every few hours to try and talk me out of the business." She said.

Tom said, "I think I have a solution to this whole problem, if you will listen to me and consider my offer."

Tom explained what he had planned in his mind and asked a lot of questions. He discovered through the questioning that Mike and Milly had kept extensive records of all trade that went through the Post. They came to an agreement and Tom asked Matthew to draw up the contracts. He said that he would present it all at the meeting tonight.

The town's people gathered at the big barn around dusk and waited for Tom and Jeremy to show up. Gerard had the place set up beforehand with three tables set in a horseshoe and he waited impatiently in the center of the end table. There were seven members of the town council and five of them had already arrived. There were benches set up facing the open end of the tables. Milly and Matthew Jenkins sat at the middle of the first bench facing Gerard and the members of the council.

Tom and Jeremy finally arrived and took their seats at the right side table. Tom was carrying a large satchel which he place on the floor.

"It's about time." Gerard said angrily. "He took a rubber ended hammer and started banging on his table. "We will come to order." He yelled. People took their seats while some stood around the edges.

When everyone was situated, Gerard started the proceedings. "We are here to discuss my emergency act for the council to take over the Trading Post."

The crowd starting yelling, "No you can't do this. Don't let him do this." Milly and Matthew sat quietly in the front row.

"It's already been decided by the council that this will be put to a vote." Gerard yelled to be heard.

Tom stood and everyone quieted down. "Can I see the proposal before I vote?" He asked.

Gerard passed the proposal around to Tom and he sat down reading it slowly. After a few minutes he said, "It says here that prices will go up twenty five percent and trade value will decrease by ten percent."

Everyone started yelling again, and Gerard started banging his hammer on the table. "Order, order, everyone shutup." After a few minutes the noise subsided. "Yes, that is the only way to get the currency back."

Tom smiled and said calmly, "But it also says in our town charter that you drafted and that we all signed off on, that any council member with a personal interest in an issue must recuse themselves from voting. That's what you made Jeremy and I do at the hearing over the altercation between Jason and the Murphy boys."

"What's that have to do with this?" Gerard asked.

"Well it's come to my attention that you and the two other members beside you are invested in the Trading Post." Tom said. "That means that you have to recuse yourselves from this vote."

People started yelling again in agreement. Gerard looked angry and the two members beside him looked shocked and leaned away from him.

"That doesn't apply here." Gerard said. "This is a major issue that affects the entire town."

Tom smiled again and said, "There is no distinction in the charter, other than an 'issue with personal interest'. It doesn't say major or minor." Tom turned to Milly and Matthew and asked, "What are Gerard's and the other members of the council's investment in the Trading Post?"

Matthew reached down into his satchel and pulled out an investment contract his father had made with the council members. He read from it, "It says that for an investment of twenty five percent of hard currency, the undersigned agree to a twenty five percent commission on profits for the next ten years, and then a return of their investment. This agreement can be extended or amended."

Tom smiled again and asked, "Can it be cancelled?"

Gerard started sputtering, but Matthew continued. "It is agreed that either party may cancel this agreement upon payment of the investment with no prepayment penalty."

"And how long has this agreement been in effect?" Tom asked.

"It was signed and dated two years ago." Matthew said.

"This is outrageous!" Gerard yelled at Tom. "There is no hard currency left. The Murphy's stole it all, and you weren't able to get it back."

Tom ignored him and continued talking to Matthew. "So Matthew, what was the initial investment in hard currency?"

Matthew read from the contract, "For the amount of `ten ounces of gold and fifty ounces of silver the undersigned will purchase a twenty five percent share of the Trading Post."

Tom looked at Milly and asked calmly, "Milly, would you consider cancelling that agreement?"

"If it means that I keep control of the Trading Post and don't have to raise prices, yes." Milly said and then turned to Gerard angrily. "Mike would never do what you're trying to do to this town. He was and honest man."

Gerard got a sly look on his face and said, "I'm only trying to keep this town going. Without the currency, we can't trade with the larger towns for the things we need. I'm doing it for everyone."

There were some 'boos' and catcalls from the crowd. Gerard

banged his hammer again and said, "Quiet! It doesn't matter you don't have the currency to cancel the agreement."

Tom looked at him with disgust and asked, "If you three aren't part of the vote, how do you think it will turn out for you? That only leaves the other four of us." He looked across the horseshoe at the other two members that weren't invested and knew he could count on Samuel, Sammy's father to vote against the measure. He knew that Gerard had made promises to Daniel to get his vote.

"It looks to me that it will be a three to one vote against the measure; instead of a four to three vote like you planned, Gerard." Tom said. Then Tom turned to Milly again and asked, "Would you consider taking on a new investor if he paid off that investment contract?"

Milly smiled and said, "If that can be arranged."

Tom reached down beside him and pulled his satchel to the table. He took a canvas bag out of it and pried it open. He counted out ten ounces of gold and then closed the bag. He took another canvas bag and opened it and counted out fifty ounces of silver. Everyone in the room was shocked into silence.

Gerard looked at him and said accusingly, "I thought you said that you didn't get the currency back from the Murphy's. What are you trying to pull here?"

Tom ignored him and said to Matthew, "If you could take this money and pay off that contract, and make up a new investment contract with Jack Anders as the investor, I would appreciate it."

Gerard yelled, "Jack Anders? Where did he get that money, steal it."

Tom stood and pointed at Gerard, "If I wasn't a civilized man, I would come over there and beat you senseless Gerard. Jack's father left him this money and all the men that went over there with me can attest to that. Jack is the most honest man I know."

Matthew got up and took the money from Tom and took it over to the head table. With a smile he laid it down and then ripped up the investment contract. He said to Gerard, "I won't need a receipt for that. The entire town saw me give it to you."

Gerard looked at the money and then scooped it up. The two men next to him looked at him angrily and he started counting out their shares.

Tom said, "I guess this meeting is adjourned, huh, Gerard. Milly, Matthew and I have a contract to prepare for Jack."

"Yes, yes." Gerard said as he counted the money.

Then Tom turned to the crowd. "Jack said that the rest of this money is to be put in trust with the Trading Post for the benefit of the town. He is willing to pay five percent to the town fund for all his future transactions." Tom took out the receipt he, Jack and Angie had signed and walked over and gave it to Milly to sign. Milly amended the amount, subtracting the money they just gave to Gerard. Matthew took out another investment contract and signed it with his mother and handed it to Tom.

Tom turned back to the crowd and said, "I'll let the men that went across the lake tell you what happened over there."

People started crowding around those men and listened to the story. The men were instant celebrities.

Jeremy pulled Tom aside and asked, "Are you sure Jack wants to be an investor in the Trading Post?"

"Once he hears what was happening here, he won't mind." Tom said. With the meeting breaking up, Tom asked Milly, "Do you have a safe place to store the rest of this money?"

"Well no," she said, "the cabinet we kept the currency in before is busted up from the robbery."

"Okay, I'll keep it until other arrangements can be made to store it."

As Tom and Jeremy walked out, they overheard the stories the men were telling the towns people. "Jack and Catherine were bushwhacked by four men. Jack killed the leader, and Catherine shot the other three."

"Really, that little girl killed three men?" Someone asked.

"Yep, she shot two of them off their horses after killing one that was sneaking up behind Jack."

"What happened to Jack? Tom said he got hurt." another person asked.

"During all the shooting, the leader's horse stepped on Jack's foot and broke it. Angie stayed to take care of it. Catherine discovered three young girls that the raiders were holding hostage. They helped Catherine get Jack back to his cabin."

"Who are they? Where did they come from? What is going to happen to them?" Questions were fired at the men.

"Their names are Elizabeth, Pamela and Mouse. No one knows Mouse's real name, because she won't talk. They all suffered trauma and abuse." One of the men said.

"Their families were killed and they were taken hostage, and Jack is going to take responsibility for them." Another of the men said.

"It's lucky that a man like Jack found them, then. He is saving our town too." A woman in the crowd said. "Is there anything that they need?"

"I'm sure they will need stuff when my son Jason returns with some supplies to help them get through the winter." Tom said in passing.

"We'll get with Angie when she gets back and prepare some things for them." The woman said.

CHAPTER 33

I sat in the living room reading to Mouse, but couldn't concentrate. *'God, I'm bored sitting around all day. There must be something I can do besides read to Mouse. Not that I don't enjoy her company.'* I closed the book and said to Mouse, "That's enough for now."

Mouse looked up at me with those big brown eyes and squeaked, "Eeep?"

"Sorry Mouse, but I need to find something to do. By the way, have you checked on the chickens yet today?" I asked.

Mouse got a surprised look on her face, said "Eeep!" and climbed off my lap and ran out the front door.

I used the crutches to get out of the chair, and hobbled into the kitchen. Pam was soaking some dried vegetables and seasoning some meat for dinner. I looked around and then had an idea. I went into the pantry where we stored dried products and saw my reloading box on the top shelf. I yelled out to Pam. "Could you give me a hand for a second, Pam?"

Pam hurried in and asked, "What do you need Jack?"

"Can you get that box down for me from the top shelf and put it on the kitchen table?" I asked.

Pam looked up at it and asked, "The reloading box?"

I had written reloading supplies on the side of the box before I put it up there. I asked Pam, "You can read?"

Pam got the short step ladder and struggled to get the box down. It was heavy. "Yes, my Mama and Papa taught me to read and write." She carried the box out to the table and set it down.

I realized that I knew very little about Pam other than her family had been killed by the Jacobs down around Spokane. I started taking the press and dies out of the box and clamping it to the table. I sorted out the empty brass and set out the powder, primers and bullets. While I was doing this, I thought about how to get to know her a little better.

When I set up the scale and powder measure, I asked Pam, "Why don't you go out with Catherine and Lizzy and do things."

Pam was quiet for a moment and finally said, "I prefer to stay inside. I can take care of the goats from here, and I don't like riding horses."

I thought that this may be a defense mechanism and she felt safer in the house. She has been through a very hard time in the last month and her bruises were still healing. I asked, "What else did you parents teach you?"

Pam got a small smile on her face and said, "My Mama taught me how to sew and spin wool. My Papa taught me how to take care of the goats and sheep and how to shear wool. Papa also taught me how to birth baby goats and lambs. Did you know that one of the nannies is pregnant?"

I said, "I figured as much since I saw MB mount her a couple times. That was about around the first of August. When do you think she will give birth?"

Pam thought for a moment and said, "Their gestation period is around 150 days, so probably around Christmas."

I was quiet for a few minutes as I thought about Christmas. *'What am I going to do for the girls for Christmas? They need some celebrations in their lives to start feeling normal again.'*

Finally, I asked, "Pam, you said you can sew? Could you take some of that elk hide in the garage that I tanned and make me some small pouches?"

Her eyes lit up and she said, "Yes, how many and how big do you need them?"

I said, "For right now I could use five that are about five inches deep with a way to secure the top."

Pam said, "I will need to get sewing supplies, needles and thread to make them."

"If you go into the closet in the back bedroom, you will find my mom's sewing box. If you need anything else, I can have

Jason get it from the Trading Post."

Pam ran up to the bedroom and rummaged around in the closet and came back down with a plastic case that was loaded with sewing things. She started sorting through them as I started resizing the brass I had set out. She had a huge smile.

As we worked, I asked her, "What did your father do? Was he always a farmer?"

Pam said, "Oh no, he was a teamster in Spokane when I was very young and finally got the money together to buy the equipment he needed to start the farm." Pam stared off in the distance and I could see tears forming in her eyes.

"I'm sorry," I said, "I didn't mean to bring up sad memories."

"My Papa was a very good man." She said hurriedly. "He always helped anyone out that needed it, and never asked for anything in return." She smiled as a thought came to her. "Every evening at the dinner table, he would ask each of us, what had made us smile that day? We would always remember back through our day and think of when we were happy and share it. I miss that the most."

"He sounds like a very good man and sharing your happy moments was a great idea." I said. "What types of happy moments did you share?"

"It was usually something simple, like playing with a new lamb, or feeding some baby pigeons in the barn rafters or chasing butterflies." She said. "Whatever brought out a smile?"

"Would you like to do that when we have our meals?" I asked.

She looked down and said, "It's silly, I don't think anyone will like it."

"I wouldn't say that. Catherine and I practice listening and clearing our minds and it frequently brings smiles to our faces."

"Can you teach that to me?" She asked.

"Sure, it helps me to keep myself centered and in the present. We have all had sadness in our past, and it's my way of letting it go and just enjoying now." I said. "We can start tomorrow."

Pam got up with a big scissors and said, "I can't wait, but now I am going to start cutting the pieces for your pouches."

She went out into the garage, and I continued with the reloading. I heard the front door open and close and after about a minute, I felt something brush by my feet. I thought someone had let Billy back inside. A moment later out of the corner of my eye, I saw two little hands grasp the far end of the table and Mouse's little head peek over the edge. I suppressed a smile and looked into the living room.

I yelled, "Mouse, would you like to help me in here?" I heard an "Eeep" from the end of the table and she ducked back down, but still kept her hands grasping the edge of the table. "Oh there you are." I said suppressing a smile. "Would you like to help me with this?"

Mouse stood up with a big smile and came around the table and climbed into my lap. I explained to her what I was doing and had her try resizing a cartridge. She had difficulty pulling the lever down with enough force, so I said I would resize the brass and primer them. It was too difficult to work with her in my lap, so I pulled over another chair and had her kneel on it and I noticed that she had dirty bare feet. I put the resized brass in a holder and showed her how to balance the scale. Once she had the scale balanced to my satisfaction, I had her move the scale weight to forty five grains. I then had her take a small powder scoop and put a scoop of powder into the pan. She stared mystified as the scale started wobbling up and down. I explained to her that she needed to add a little more with a tiny spoon until the scale was balanced again. She overloaded it the first couple tries, but finally figured it out. Once she had the correct measure of powder, I had her put the small funnel onto a cartridge and pour it in. During this whole process, she had her little tongue sticking out of the side of her mouth slightly, in concentration. I kept resizing and priming and let her take over the charging of the powder. It was slow going, but after about a half hour, she was getting very good at it. I started seating the bullets on the brass she had charged with powder and measured their length with a caliper to make sure they would fit in the gun. Together we reloaded fifty .308 rounds.

While we were reloading, Pam came back in with some pieces of leather and worked on her pattern on the other side of the table. Every once in a while I would see her look at Mouse and smile at Mouse's concentration. This was a good start at normalcy. I heard Catherine and Lizzy come back on the horses and put them up in the garage.

Lizzy came in and said excitedly, "We shot four grouse and we saw some wild pigs."

Catherine followed her in a minute later, and saw what we were doing and smiled at Mouse. She said, "We are running low on shotgun shells. Do you reload those too? I kept the shell casings."

I said, "No, I put them on the list for Jason to bring back, but thanks for saving the casings. We will trade them in to be re-loaded by someone else."

"Did Lizzy tell you about the wild pigs?" Catherine asked. "They were huge. Probably about 300 pound each. There were some little ones too."

"Yes, she did, but if you try to hunt them, aim for their head, and then watch out for the others in the herd. They can be really dangerous." I said in warning. "I wish I could go along with you, but just be extra careful with them. Actually could you wait until Jason gets back to go?"

Lizzy asked, "Can Catherine teach me to shoot?"

"Of course she can." I said. "I think all of you need to learn to shoot."

Pam said quickly, "I don't want to learn it."

I looked at her and could see that she was afraid. I said, "I would like you to try Pam. If nothing else, I want you to learn how to handle a pistol. The way things are, you may need to de-fend yourself someday."

"But I don't want to hurt anyone." She replied.

"You may not have a choice." Catherine said. "If I hadn't learned, those men would have killed Jack and you wouldn't be here."

Pam looked surprised at Catherine's comment and a little shocked. "Okay," she said hesitantly, "I'll try with the pistol."

Catherine and Lizzy cleaned the grouse and hung them in the cold cellar and then went to brush down the horses. Pam started dinner while Mouse and I put the reloading supplies away on a lower shelf. I went into the living room and put some water in the big kettle to boil, and put some buckets of water in the bathroom. I was starting to get around pretty good with one crutch. When I had everything set up, I called Catherine and Lizzy in and asked them to give Mouse a bath. She was starting to stink and her feet were filthy. While they were in the bathroom, I asked Pam if she would be able to make Mouse some moccasins.

Pam's eyes lit up again, and she said, "Yes, I made those for my brother all the time."

"Could we keep it a secret and give them to her as a gift?" I asked

Pam said, "I need to guess at the size, but I think I can do it."

When Catherine and Lizzy brought Mouse back out, she was clean and full of energy. Pam set dinner on the kitchen table and we all sat down to eat. Before we started, I asked everyone to tell me what had made them smile that day. Catherine and Lizzy looked at me funny, so I asked Pam to start.

Pam closed her eyes for a minute and then said smiling, "It made me smile today thinking about my Mama and Papa. Thank you, Jack."

I looked at Mouse and asked, "What made you smile today Mouse?"

Mouse looked down and thought a second and then looked up and pointed at me with a big smile. "Eeep."

"Thank you Mouse, I'm happy I can make you smile." I said.

I looked at Catherine and she shrugged. I said, "Give it a try."

Catherine thought for a second and then said smiling, "When Lizzy and I went out on the horses, I got Black up to a full gallop in the meadow out back and he is really fast. I was smiling the whole time.

"How about you, Lizzy?" I asked.

Lizzy had been thinking while everyone else was telling what made them smile and quickly said, "I thought about Jason today and it made me smile."

I got a big smile on my face and said, "It makes me smile that the five of us can still find some happiness in our lives in simple things and even though the smile you remember was in the past, it can still bring you the happy feelings you had when you smiled. Thank you, Pam, for telling me how your father did this at dinner every evening. I think we will do it every time we sit down to eat."

CHAPTER 34

J ason showed up four days later with Sammy in tow. They had all the supplies I had requested and some extras sent over by Angie. Jason handed me an envelope and said it was from his father. He had a cryptic smile on his face. While the kids unloaded the canoe and put the supplies away, I took the letter into the den and sat at my father's desk and opened it. Inside were a letter from Tom and two documents. I set the documents aside and read Tom's letter first.

Jack,

I hope this letter finds you well and on the mend. I don't know how to start, so I will start the way you would, straight at it. You are now part owner in the Jenkins Trading Post. To explain, when I got back, Gerard Perot, the head of the town council was trying to take over the Trading Post. He tried to pass an emergency act that would have killed trade in our town, and lined his pockets with whatever money came through the Trading Post. I hadn't told anyone about the money you sent over, and all the men kept quiet until we had a town meeting. I approached Milly Jenkins and her son Matthew beforehand to determine what could be done. Needless to say, I used part of the money you sent over to buy out the investment contract that Perot and a couple other members of the council had made with Mike Jenkins a couple years ago. I can give you more details, the next time I see you.

Enclosed you will find your investment contract signed by Milly and Matthew Jenkins for the money I used to buy out the old contract. I signed for you as proxy. This is your copy to keep and Milly has a copy, with a duplicate she gave to me to hold, since I signed for you. The second document is the receipt for the money you put in trust with the Trading Post, minus the amount of the investment contract and the cost of the supplies we sent over. You can compare the amounts and see that you still have quite a bit of money left. I am holding the money until we can set up a secure place to put it at the Post. I hope I made the right decision, but knowing you, I think I did.

Tom Gray Wolf

PS. Angie sent a package over for the girls. There are some second hand clothes that should fit each of them. I trust Angie to get the sizes right. She also sent over some colored pencils and paper that she thought Mouse would like. If there is anything else you need, send a list back with Jason and Sammy.

I smiled to myself and thought, *'Tom knows me so well. I would have done the same had I been there myself. It's been a long time since I was in the trading business, but I think I will just be a silent partner and let the Jenkins run it like they always have. I have four girls to raise, and that will keep me busy enough.'* I got out a pen and some paper from my father's desk and started to compose a couple letters back, the first letter to Mrs. Jenkins and the second letter to Tom.

Mrs. Jenkins,

First, let me send my condolences at the loss of your husband. I only met him the one time I was in the Trading Post, and found him to be a very personable and honest man.

I understand that I am now an investor in the Trading Post. I believe it was the right decision for Tom to invest some of the money I sent over to help the town out. I leave the business end of it in your capable hands. If there is anything more that I can do, please let me know.

As I wrote this, a thought came to mind. It involved Catherine and the girls.

I would like to amend the investment contract and trust agreement though. I would like to put it in the following names:

Catherine Lea Barstow	Elizabeth Duncan
Pamela Todd	Mouse (name unknown)

This new contract will take my name off, and put a one fourth interest of my investment in each of these names. I leave it to you to write up the revised contract and trust agreement, and I would like copies sent to each of the girls.

As far as the extra money I put in trust at the Trading Post, use what you need to keep the store stocked and prices even so the towns people don't suffer from the tragic events of a few weeks ago. Tom tells me that storing the money may be an issue. Please use some of the money to buy a proper safe and have it delivered to the Trading Post on one of your supply runs. I would also be willing to spend some of the money to pay for a guard to be present whenever there are strangers in town. That's all I can think of, but if there are any other issues you need help with, don't wait to contact me, I trust you to take care of them.

Sincerely,
Jack Jesse Anders

That letter finished, I sat and thought for a few minutes about what I had just done. *'I had just made four young girls the richest women in the territory.'* I have lived most of my adult life without any money in my pockets at all. I have always been able to live off the land, and trade for whatever I needed. I no longer had the option of trading my services in raider protection, but the money my dad left negated the need for that. I felt good about what I had just done, for the girls and for the town, so I started a letter to Tom.

Tom,

Don't worry, I think you made the right decision for me and trust the town will benefit. I have enclosed a letter to Mrs. Jenkins, and I would like you and Angie to read it before you deliver it to her. Since you are Catherine's relatives, I know you will look out for her and the girls' interests. If anything should happen to me, I know she and the girls will have a place to go and this will provide for them. I only say this, because I doubt my brother Jim will give up trying to find me.

Sorry for the negative attitude, but I love these girls to much to take the chance that they wouldn't be taken care of. I am the happiest I have ever been, broken foot and all.

Mouse came running into the den wearing new clothes and carrying a bundle. She climbed into my lap and pushed my letters aside and opened the bundle. Inside were the colored pencils and paper. "Eeep!" she said with a huge smile.

"Did Auntie Angie send you some presents?" I asked laughing.

"Eeep." Mouse nodded and said smiling.

"Well, would you let me finish my letters and then we can draw something with your new pencils." I said.

Mouse closed the bundle up and climbed down and went over to my dad's easy chair and opened it up again. I thought for a minute about the letter I was writing and decided to add some.

Angie, thank you for the presents for Mouse, she is very happy with the colored pencils and paper. She just interrupted me from writing this letter to show me, and I thank you for the

clothes. I was wondering how I was going to provide those for them. Though, I did discover that Pam is very good at sewing and making clothes. She is making Mouse some moccasins.

All the girls are adjusting pretty well to their new situation. Lizzy did tell me something about herself that I think will affect Jason, but I will let him tell you. I will talk to him if it becomes an issue though.

That's all I have for now. When you read the letter to Mrs. Jenkins, you will understand the rest.

Sincerely,
Jack

I folded the letters and placed them in the envelope that Jason had given me and put it aside. "Okay Mouse let's play with your present." I said.

Mouse jumped out of the chair and raced back over to my lap. I showed her how to draw stick figures and let her try. She got pretty good after a few tries. I drew one with big brown eyes, and ears that stuck out and wrote Mouse beneath it. "That's you." I said.

Mouse drew a taller figure with brown hair and blue eyes holding hands with the figure I had drawn. She pointed at me and at her name. "Eeep?" she asked.

"You want me to write my name?" I asked.

Mouse nodded, so I wrote 'Jack' below the taller figure. "That's how you write my name." I said.

Mouse looked at it and then tried to write it. Her tongue was sticking out of the corner of her mouth as she tried to duplicate my name. She got a close approximation after a couple tries. Then she tried writing 'Mouse' beside it. We kept at it until dinner was ready.

◆ ◆ ◆

We all sat down to dinner and I had everyone tell something that made them smile that day. Jason and Sammy looked apprehensive, but joined in. While we ate, Jason cleared his throat.

"What do you think of the letters I brought you?" Jason asked with a smile on his face. He was sitting beside Lizzy and I could tell they were holding hands beneath the table.

"I'm glad you brought that up." I said. "Girls, Jason has been itching to say that since I read them, so I'll let you know why he is grinning. Some of the money I sent back with Tom was used to buy an investment in the Trading Post."

"Why?" Catherine asked.

"Because the town council was trying to take over the Post from the Jenkins." Jason said.

"It wasn't the town council." Sammy interrupted. "It was Gerard Perot."

"It is being used to keep the town going Catherine." I said. "Without that money, trade would die, and people would horde supplies, and the town would suffer."

"But that's your money Jack. How can they use it without your permission?" Catherine asked.

"Tom did exactly what I would have done had I been there, and it wasn't that much money." I said.

"What are you going to do with owning part of the Trading Post?" Catherine asked skeptically.

"I will figure something out." I said and then kept quiet as the kids all starting talking about what had happened at Ten Pines.

After dinner, Lizzy asked Jason if she could talk with him on the porch. They went outside and sat on the swing together. Lizzy was quiet for a few minutes and then spoke to Jason.

"Jason, I like you a lot, but I have something to tell you, you're not going to like." Lizzy said quietly not looking at him. "I'm married."

Jason felt a knot in the pit of his stomach, just like when he found out that Catherine was his cousin. He heard Jack's voice in his mind, *'just listen and don't jump to conclusions.'* He kept his doubts off of his face as best he could and listened as Lizzy told him the story she had told to Jack a few days earlier. He felt anger as he listened to what had happened in her life before they met. When she finished, she looked at him out of the corner of her eye to see how he was responding. Jason sat looking straight ahead and then reached over and took her hand.

"I don't care." Jason said. "I love you."

Lizzy turned and melted into his arms. They held each other tightly. After a few minutes, Lizzy said, "I wasn't going to tell you, but Jack said that I should, if I cared about you."

"Well, if there is one thing I know," Jason said, "it's that Jack is usually right. I'm glad you told me. So where do we go from here?"

"I don't know." Lizzy said. "Let's talk with Jack."

They went inside and found me reading to Mouse. I looked up at them and then asked Mouse to go into the kitchen and see what Catherine, Pam and Sammy were doing. Mouse gave a disappointed 'Eeep' and climbed down from my lap. She went into the kitchen with a backward glance at Lizzy and Jason.

"Looks like you two have something to ask me." I said to Lizzy and Jason.

"I told him what I told you Jack." Lizzy said.

"What can we do about it?" Jason asked quickly.

"Right now there is nothing you can do about it." I said. "If you want to pursue it, someone will have to go back to Spokane and find her husband. I don't think it is necessary though. Where did you get married Lizzy?"

"Nowhere!" Lizzy exclaimed. "My father took me to Charles farm and dropped me off when he picked up the mule he traded me for. He said I was Charles wife now before he left."

"Well, it doesn't sound like a legal marriage to me." I said. "I'm sure if you two decide to get married someday it shouldn't be an issue."

They both blushed and glanced at each other. It was harder to tell on Jason with his darker complexion, but I was getting to know him pretty well.

"You don't have to decide right this minute." I said. "I think you should get to know each other better first. You never know Jason, Lizzy might eat crackers in bed."

"No I don't." Lizzy said indignantly.

"It's just an expression from when I was younger." I said. "It means that you each may have something that you don't like about each other. Take your time and be happy now."

CHAPTER 35

The next day, the kids planned a pig hunt. The herd of pigs had their territory about 2 miles to the south, where a creek fed out of the mountains to the west down to the lake. Catherine estimated that there were about fifteen pigs in the herd. She cleaned the .308 and grabbed a handful of the rounds Mouse and I had reloaded. Jason got out his bow and a dozen arrows. Sammy took the shotgun and a box of double-aught buckshot that Matthew Jenkins had included in the case of shotgun shells I had purchased. They saddled up the horses and Jason rode double with Lizzy behind him on Betty. Sammy rode Zack with just a blanket over Zack's back. It was around ten o'clock when they were ready to leave.

I hobbled out onto the porch and said to Catherine, "Make sure you have an escape route planned. Wild pigs can be vicious and very unpredictable when they are threatened. Shoot a small one if you can and aim for their head if you can. The meat will be better than an old boar or sow."

"Don't worry," Catherine sounded exasperated, "We will be safe and it will be nice to have some ham and bacon to eat."

"Don't count your pigs before you have them." I said with a smile. "I'm serious about how dangerous wild pigs can be though. Have a safe hunt."

Catherine led the way and they rode south. When they were about a quarter mile from where Lizzy and Catherine had seen the pigs, they dismounted and tied the horses to a fallen tree that had a lot of grass growing around it. Catherine started out and Jason followed with Sammy bringing up the rear. When they were about a hundred yards from the river, Catherine stopped and pulled out the binoculars. She scanned the area where they had last seen the pigs.

"I don't see them anywhere." Catherine whispered to the rest.

Jason looked at the terrain and whispered back, "There is a gully over there by the river. Pigs like to wallow in the mud. Maybe we will find them there."

They crept forward and when they got to the edge of the gully, they heard the pigs grunting below them. The brush was thick, but the pigs had made trails through it. Catherine looked through the binoculars again, but the brush was too thick to see through. She handed them to Jason and he looked and then shrugged.

"Looks like we are going to have to go in after them." He whispered.

"I don't know," Catherine said, "those trails are pretty low. We would have to crawl on our hands and knees."

"I've done it before for deer and elk." Jason whispered.

Catherine thought about it and images of catching the chickens came to mind. The trails were low just like the chicken trails through the hedge in Nordman.

"I've got a better idea." Catherine whispered back and then told them the story of how they had caught the chickens.

Jason's eyes lit up and he whispered, "That's a great idea, but who is going to go around and scare them this way?"

Sammy whispered, "I'll go around to the other side of the creek and shoot off a couple rounds with the shotgun. That ought to scare them."

Catherine looked at Jason and asked quietly, "Where should we set up?"

Jason looked around and then stood up behind a tree trunk to get a better view. "I'll set up behind that big tree there at the entrance to that trail, and Catherine you need to be farther back with the rifle, so you set up on top of that little cliff over there. That will give you a clear shot at those two trails."

"What about me?" Lizzy whispered.

"You go around with Sammy and start yelling when he

shoots the shotgun." Jason said.

"But I want to be with you." Lizzy protested.

"It's too dangerous." Jason said. "I am going to be the closest to where they come out. I don't want you to get hurt."

"But…" Lizzy started.

"No!" Jason said adamantly. "It will be better if you help Sammy make noise."

"Uughh…" Lizzy whispered. "That's no fun."

Jason smiled at her and chose his next words carefully, "Please, I would feel safer not worrying about you beside me if something bad happens."

"Okay, if I have to." Lizzy whispered reluctantly.

They made their plans. Sammy and Lizzy headed west to cross the creek about a quarter mile upstream and then headed back to the gully. Jason crept down to the big tree and stood behind it with an arrow nocked. Catherine climbed up onto the small cliff and lay down, placing the rifle on top of her daypack. Jason was only about twenty yards from the trail he was watching. Catherine was about fifty yards away and ten yards above the two trails she was watching. She looked over to her left and could see Jason standing behind the tree another fifty yards away from her. She waved at him and Jason waved back.

They waited patiently for about a half hour, listening to the pigs grunting and some of the little ones squealing in the gully. Suddenly, there was a loud whistle from the other side of the gully. Jason and Catherine got ready. Lizzy and Sammy started yelling loudly, and then they heard Sammy shoot the shotgun twice. The gully erupted with squealing pigs. Three huge pigs came out of one of the trails Catherine was watching, followed by two little ones. Catherine aimed at the rear one and led it slightly. She eased the trigger and felt the surprise when the gun went off. The rear pig tumbled into a heap. She turned and looked over at Jason, but she couldn't see him. Catherine stood up to get a better view and saw Jason running up the trail with a big boar chasing him. The boar was about thirty feet behind him and catching up. Catherine swung the rifle up and led the boar by about a foot and pulled the trigger. Nothing happened. "Shit". She realized she hadn't chambered another round. Jason flung his bow to the side and jumped up into another big tree. Catherine quickly chambered a round. Jason was only a few feet ahead of the boar when he reached a branch about eight feet off the ground. He swung up onto it and looked down laughing. The boar grunted around the bottom of the tree, but Catherine couldn't see it to get a shot. Jason tore a dead branch off the tree and flung it at the boar. He hit the boar in the snout and it squealed. The boar lost interest and went off looking for the rest of the herd.

Catherine yelled, "Are you all right Jason?"

"Yeah, but my heart is pumping like mad." Jason yelled back laughing.

They heard the shotgun go off again. Sammy yelled from across the creek. "Hey guys I just shot a little one, and he has an arrow sticking in his butt."

Jason laughed and yelled back, "That's the one that I tried to shoot, but it was being pushed out of the brush backwards by the big boar that chased me."

"Are you all right Jason?" Lizzy yelled concerned.

"He's fine." Catherine yelled laughing. "He went up a tree like a squirrel."

Lizzy and Sammy had to drag their pig down the creek until they could get around the brush. They all gathered together at the tree Jason had swung up into. Lizzy ran up to Jason and hugged him tight. Jason hugged her back, laughing. Lizzy stood back and looked at him. Other than some scraps on the palms of his hands from the tree bark, he looked fine.

"Dammit Jason, don't scare me like that." Lizzy said angrily, punching him in the shoulder.

"Sorry, but now you see why I had you go with Sammy." Jason said with a grin on his face.

"Stop smiling." Lizzy said. "You could have been killed."

"He's smiling, because he was scared shitless." Sammy said

with a grin.

"You got that right." Jason said.

Catherine and Sammy went over to the pig she had shot and dragged it back to the tree. Jason and Sammy started gutting them. Jason looked at the one Catherine had shot and saw a bullet hole behind the right ear and the exit wound out the left ear.

"Damn Catherine, nice shot." Jason said.

"Well Jack did say to shoot them in the head." Catherine looked at the one Jason and Sammy had shot. It had an arrow in the butt and buck shot had torn up its left shoulder. "Not in the butt." She said laughing.

"I want to learn to shoot like that." Lizzy said.

Lizzy and Catherine hiked back and brought the horses down. Black got a little skittish around the dead pigs, but Betty and Zack stood unconcerned. They tied one pig on the rump of Zack, and the other onto Betty. Lizzy rode behind Catherine on the way back. Sammy rode in front of the pig on Zack.

Sammy asked on the way back, "Should we tell Jack that Jason got chased by a boar?"

"Oh he'll know something happened." Jason laughed. "Better to be honest about it and learn from the experience."

"Yes, always be honest with Jack." Lizzy said with a thoughtful smile.

We had heard the shots in the distance from the cabin, and I knew that the hunt had been successful. They showed up a couple hours later joking and laughing as they rode up. Mouse, Pam and I were sitting on the porch and could see the two pigs on the horses behind Sammy and Jason. They looked to be about a hundred pounds each though one looked a little tore up.

"You were successful." I said.

"Not without some excitement though." Jason answered. "I got chased up a tree by a big boar. I think from now on, I'll hunt dangerous game with a rifle like Catherine."

Mouse ran down to see the pigs and smiled up at Sammy. "Eeep." She laughed jumping up and down.

I had the kids take the pigs over to the tree we used to hang deer and elk, and had Pam bring them a couple buckets of hot water I had had her heat up earlier to wash them off with. Jason and Sammy went to work skinning them, and Pam gathered up the skin as they cut it off.

"I'm going to make fried pork rinds from this." She said with a smile.

"Mmmm... that sounds delicious." I said. "We used to be able to buy that in the store when I was your age, Pam."

"Really?" Pam asked.

"Yeah." I said thinking back. "Fried pork rinds, potato chips, Cheetos, corn chips; all kinds of fried snacks."

"What are Cheetos?" Sammy asked.

"They were puffed cheese crisps that turned your hands orange when you ate them." I said.

"Mmmm.. that sounds good." Pam said. "Can you show me how to make them?"

"Sorry Pam that I don't know." I said.

"Well, I can make potato chips." Pam said. "My mom used to make them all the time from the soft potatoes that we didn't use for planting."

"Then it sounds like we should plan a little celebration." I said. "We need to celebrate Mouse's birthday next week."

"Eeep?" Mouse questioned in surprise.

"Yes, Mouse. We don't know when your real birthday is or how old you are, but we are going to celebrate your birthday on November 1st."

Mouse looked thoughtful and then held up both hands. I got the message and asked her, "You are ten?"

Mouse nodded and gave out an excited "Eeep."

"Then we will celebrate your eleventh birthday next week, okay?" I asked. "Lizzy and Pam when are your birthdays?"

Lizzy said, "Mines on April 22nd. I'll be eighteen."

Pam said, "I just had my birthday on October 3rd. I'm fifteen."

Lizzy looked at Jason and asked, "When's your birthday."

"The same day as yours." He said smiling at her surprised look. "Just kidding, but mines very close to yours. Mine's on April 20th, and I'll be eighteen."

"So you're two days older than me." Lizzy said grinning.

"Yeah, I'm an old man." Jason said laughing.

I watched the interaction and thought, 'good, they are all forgetting about the past and getting on with life.' The boys butchered the pigs and we hung the hams and bacon in the smoke house and we took the chops down to the cold cellar. We had a good supply of meat now and it should get us through most of the winter. We would probably have to make a hunt again sometime in February. By then, I would be out of this cast and be able to go along.

We had fresh pork chops for dinner, and when I asked everyone what made them smile that day, the hunters all related the happiness and relief they felt when the hunt was over. Pam said that the listening lessons I was giving her made her smile, and Mouse said "Eeep," and held up ten fingers and then one with a huge smile on her face.

"What about you Jack?" Catherine asked.

I looked around the table and said, "This makes me smile."

That night was the first night that I slept with Catherine again. I was able to negotiate the stairs slowly and it felt good to lie down in a bed again instead of the couch. Catherine got undressed and crawled in next to me. She kissed me lightly on the lips and hugged me.

"I like this." She said. "I missed having you next to me. Do you think...."

"No, I don't think." I interrupted. "What the girls have been through before they came here..." I stopped and shrugged. "I don't think it would be appropriate."

"Jack, Lizzy and Pam know I love you and you love me." She said. "They won't care."

We both felt the end of the bed move and Mouse crawled up

and pushed between us. "Eeep?" she asked.

"Well I guess that settles that." I said. "Yes Mouse you can sleep with us."

"Uughh!" Catherine whispered aggravated. "Okay Mouse but just tonight."

CHAPTER 36

We settled in to a routine and the following week, we had a birthday party for Mouse. We didn't have any cake, but Pam had made potato chips and fried pork rinds. Lizzy and Catherine dressed Mouse up after a much needed bath, and we all sang "Happy Birthday" to her. Mouse couldn't stop smiling.

After lunch, we all sat in the living room and gave Mouse presents. I handed Mouse the moccasins that I had Pam make for her. Mouse looked at them and smiled happily. Catherine helped her put them on and showed her how to tie the leather laces around the top. They covered her feet and ankles. Jason gave Mouse a knife with a deer horn handle and a four inch blade. It was in a nice sheath with some beadwork on the leather. Catherine gave Mouse some of her comic books.

Lizzy walked up to Mouse, hugged her and said, "Mouse, I don't have anything to give you but a hug and to ask you if I can call you my little sister."

Mouse got a surprised look on her face, smiled and said, "Eeep," and gave Lizzy a tight hug back.

Sammy gave Mouse a belt that he had punched extra holes in so it would fit around her. He put the knife sheath on it and then buckled it around her waist. It was way too long so he wrapped the end around the belt a couple times to keep it from flapping. Mouse looked down at it with a huge smile on her face.

Pam gave Mouse a hug and started to say that she didn't have anything to give her either, when I stopped her.

"Mouse, Pam made those moccasins for you. I just provided the leather." I said.

Pam gave me a grateful look as Mouse gave her a big hug.

Mouse stood still for a second and then to everyone's surprise said, "Thank you," in a squeaky high pitched voice just above a whisper.

By the end of that week, the weather started changing. By mid-afternoon every day, the wind picked up and clouds started coming in. I talked with Jason and Sammy about getting back to Ten Pines. Jason said he wanted to stay, but Sammy said he had to get back. I told Jason that Sammy shouldn't head back across the lake alone and that he should head back with him. They could plan a trip back here after the lake froze over. We decided that they would leave the following morning if the weather was okay.

That evening, Lizzy and Jason sat on the porch talking quietly for a couple hours. The rest of us sat in the kitchen playing Monopoly. I could tell that Jason was looking for a way to stay, but Lizzy had told him that it was better if he helped Sammy get back. After Lizzy and Jason came back in, we all went to bed.

The following morning it was calm, so Jason and Sammy prepared the canoe for the trip back. I gave Jason the envelope that had the return letters inside, and shook hands with him and Sammy.

"Thanks for bringing the supplies over boys." I said. "And thanks for the pigs you helped get. That will go a long ways with three extra mouths to feed."

"You're welcome Jack." They both said.

"We'll head back around Christmas and I think I can talk Mom and Dad in coming too." Jason said.

"That would be great." Catherine said smiling.

Lizzy came down and gave Jason a long hug and then attempted a kiss on his cheek. He turned quickly and kissed her on the lips. She blushed a deep red and all her freckles stood out. Everyone smiled at them. Pam handed Sammy a package and said it was some leftover breakfast for their trip back. Mouse gave them each a hug and then came over to stand beside me. Lizzy and Catherine helped push them off and stayed on the beach as they paddled off.

I inspected the garage and had the girls muck out the horse and goat droppings. I checked the potbelly stove in the corner and had Mouse clean out the old ashes. I checked the damper with a burning stick to see if the smoke would clear the garage. It didn't, so I had Catherine climb on the roof and take the top off and look down the pipe. She yelled down that it was plugged at the top by an old bird nest. She cleared it out and I checked it again and the smoke cleared through the chimney. I told all the girls that when it got a lot colder, we would have to keep a fire burning in the stove every evening to warm the garage up. The horses and goats could survive pretty cold temperatures, but I preferred to keep them comfortable. That afternoon, it got overcast and started to snow.

We settled in for winter. Every day, I gave Mouse reading and writing lessons, and let her draw her pictures. She started tracing characters out of the Dr. Seuss books. Catherine and Lizzy took a few hunting trips and brought back some rabbits and grouse. Pam had taken over the kitchen and prepared all of our meals. When she wasn't cooking, she would sit and sew. Catherine gave her the green cloth that Marge and Janice had given her.

I hadn't had a domestic life since I was sixteen, and I was getting comfortable having the girls take care of everything. That bothered me.

It started snowing hard the following week, so I had Catherine and Lizzy help Mouse get the chickens into the shed. By the end of the week, we had two feet of snow on the ground. Catherine had to shovel a path from the back of the cabin to the shed for Mouse. We still had six weeks to go until Christmas, so if the chores were done, everyone sat around and read or worked on little projects. Catherine and Mouse reloaded the rest of the .223 brass, and some of the .375 pistol cartridges. Winter was always boring. Pam sat and sewed and started teaching Catherine and Lizzy to sew.

The Murphy's just made it to Spokane when the snow started. Being as lazy as they were, they decided to postpone their trip to Lewiston until spring. They found a couple rooms at a hotel, and settled in.

"Pa, if we stay here until spring, we'll spend all the money we took from Jenkins." George said as they sat in their room one evening.

"Well, we'll just have to steal it back when we leave." Murphy said.

"But we don't know where they keep it." Andrew replied to his father's comment.

"That's your job Andrew." Murphy said. "I want you to get real friendly with the barmaid downstairs over the next couple of months and find out where the money is kept."

Andrew laughed and said, "She is kinda cute, and she has been smiling at me a lot. That shouldn't be a problem."

"Well, have your fun and get the information we need. It's going to be about four months before we can head out. We have enough money to last that long, and I plan to play cards with some of the locals in the meantime." Murphy said.

The Murphy's made their plans and settled in for a long winter. They weren't well liked by the locals, but Murphy was always able to get a couple of the local business men to play cards with him, and he was careful not to take them for too much. He wanted a steady stream of cash coming in while they waited the snow out.

The snow storm hit Lewiston at the same time, and Jim had his men gather all the supplies they could to wait out the winter. He had about seventy men in his gang now, and they stole everything they could from the locals. There were a large number of funerals that winter as the gang killed anyone that stood up to them. The rest of the locals hunkered down to wait out the season and made their plans to leave when spring arrived.

"Brian, get in here." Jim yelled.

Brian was sitting in the kitchen drinking tea when Jim yelled for him. He got up slowly and walked into the living room. Jim was sitting on the couch in his underwear with just a bathrobe opened in the front. His huge belly was hanging over. There was a different young girl cowering at the other end of the couch, crying. She couldn't have been more than fourteen. She had a bruised right cheek. Most of the girls Jim got these days were from a brothel in town that a woman named Maggie ran. They were mostly kidnapped girls that she bought from the raiders. She provided Jim with girls whenever he asked, more out of fear of Jim than respect for him.

"What's up boss?" Brian asked.

"Any word from the Jacobs boys?" Jim asked.

"Nope, and I don't think we'll be hearing anything until spring now with all this snow." Brian replied.

"Well if that's the case, we'll wait until the snow melts and the ice breaks on the rivers and then head to Bonners Ferry. We'll probably run into them on the way back." Jim said. "And if they haven't found my brother, I'm going to be pissed."

"I'll let you know the minute I hear anything." Brian said, thinking 'What an ass. Jack hasn't been around for seven months, and Jim is still fixated on him.'

"You're damn right you will." Jim said angrily. "That'll be all. Get out."

Brian left out the back door and headed down to the hotel he had a room at. As he trudged through the snow, he thought, 'Bonners Ferry is going to be the last trip I take with Jim and these men. I'm going to sneak off from there and head to Calgary and get *away from all this bullshit. Why, why didn't I leave when Jack left? I would have been a better brother to Jack than the asshole he has as a brother. If Jack's still alive, I'll do what I can to help him, even if it means killing Jim. Damn Jim scares me. I don't know if I got the balls to stand up to him.'* Thoughts like that plagued Brian daily.

As winter took hold, Jim had Brian and a couple of his other lieutenants lock up all the guns from his men. They had started killing each other in drunken brawls or over a girl. They lost five men the first month of winter. This didn't stop the fights, and a few men left because they wouldn't give up their guns. Jim was feared by all of them and he told them that if anyone was killed in a brawl, the other men in the brawl would be hung. It took two hangings to get the men to stop fighting. It proved to be a long winter for Brian.

CHAPTER 37

The cold hit hard the first two weeks of December, and the lake froze quickly. We stayed inside most of the time, and tried to find things to keep us occupied. The cast on my leg was itching like crazy, so I made a scratcher to reach down inside to relieve the itchiness. By the time Christmas was approaching, the girls were going stir crazy. They got into shouting matches over little things, like messes and things out of place. I spent a lot of time refereeing their disputes.

Two days before Christmas, Lizzy and Catherine were in the garage mucking the stalls and feeding the animals. They heard some yelling coming from down by the lake and went outside. Jason was running up the slope followed by Tom and Angie. Lizzy ran out to him and they hugged each other tightly.

"Damn, I missed you." Jason said smiling.

"I missed you too." Lizzy said laughing.

I came out on the porch and welcomed Tom and Angie. They kicked the snow off their feet and took their backpacks and coats off and we went inside. Pam quickly went about making a pot of tea to warm them up. Tom and Angie stood by the fireplace to warm up, but Jason was on the couch with Lizzy and sat smiling at her.

"I'm glad you guys could make it over." I said. "These girls are driving me crazy."

"That's what you get for being a nice guy." Tom chuckled.

Catherine hugged Angie tightly and said, "I'm glad you are here Angie, I've missed you."

"What about me?" Tom said with a fake sad look on his face.

Catherine walked over to him and gave him a big hug. "Oh, I

missed you too, Uncle Tom."

Mouse was peeking in from the kitchen, and Angie went to her and hugged her. "My, my Mouse you are getting so big." Angie said laughing.

I looked at Mouse and thought, *'Big? She's still less than four feet tall and probably only weighs sixty five pounds.'* Then I realized that Angie was trying to include Mouse in the group. Mouse joined Angie on the couch next to Lizzy and Jason. Mouse showed Angie her drawings she had made and Angie acted satisfyingly impressed.

We settled in for the evening talking about things that had happened over the past seven weeks. Tom told me that they were able to get all the trenches dug for the stockade, and had set at least fifty percent of the logs. Angie spent time with the girls, especially admiring the moccasins that Pam had made for Mouse. Pam showed her some other things she was making, but kept them hidden from the rest of us. It was a relaxing evening, and it started snowing again.

Having guests had the girls on their best behavior. Angie mothered them, and it left time for Tom and I to talk.

"Do you think you will be able to finish the stockade this spring?" I asked Tom.

"It should go fast after it thaws." He said. "We cut all the logs for the rest of the walls, but we don't want to set them until we can pack the ground around them."

"How do the townspeople feel about it?" I asked.

"Most all of them are for it, but Gerard Perot tried to stop it from happening. He pissed so many people off, that there was a referendum to remove him from head of the town council." Tom said.

"How did that go?" I asked. I didn't know Perot, but from what I had heard so far, I didn't think he had the town's best interest at heart.

"He was voted out by over 90 percent." Tom said laughing. "After his attempt to take over the Trading Post, he lost all trust."

I could tell that Tom didn't like Perot at all, and I trusted his ability to read other people's character.

"So who took his place?" I asked. "You?"

"God no!" Tom exclaimed. "They tried to talk me into taking the position, but I hate politics. Jeremy took his place. He has a better disposition for it."

"Well, as long as the best interests of the town are being met, I trust it was a good choice." I said.

"By the way, since we are talking about Perot, I have the investment and trust agreements from Milly Jenkins for you." Tom said taking a large envelope out of his pocket.

I opened it and saw four smaller envelopes inside with each of the girl's names on them. Catherine came out of the kitchen and asked, "What's that?"

I closed the envelope and said, "It's just the investment agreement for the Trading Post."

"Can I see it?" she asked.

"Not now, later." I said looking at Tom who had a big grin on his face.

"Why not now?" Catherine asked curiously looking at Tom.

"Because I said so." I said a little too quickly.

"Okay, okay, chill." Catherine said frowning.

"Sorry, but it's private." I said trying to calm my outburst.

"Okay I said. Keep your little secrets." Catherine said not entirely satisfied.

Tom and Angie took the front bedroom, and Jason took the couch, while Lizzy and Pam stayed in the back bedroom. Mouse had made a habit of sleeping between Catherine and me, much to Catherine's frustration.

The next day was Christmas Eve, and Jason, Lizzy and Catherine went out and cut down a small Christmas tree. Angie had gotten some popcorn from the trading post, and she had Pam and Mouse make popcorn strings to wrap around the tree. I had

Mouse climb up into the attic and bring down an old box of Christmas ornaments. That afternoon, we all took part in decorating the tree. Tom held Mouse up to place the Angel on the top of the tree. Everyone cheered, and Mouse blushed.

After dinner that evening, Angie inspected my foot. She asked me to wiggle my toes. I did, and she wanted to know if I felt any pain. I told her no, it felt fine. She had Catherine bring her a garden shears from the garage, and cut the cast off. Everybody covered their noses from the smell. My foot still had red lines from the incisions Angie had made to reset the bones. She took out nail clippers and cut the knots on the stitches she had used to hold the cuts closed, and then washed my foot and calf off with hot soapy water.

"I don't want to pull the thread out of the stitches. They should work their way out on their own. It will itch when they do, but if you soak your foot in hot water you'll be fine." She said.

I stood up and walked around the couch. My foot was a little stiff, but it was a relief to have the cast off. Mouse ran upstairs and came back down with the wool sock for my left foot and handed it to me.

"Thank you Mouse. My foot is a little cold with the cast off." I said appreciatively to her.

"I'll resew the seams in your pants tomorrow." Pam said. She had opened the left seam in my pants from the knee down before, so I could get them on and off.

"It can wait Pam, tomorrows Christmas, but thank you." I said to her.

The next morning, Mouse was up before the sun came up and was running up and down the hall waking everyone up. "Eeep, eeep." I was lying next to Catherine holding her since Mouse had crawled out of bed, when Mouse ran in and jumped on the bed. "Eeep."

"Oh Mouse, not now." Catherine said in exasperation. It was the first time we had been close in a month.

"I don't think we can ignore her." I said. I heard everyone else getting up and smiled at Catherine. "We can take a nap later."

"You know I want more than a nap." She said as she hugged me hard and wouldn't let go.

We disengaged a few minutes later and got up and dressed. Mouse was running up and down the stairs trying to get everyone to come down. Everyone slowly made their way down and Mouse was finally satisfied. Jason was sitting up on the couch rubbing his eyes and yawning. He woke up quickly when Lizzy sat down next to him. Pam went into the kitchen and whipped some eggs to make scrambled eggs for everyone, and Angie and Catherine stoked the fire and started some bacon frying. Tom and I went into the kitchen and made some tea from a pot of hot water that Lizzy brought out. Mouse ran from the kitchen to the living room checking on everyone. Billy followed her as she scooted around the house. I put my moccasins on, thankful that the cast was finally off, and went into the garage and fed the animals. I checked the stove and added some kindling to heat the garage more. It may be Christmas for us humans, but the animals deserved some comfort too. Then I noticed a new arrival.

"Hey everyone, come out here and see what Santa brought us." I yelled.

Mouse and Pam came out first, followed by Tom and Angie, then Jason, Lizzy, and Catherine.

"What did Santa leave us?" Catherine asked.

I reached into the goat pen and held up a new born female baby goat. It couldn't have been more than four hours old and was already standing and walking.

Mouse came over to pet it, and I handed it to Pam. Pam cuddled it and smiled the biggest smile I had seen on her yet. Everyone gathered around to pet the newborn, and I asked Pam what she was going to name it.

Pam looked thoughtful and finally said, "I think we should

name her Angel since she was born on Christmas day."

That met with everyone's approval, and the mother goat started bleating for her baby. Pam put Angel back into the pen and it hopped stiff legged over to its mother. We all went back inside.

We all sat in the kitchen and ate a big breakfast, and made small talk. Mouse couldn't sit still and wouldn't eat until I told her that there would be no presents unless she cleaned her plate. She gobbled the rest down and sat fidgeting while the rest of us finished. After everyone finished and we had cleaned up, I looked at Mouse and asked, "What do you think we should do now, Mouse?"

In a squeaky little voice, Mouse said. "Presents!"

It surprised Tom and Angie, but the rest of us knew that Mouse could talk when she wanted to. I said, "Okay, let's go into the living room and open presents."

Mouse bolted from the kitchen and ran into the den. She came back with her drawing supplies and sat on the floor. I went upstairs and got the envelope and the leather pouches that Pam had made for me. Tom, Angie and Jason got their backpacks from beside the door and sat down. Pam went to her bedroom and grabbed some bundles and came back down and sat next to Mouse on the floor. Lizzy and Catherine went into the garage and came back with some bundles. I guess that I wasn't too attentive over the last seven weeks, because I hadn't noticed anyone making presents besides Pam. Of course, Catherine and Lizzy were always out and about during the day.

I sat down, and asked Mouse if she wanted to start? Mouse opened her papers and took the top one and gave it to me. It was a picture of a tall brown haired man with blue eyes and a cast on one foot holding hands with a little mouse eared girl, holding hands with a tall black haired girl, holding hands with a red haired girl, holding hands with a yellow haired girl. Below each stick figure in her childlike hand, was written Jack, Mouse, Catherine, Lizzy, and Pam.

"I love it Mouse." I said with a big smile, thinking that this is how my parents must have felt when I gave them pictures like this when I was little. "Thank you very much. I'm going to put it up on the wall in my bedroom, so I see it every morning when I wake up."

Mouse hugged me and said in her quiet squeaky voice. "I love you Jack." It brought tears to my eyes as I hugged her back.

Mouse then handed out pictures to everyone, even Billy who sniffed it and then lay down on it. She told everyone that she loved them and they each hugged her. There wasn't a dry eye in the room other than Billy.

Pam was next, and took out a hooded coat she had made for Mouse from the green cloth that Catherine had given her. She had Mouse try it on, and it was a little big, but it was perfect. It had ties to close the front. Mouse pulled the hood up and smiled from ear to ear. Pam gave me a plaid shirt, and gave me a little hug. Pam was still uncomfortable getting close to men.

"Thank you Pam, it's perfect." I said trying it on.

She gave Lizzy and Catherine shirts she had made out of some old flowered sheets. They all hugged tightly and thanked her, and then they went into the bathroom to put them on and came back out so everyone could see.

Lizzy and Catherine had worked together on their gifts, and gave Mouse a new belt they had made out of elk hide that was more her size. They gave me a new leather scabbard that I knew would be perfect for the AR, and it even had ties on it so it would attach to the side of my saddle. Then they turned to Jason and asked, "Did you get it?"

Jason smiled and nodded, and rummaged in his pack and pulled out a box. He handed it to Lizzy and Lizzy gave it to Pam. Pam opened it and it was full of different color spools of thread and all different size needles. Lizzy said, "That is from all three of us."

Pam's eyes lit up and she squealed, "Oh thank you, thank you, Lizzy, Catherine, and Jason. I love it."

Tom and Angie gave them each some new clothes, pants, underwear and shirts, and Angie gave Mouse an extra present.

Mouse opened it and squeaked with joy. It was a box full of color pencils, colored chalk, charcoal sticks and paper.

It was my turn, and I handed them each a leather pouch that Pam had made for me. They looked at them curiously until I said, "Open them."

They each untied the tops and poured out the money I had put in each one. I had split the remainder of the coins that my dad had left, that I had kept, in five equal amounts and put it in each pouch. Tom and Angie looked on in surprise, and Jason looked jealous, so I threw him the fifth pouch.

"You don't need to give me this." He said.

"I don't need any money." I said. "I've got everything I want right here. Besides, I've lived most of my life without any, so why should I change now?"

Mouse was playing with her coins, and then I took the en velope out of my pocket. The girls looked at me curiously, while I opened it and took out the four envelopes inside. I looked at the names and handed each of them their envelope. Catherine, Lizzy and Pam opened theirs immediately and started reading. There were two letters of agreement in each one. I had checked them to make sure they were accurate.

"Does this mean what I think it means?" Catherine asked in shock.

"What do you think it means?" I asked her smiling.

"I own one sixteenth of the Trading Post?" she asked. "And what is a Trust Agreement?"

"Yes." I said. "You each now own one sixteenth interest in the Trading Post and one fourth of the money I sent over with Tom to be held in Trust."

Pam and Lizzy sucked in their breath in shock and stared at the papers. Mouse didn't know what was happening, but she knew it was important.

"It says here that you, Uncle Tom and Aunt Angie are the Trustee's until we come of age. What does that mean?" Catherine asked.

"It means that we will watch over it for you until you are

eighteen, which is still a rule that I don't agree with, but it is still the law." I answered.

All four girls ran up to me and gave me a big hug. This time Pam didn't hold back, and I hugged her back.

CHAPTER 38

Tom, Angie, and Jason stayed until January 2nd. They threw me a surprise birthday party on the 1st, but I had an idea it was coming because of the way Catherine started sneaking around and whispering to everyone. Tom and I had a lot of time to catch up and Angie and the girls kept themselves busy cleaning the house. Jason followed Lizzy around like a puppy and helped with all the heavy lifting. He didn't want to leave, but Angie made him go, to Lizzy's disappointment.

It was just the four of us again, and we settled into a routine. Every day, I taught Mouse to read. Pam made our meals with help from Catherine, and then sat around most of the day sewing. She continued teaching Catherine and Lizzy to sew. Catherine and Lizzy went hunting a couple times a week if the weather was good. I even found my dad's old ice auger and we did some ice fishing. It helped make our meals less predictable. There's only so much you can do with venison, pork and smoked fish, but Pam was an excellent cook.

It turned out to be a pretty mild winter. It snowed another five or six times, but only dropped about six inches each time. The wind blew most of the snow off the lake. The snow along the path to the shed was already over Mouse's head. We started getting fewer eggs, so we cooked a few of the chickens to Mouse's dissatisfaction. I had her pick her least favorite chickens for the pot, and it helped a little.

Time seemed to stand still, but I was happier than I had ever been. Catherine still tried to get me to have sex with her, but I resisted. Though, it was getting tougher to do, not because we didn't have opportunities. I still felt I was too old for her. As winter went on, Catherine became more distant from me. She started turning away from me and stopped kissing me good morning and good night. So I decided that it was time to talk. Always forward.

"Catherine?" I whispered to her one night over Mouse's little snores. "We need to talk."

"About what?" She asked with a hint of sarcasm.

"You're ignoring me." I said.

"Really, I hadn't noticed." She replied.

"Well, I have noticed, and I want you to tell me why." I said, even though I knew the reason.

"Because you don't love me!" She said with a shudder in her voice.

"You know that's not true." I said.

"Okay, you won't love me." She replied and started crying. "You always come up with a reason not to make love to me, even when we are alone."

"Catherine, I love you more than I have ever loved anyone, but I am too old for you." I tried to justify to myself.

"You always say that, but it doesn't matter to me." She said still crying.

"But I care what others would think about you and me if we did." I tried to sound reasonable, but my arguments were getting fallacious even to me.

"I don't care what anyone else thinks." Catherine said angrily, finally stopping her crying. "Even Angie knows that I love you."

"Well I'm sorry, but I can't come to terms with that." I said. "I hope you will understand and accept it someday."

"I'll never accept it, or quit trying." She said angrily and then turned away from me.

I realized that our conversation was over and I hadn't fixed a thing. I probably had made it worse. 'Well', I thought, 'time heals all wounds. Who am I kidding, love is not a wound.' I had a hard time going to sleep, and I could tell by Catherine's breathing that she wasn't sleeping either. For the first time in my life since the 'Big Shit', I didn't know what to do. After hours of lying there awake, I got up and went downstairs and sat in front of the fire. I stared at it hoping it would give me some answers. A little while later, Catherine came down the stairs and wrapped her arms around me from behind and laid her head on my back.

"I'm sorry Catherine; I know I made things worse." I said quietly. "I do love you."

"I know, but you really piss me off." She replied. "But you're right, I have been ignoring you. I was hoping that you would come to me, but I don't like trying to manipulate you."

I pulled her around and kissed her on the lips. She melted into my lap and I felt myself letting go.

"Stop." I said. "I still can't."

"God you're a stubborn old bastard." She said angrily and got off my lap and stomped back up the stairs.

'Oh well, that didn't go any better.' I thought.

Around the first of March, a strong Chinook wind hit us and the snow started melting quickly. Jason had been coming over every couple of weeks and staying a few nights, but when the winds hit, the lake ice started cracking and after a couple days, was too soft to cross. The creeks were overflowing from the snow melt, and running out onto the ice of the lake. After a week, most of the snow was gone, except in shaded areas. We let the horses, goats and chickens out during the day, though it still dropped to freezing at night. By the third week of March, most of the runoff had slowed down and the lake ice started drifting to the south end of the lake. The higher elevations were drying out, and I hoped that it wouldn't end up a dry year, for fear of a fire season. There had been a few dry years since the 'Big Shit', and some of the forests in lower Idaho and western Montana had burned.

Catherine decided it was time to talk with me again. We had been avoiding each other for weeks. She came into the living room one evening and told me she wanted to take a trip to Bonners Ferry.

I thought about it and said, "We only have three horses, and we would be gone for a week at least. We can't all go, and I don't feel comfortable leaving anyone here alone."

Lizzy said quickly, "We don't have to go. Besides, Jason should be heading back over after the ice clears on the lake."

Pam jumped in and said, "I don't like riding horses anyway, if I don't have to. Someone has to stay and take care of the goats and chickens."

I could see that this was an orchestrated effort on their parts. Obviously Catherine had already talked to them about it. Mouse was the only one that didn't look happy at the idea.

"We'll be alright for a week alone." Lizzy said looking at Catherine and avoiding my gaze. "And I'm sure Jason will be over in a couple of days."

"Well I guess you girls already have this all planned out, so when do you want to leave Catherine?" I asked.

"In a couple days," She said, "that will give more time for Jason to head over."

"Okay," I said, "everyone make out their shopping lists and we'll leave in two days."

As the weather dried in Spokane, Murphy felt it was time to leave. He had heard stories of a large group of raiders that took over Lewiston and thought it would be a good idea to head there. He had Andrew get the barmaid up to his room, and waited outside the bedroom until Andrew had her in his bed. He, George, and Bob entered the room and together they tied the girl up to the bedposts. They had her naked, spread eagle on the bed, and he took out his Bowie knife and held it to her throat.

"Tell me where the owner keeps his money." Murphy said with an evil look on his face.

The girl was terrified, and blubbered, "He has a safe in the basement storeroom. He keeps it behind the racks on the west wall."

"Now that's a good girl." Murphy said and then he wrapped a gag around her head and mouth to keep her quiet. "She's your girl Andrew, so you can go first." The four of them took their turn raping her. When they were done, it was just past 2 AM. He sent Bob and Andrew to the stables to get their horses ready. The girl was blubbering, and he looked at her and said, "You don't have to worry sweetie. We're leaving, and you won't have to think about what just happened." He took out his knife and cut her throat.

He and George went down the stairs quietly and snuck into the owners rooms. They found him in bed with his wife, and holding a knife to the owner's wife's throat, told the owner to take them down to the safe and open it for them.

"We just want the money." He said reasonably. "If you co-operate, we'll just tie you up and the barmaid can untie you in the morning."

The owner was frightened and complied with Murphy. He took them down into the basement and pulled the racks off the west wall that hid the safe. George held his wife with the knife to her throat so he wouldn't try anything stupid. When the owner finished entering the combination and started opening the safe, Murphy stopped him and pushed him back. Murphy opened the safe and took out the pistol that was on top of the bags of money.

"You should have told me that you had a pistol in here." Murphy said smiling. He then turned and stabbed the owner in the stomach with his knife. At the same time, George cut the wife's throat. The owner went down screaming. Murphy grabbed him by the hair and cut his throat. He went back to the safe and pulled out two full bags of money and threw them to George. George put them into a backpack, and then Murphy closed and locked the safe.

Murphy put the owner's pistol into his dead hand and

wrapped the fingers around it.

"That should make anyone that finds them think it was a robbery gone wrong." He said.

They walked out of the establishment and mounted the horses waiting for them and headed south. No one was around to see them at 3 AM.

It was drying up in Lewiston at the same time, and Jim was getting bored fucking a different girl every week. He wanted to find his brother and the black haired girl that he knew his brother stole from him. At the beginning of the second week of March, he ordered Brian to pick some men to ride north and look for Jack. He knew it would take a couple of weeks to get up to Priest Lake, and was anxious to leave immediately. He sent for Murphy and his sons. Murphy had shown up the week before with bags of money and met with Jim to cement a relationship with him. Murphy was a ruthless bastard, and Jim understood that.

"I'm leaving to look for my brother and I'm taking some men with me. I want to leave you in charge while I'm gone." Jim told Murphy.

Murphy got an evil grin on his face and said, "I'll be glad to watch over your interests here while you're gone. My sons and me will make sure it's all still here when you get back."

"I'll be taking your sons with me." Jim said. "That way you won't get any bright ideas of taking over here."

"You don't have to do that." Murphy said with a worried look.

"I don't have to do a lot of things, but they'll be going with me to keep you honest." Jim said with an evil grin of his own. He loved putting people in their place, and he didn't trust Murphy, but he didn't have any other men that he felt could hold his group together. "If you don't like it, you are welcome to leave. Your sons are going with me if you agree to stay."

Murphy knew that his sons would be hostages to insure that he didn't try to take over, but he also knew that he had little choice in the matter. Jim had 80 men, and he only had himself, Bob, and his sons. To leave now would reduce his chances of getting rich preying on people. He put a smile on his face and said, "Okay, it'll be a good experience for them."

CHAPTER 39

J im and his men headed north, and made good time. He had thirty four men with him. Brian came along, but kept pretty much to himself. Jim didn't trust Brian with anything but organizing his men. By the third week of March, they made it to Coolin. That evening, Jim called Slim, one of his lieutenants and told him that the next day he wanted him to take three men and head up the west side of the lake to check the cabin his parents used to own.

Brian overheard this conversation, and worried that Jack would get surprised by these men. He thought, *'I should do something to warn Jack.'* He thought of volunteering to go along with those men, but, that was far as it went. He was still too frightened of Jim and he knew that Jim was starting to not trust him with anything anymore.

The next day, Slim and three men headed northwest. The rest of the group headed up the east side of the lake. They made it to Boville that afternoon, and when they rode up, they were met by Big Bo. Jim looked him up and down and thought, *'that's the biggest man I've ever seen.'* Jim looked beyond the man and saw that there were guns sticking out of the three houses.

"Can I help you men?" Bo asked not looking a bit frightened, and holding his shotgun cradled in his arms, making sure not to point it at anyone.

"Yes you can." Jim said, "I'm looking for my brother Jack Anders. Did he pass through here last year?"

Bo thought he should be careful with his answer, but didn't want these men to have a reason to start a fight. He looked over and saw George Murphy towards the middle of the group.

"How's your mother doing son?" He asked looking at

George.

Jim turned to look at George and asked, "You been here before boy?"

"Yeah, and he knows that I don't have a mother." George said. "The men from Ten Pines showed up while I was talking to him and he knows we robbed the Trading Post."

"Well that's true, boy." Bo said and then decided to fabricate a little lie. "But the men that showed up told us that a group of men called the Jacobs attacked Jack up by his cabin on the northwest side of the lake. He killed them all, and then headed up to Calgary to get out of the area. I think you should head up there to look for him."

"Was there a girl with him when he came through here?" Jim asked.

"Nope, he was alone when he stopped here last year." Bo lied again.

"If I was to question the rest of the people here would they tell me the same story?" Jim asked.

"Sir, I think you and your men should leave us be." Bo said sternly.

"And if I don't?" Jim asked with a smile.

"Then you'll be the first one to die." Bo said smiling back.

Brian whispered to Jim, "These people don't have anything we need. We should continue north like we planned."

Jim thought for a few minutes, letting the tension rise, and then turned his horse and said, "Come on men. We should make it to Bonners Ferry in about a week. We can stop there and rest and wait for Slim to catch up with us."

Bo understood from that comment that Jim had sent some men to the cabin. The men all galloped away, and Bo turned and went back to talk with Marge, Ben, and John.

Marge came out and said, "That was foolish lying to him like that."

"We got the boat ready, and we can leave in the morning. We should be able to reach Jack's cabin before anyone can ride around the lake and we can warn Jack." Bo said ignoring the comment.

"There's still a lot of ice jammed up on the lake." Ben said. "It'll be tough going."

"I know, but we have to try." Bo said. "I'll take Little Bo, and a couple of the other boys to run the bikes, and I can use a pole to push the ice out of the way. It should only take a little over a day to get there."

"I'm going to." Marge said with finality. Bo knew better than argue.

Jim and his men made it to Ten Pines two days later, to the ringing of a bell. As they rode up, he saw that there was a stockade around the center of town, and people were running from the outlying houses into it. They rode up and stopped outside the main gate. Jim recognized Tom Gray Wolf standing behind the wall on a platform beside the gate. There was no one else in sight.

"Hello Tom." Jim said.

"Jim, what can I do for you?" Tom asked, cradling a rifle in his arms.

"How about letting us in?" Jim asked casually.

Tom looked over the group, and noticed the Murphy boys. "You can come in and watch us hang the Murphy boys for murder and robbery." Tom said angrily.

George and Andrew Murphy looked frightened and moved to the rear of the group of men.

"Now, now, no reason to get all pissed off Tom." Jim said and then asked. "Have you seen my brother around?"

"Not since he killed the Jacobs gang." Tom said. "Haven't seen him since."

"We heard from Boville that he headed up to Calgary. Is that true?" Jim asked.

"Don't know." Tom said. "Like I said, haven't seen him."

"Well, it'd be right neighborly if you would let us in to rest our horses and get some hot food to eat." Jim said reasonably.

Tom put his fingers in the corners of his mouth and whistled. Sixty men, young boys, and women stood up on the platforms they had been crouched down on and suddenly there were sixty rifles and shotguns pointed at Jim and his men. Their horses got skittish as the men reacted to the sudden change in the situation.

"I think it would be better for you and your men to leave." Tom said with a smile.

"Not a very nice way to treat an old friend." Jim replied.

"We've heard what you've been up to Jim. Unless you want to die here, I suggest you move out now." Tom said forcefully and pointed his rifle at Jim.

Jim smiled and shrugged. "Have it your way, but if I find out you've lied to me, I'll come back here with all my men a burn this place to the ground." He then turned his horse and rode off with his men following him. The Murphy boys kept men between themselves and the guns on the stockade.

Tom watched them ride off and then issued orders for half the men to stay on the wall and keep watch. He called Jason and Sammy over and said, "Get in a canoe and head across the lake and warn Jack that Jim's in the area. I don't have to tell you to hurry."

Jason and Sammy ran down to the beach and threw their guns and Jason's bow and arrows into the canoe and took off straight across the lake. They didn't want to head north for fear that Jim's men would see them. They paddled hard.

Slim and the men with him made it to Nordman the night before, and made camp. From the map Jim had made for him, he knew they should make it to the cabin by the next afternoon. They planned to case the area first and surprise anyone there.

The next morning they left at first light, and traveled a game trail until they could follow the beach. By mid-afternoon,

Slim knew they were getting close and stopped the group. He climbed the bank and moved through the woods until he could see the cabin. He stayed back and took out a pair of binoculars and studied the cabin. There were goats and chickens, but no horses. Looking through the windows, he saw three young girls, but no sign of Jim's brother Jack or the black haired girl. He hiked back to the men and told them what he saw.

"Jim's brother isn't here, but we can have some fun anyway." Slim told the men; who grinned at the idea.

They walked the horses down the beach until they were below the cabin and Slim told the youngest, Seth, to stay with the horses. They walked up to the cabin and up onto the porch. Mouse had been looking out at the lake at that moment and let out a loud "Eeep!" Lizzy looked out and saw the men coming up from the beach.

"Quick Mouse, go hide in the den." Lizzy told Mouse. Mouse made it to the den door just as the men came onto the porch.

Pam came out of the kitchen drying her hands and asked, "What's going on?"

Lizzy bolted for the stairs and yelled, "Pam, run!"

Slim kicked in the door to the living room and rushed into the cabin. He saw the den door close, and one girl running up the stairs, with another running into the kitchen. He pointed one man to the den and the other up the stairs, and then took after the one that ran into the kitchen.

Mouse hid under the desk, and pulled out the knife that Jason had given her. She was terrified. The den door opened, and she heard footsteps.

"Hey little girl come on out. I ain't going to hurt you." She heard a man say.

She heard the footsteps coming around the desk and saw the man's feet stop by the opening under the desk. She gripped the knife tight. The man bent down and looked under the desk.

"There you are." He said smiling.

Mouse lunged forward and stuck the knife into his throat and up under his chin. She pushed with all her strength and felt warm blood run down her arm. She twisted the knife and pulled it back. The man fell to the floor grabbing his throat, and blood bubbled out of his mouth.

Slim ran after the blonde girl running into the kitchen, but she made it out into the garage before he got around the kitchen table.

Pam ran out into the garage and then out the garage door and around the side of the house. Slim was about thirty feet behind her. He came around the side of the house and saw the girl kneeling down beside a goat, hugging its neck. He stopped about ten feet away.

"Hey girl, why don't you come with me?" Slim said.

"Get him MB." Pam yelled.

The goat lunged forward with two hops and slammed its horns into Slims chest. With an 'Oooff!', Slim went over backwards and stopped coming up in a sitting position gasping for air. MB turned and kicked back with his hind feet and cracked Slim's skull. He was dead before he fell over.

Pam ran up and hugged MB. "Oh thank you MB." Then she heard a shot from inside the house.

Lizzy ran up the stairs to the back bedroom, and grabbed the shotgun from behind the door. She heard one of the men coming up the stairs. She loaded a round and came back out of the bedroom just as the man reached the top of the stairs. She pointed the shotgun at him and yanked the trigger. The double ought buckshot hit the man square in the chest and he went over backwards and down the stairs. Lizzy didn't wait, she ran down the stairs and into the den. She saw the man gagging on the floor and Mouse climbing out from under the desk.

"Are you alright Mouse?" Lizzy yelled, shaking with adrenaline.

"Eeep." Mouse replied.

"Pam!" Lizzy screamed.

Jason and Sammy pushed hard, and their arms were burning. They made it across the lake and were heading along the west shore towards the cabin. Sammy noticed the horse tracks along the beach, and they pushed harder. When they were about a quarter mile away, they saw four horses with a man standing beside them watching the cabin. They continued until they were about a hundred yards away, and beached the canoe quietly. Jason nocked an arrow and had Sammy follow him along the beach with his rifle. He didn't want to shoot and make any noise that would warn the men they were coming.

Seth stood on the beach beside the horses, and saw Slim running around the house after the blonde girl. He was hopping back and forth on his feet, yelling, "Get her Slim." Suddenly, he felt something hit him hard in the back. He looked down and saw a foot of a bloody arrow sticking out of his chest. Jason and Sammy ran past him before he even realized he was dead and fell over. Jason heard a shot come from inside the cabin. Desperate, he ran up the slope and heard Lizzy yell, "Pam!"

Pam came around the side of the house with MB and saw Jason and Sammy. Jason yelled, "Lizzy are you alright."

Lizzy and Mouse came running out of the house and Lizzy fell into Jason's arms. Mouse ran over and grabbed onto Pam. Sammy looked around the side of the house and saw the dead man.

Lizzy, Pam, and Mouse were crying and shaking. Jason looked them over and saw the blood on Mouse's arm. "Are you bleeding Mouse?"

Mouse shook her head and then they heard someone yelling from the lake. "Halloo the cabin."

CHAPTER 40

J ason, Sammy and the girls turned to the lake and saw a huge boat floating about a hundred feet offshore. Jason recognized Bo Jensen standing towards the back of the boat with his wife Marge beside him. Bo lowered a rowboat into the water from the back of the boat and he, Marge and a large boy got in and rowed to shore.

"Halloo Mr. Jensen." Jason yelled back.

The rowboat came ashore and Marge headed up to the cabin with the large boy. Bo walked over to the horses and looked at the dead man beside them, and then headed up to the cabin.

"Is everyone alright?" Marge asked as she approached the group.

The girls were still crying, but more out of relief than fear. Mouse clung to Pam and looked up at the large boy smiling down at her.

"We just got here a minute ago." Jason replied.

"We saw you from the lake, but we didn't want to make any noise until we could see what was happening." Bo said. "What happened here?"

Lizzy and Pam started talking at the same time, and Marge stopped them. "Bo, little Bo, check the area and make sure there aren't any other men around." She continued. "Where are Jack and Catherine?"

Bo, little Bo and Sammy went around the cabin and looked for signs of any other raiders, while Jason waited with Marge and the girls.

While they were looking, Lizzy answered, "Catherine and Jack left two days ago, headed for Bonners Ferry. They should be getting there any time now."

Bo and the two boys returned just as Jason was saying, "Nooo…, his brother Jim left Ten Pines about three hours ago headed that way with thirty men. We have to do something."

"If they have a two day lead, there isn't much we can do." Bo said sadly. "We need to take care of you girls now."

◆ ◆ ◆

Bo, little Bo, Jason and Sammy dragged the two bodies out of the cabin, pulled the one by the lake up, and dragged the one beside the garage around. They stood trying to decide what to do with them, when Lizzy had an idea.

"Put them on the horses and take them down and throw them to the herd of pigs just south of here. They're garbage any- way. Sammy knows where." She said.

They discussed the idea, Marge wanting to give them a Christian burial, but Lizzy was adamant that they would not be buried on Jack's land. Marge finally relented and Bo and Sammy took the bodies to where the pigs hung out. While they were gone, Marge had the girls pack their things and had little Bo and Jason row them out to the big boat. When Bo and Sammy re- turned, Sammy asked what they should do with the horses. He didn't want to let them go, because they were worth something, along with the saddles and gear.

Bo said, "We could string a line and have them swim behind the boat."

Jason stopped him, "I don't think they could make it that far across the lake without drowning. I know they can swim, but only for short distances."

"I'll take them around the north end of the lake and then down to Ten Pines." Sammy said. "It should only take me a day and half."

"I'll go with you." Jason said.

"No, you need to stay with Lizzy and the girls." Sammy re- plied.

"Little Bo will go with you." Marge said. "You shouldn't go

alone. That's settled."

While they prepared to go, Marge made them some supplies from the pantry to take along. When they were about to leave, one of the other Boville boys rowed Pam back ashore.

"We can't leave the goats." She said anxiously. "MB saved my life, and I can't leave Angel."

With Pam's help, Bo and Jason got the goats out to the boat, but they had to hobble and blindfold MB for the trip. Even though MB trusted Pam, he wanted nothing to do with getting into a rowboat.

When everyone was settled, Sammy and little Bo left, headed north. Jason went back to the cabin and tried to shut the door, but had to leave it slightly ajar. He decided he would come back later and fix it. He went down and got his canoe and rowed it out to Bo's boat and they pulled it behind.

On the trip across the lake, Pam kept the goats quiet and listened to Bo's story of their trip north and the reason they were late. They had trouble getting through the ice, and when they were about to Nordman, a couple of the chains on the bicycles broke and they had to stop for the night south of Nordman and find replacement chains by going through every garage they could. They didn't see the four men that were headed north, but they were probably in the same area at the same time.

The big boat made better time crossing the lake than a canoe would, and arrived just after it got dark. Bo steered it up to the long dock Ten Pines had, and tied it off. A few people were fishing from the dock when they arrived and sent word to Tom.

Tom and Angie came down to the dock and looked at the mayhem that was taking place getting the goats off. Tom walked up to Bo and looked up at him and then shook his hand.

"What you doing up here Bo?" Tom asked. "And where's Jack

and Catherine?"

"They headed to Bonners Ferry a couple days ago, the girls said." Bo replied. "His brother Jim passed by Boville a couple days ago, and we were headed up to the cabin to warn Jack."

"Oh no, Jim went through here today." Tom said anxiously. "I should have stopped him when he was here. We could have killed them all."

Angie said angrily, "Tom, you are not a murderer and you know that people other than Jim and his gang would have gotten hurt."

"But if anything happens to Jack and Catherine, it's my fault for not stopping Jim here." Tom said unhappily.

"There's nothing we can do about it now, let's get these people a place to stay while they are here." Angie said. "How long do you think you'll be staying?" She asked Marge.

"We'll stay until our son and Sammy get back and maybe until we hear from Bonners Ferry." Marge replied.

Angie made arrangements for Bo and Marge to stay with Jeremy and Elizabeth, and farmed out the two boys to another house. She took the girls up to their house and made up the guest room for them. She started making dinner for them, and Pam joined her in the kitchen to help.

"Pam, are you alright?" Angie asked seriously as they worked together.

"I am now." She replied. "But I was terrified earlier. I know I'm going to have nightmares, but I'm more worried about Catherine and Jack."

"Jack knows how to take care of himself, and he will protect Catherine." Angie replied. "How is Mouse doing?"

"Not so good. She has been talking since Christmas, but now all she can do is 'Eeepp' again." Pam said. "I'm worried about her."

"I'll talk to her and let her know she is safe again." Angie said as Marge walked in.

"I got the boys settled, and Bo, Tom, and Jeremy are talking about sending some men up to Bonners Ferry. Can I help in here?" Marge asked.

"Marge, if you could help Pam, I need to talk to Mouse." Angie said.

Angie went out into the living room and found Mouse sitting in the easy chair crying and humming in a monotone. Angie picked her up and settled into the chair with Mouse on her lap. Mouse looked up at her with tears streaking down her face and let out an 'Eeepp?'

"It's okay Mouse, you're safe now." Angie replied.

Mouse hid her face in Angie's bosom, shuddered and whispered "Jack? Catherine?"

"I don't know Mouse, but Jack can take care of himself and Catherine." Angie replied.

Mouse held Angie tight and shuddered, crying herself to sleep. Angie got up slowly and took her into the guest room and tucked her into bed.

Two days earlier...

Catherine and I left just after sunrise for Bonners Ferry. Catherine had a list of the things the girls wanted her to buy for them and they all decided to settle up payment after she got back. It was turning into a beautiful day, and we talked and laughed as we rode. It reminded me of last year when we traveled together from Elmira to the cabin. I realized that's when I fell in love with her. We didn't have the distractions of taking care of the cabin, planning a garden, hunting, or dealing with anyone else. Billy followed for a while, and then took off after some scent. He always caught up with us during the day.

Catherine turned to me and smiled, "I love this, just you and me and nothing to worry about, but where to camp."

I smiled back at her, "Just like our trip from Elmira."

"I was just thinking about that." She said with surprise.

"Me too." I said laughing.

"Do you think our lives will ever be that simple again?" She asked.

"Just like the trip from Elmira. I still can't predict the future, and I'm really enjoying the present." I replied. "Our lives will be what we make them to be. I read that on a fortune cookie once."

Laughing, Catherine asked, "What's a fortune cookie?"

I smiled at her, loving her more by the minute and replied, "Doesn't matter, I just enjoy this time with you."

"Jack, will you marry me?" She asked suddenly. "I want to spend the rest of my life with you."

"What?" I was taken off guard, and thought *I keep messing this up, how do I answer her'*?

"Is that your answer?" She asked getting an angry look on her face.

"No, you just took me by surprise." I said stalling while I thought.

"So your answer is No?" She asked angrily.

"No, I mean... dammit what can I say?" I stuttered.

"You can say yes you will." She replied still angry.

"But.. but.. Dammit, I love you Catherine." I kept stuttering and felt like a fool.

"Well, if you won't marry me, will you at least make love to me? There isn't anyone else around for you to feel ashamed in front of." She continued pressing me.

It was early afternoon, and I couldn't think of an answer, so I said, "Let's set up camp over there for the night."

"Damn you Jack!" Catherine said in frustration and pulled Black ahead of me and galloped to the clearing I had indicated. She got down and started taking Black's saddle and pads off. She wouldn't look at me.

'There I go again, ruining a perfect day'. I thought to myself. I took care of Betty and Zack, and started setting up camp. Catherine wouldn't talk to me, so I walked to a bluff, and found a log. I had to think this thing through.

I sat against the log and closed my eyes and started listening to everything around me. It has been a while since I've taken the time to center myself. I breathed slowly and listened. It was a quiet afternoon, and the sun was warm on my face. I quit trying to identify the sounds I heard and just listened. When I felt a calm come over me, I asked the question. *'Should I have sex with Catherine'?*

My mind immediately said, *'It's wrong, she is too young.'* I stopped that thought and asked who says it's wrong and why? *'Society'* was the only answer I could think of. *'But what is society but peer pressure? After the world I knew before ended, there were rules and restrictions against sex between an older man and a quote "child". The "child" had to be at least eighteen; otherwise it was considered statutory rape. But isn't rape forced on another? Sex freely given by both parties is consensual. I asked myself, isn't it Catherine that wants this so much? IIa, I want it just as much. So between us it is consensual and she is definitely not a child'.*

Then my mind said, *'Then why does society consider it wrong for two consenting people that are in love to share physical intimacy.'* I stopped myself here as my brain said *'Not two consenting people, two consenting adults.'* I then had to ask myself, *'What is an adult?'* I believed that an adult was a person that knew right from wrong and also a person that was able to take care of themselves. During my time with Catherine, I discovered that she was more than capable to make the right decisions and could definitely take care of herself. This was not true in the beginning when I first met her, but she had learned so much during our time together.

Society tries to control those under its power. By restricting who you can love they have control. You can only love someone of your same race, or your same country, or of the opposite sex, or your same religion otherwise you are ostracized. *'What a crock of crap. We are all humans, and love is love, no matter who you feel it for.'* I strayed a little in my thoughts here, because love and sex are two different things. Though physical intimacy compliments love, love is not required to have sex. I have been intimate with women in my past that I didn't love the way I love Catherine, but it fulfilled a need in both parties.

'Now what about religion,' I thought. I was brought up as a Christian, and felt that religions of the world were more divisive than just about people loving one another. Every one of them says that their religion is the true religion and every other religion is wrong. How can so many people be wrong? Jesus said *'Love thy neighbor'. Did he just mean the person next door, or did he mean anyone else that resides on this earth?* I believe that love is everything, and restricting love to one group and hating other groups, causes most of the problems that the world has faced. Or is this religions way of controlling people also?

So regardless what other people think based on their society or religion, it all comes back to *'Do I love Catherine in a way that precludes intimacy?'* The answer is NO. Society and religion has conditioned me to feel guilty if I have sex with a girl (young woman) under the age of eighteen. Well society is gone and most girls her age are already married and starting families.

So have I decided? I love Catherine with all my heart, and I know she loves me with all her heart. I can hardly wait to see her, talk to her, listen to her, sit next to her, hold her, be with her, or make her smile. I know that the first time we met and she offered to sleep with me, it was out of gratitude for saving her. But we have grown so close in the past year that I can't see my life without her in it. So have I decided?

Just then as if on cue, Catherine joined me. I opened my eyes and smiled at her. She smiled back and my heart raced. She asked, "Have you decided?"

I said, "Yes, and yes." Then I wrapped my arms around her and kissed her lightly on the lips. She has kissed me on the lips many times, but this was the first time that I kissed her first. She melted into my arms and kissed me back.

I smiled and said, "Would you like to skip dinner?"

"Yes I would." She said breathlessly.

CHAPTER 41

We walked back to our camp. I had my arm around her shoulder and she had her arm around my waist. I could feel the warmth of her body where it touched mine. The closeness was intoxicating, now that I didn't resist our desire. We reached our camp and I could see that she had already spread out our bedrolls together. I looked at her and raised my eyebrow and she smiled up at me and said, "I wasn't going to take no for an answer again."

I just smiled and kissed her again, this time pressing my tongue against her closed lips. She stiffened for a second and then opened her lips against mine. I explored her mouth and the taste of her with my tongue. She grinned and I pulled back a little.

"That was new." She whispered huskily. "I like it."

I picked her up and laid her gently on the bedrolls. She lay looking up at me, as I slowly unbuttoned her shirt. I opened her shirt and looked at her beautiful firm breasts. I leaned over and kissed her again, this time with her exploring my mouth. I broke the kiss and kissed her neck and nibbled on her ear-lobe. She giggled and said, "That tickles." I smiled at her and then took her nipple in my mouth. She pressed up against my mouth as I sucked and licked her nipple. I backed away slightly and blew on her wet nipple. Catherine shivered and pressed her breast back into my mouth. I nibbled on it lightly, and she let out a moan and said, "Don't stop."

I reached down and loosened her belt and unbuttoned her jeans. I reached in and ran my fingers over her pubic mound. When I touched her lower, I discovered that she was already wet. She raised her butt up and I pulled her jeans off. I rubbed my hand across her wetness and slipped my finger inside her. She gasped and arched her back. I suckled on her nipple again for a few seconds and then kissed down to her belly button. I licked her belly button and she giggled again and tensed her firm stomach.

Then I crawled down between her legs and kissed her wetness. She looked at me funny, and I said, "It's okay." I licked her and she gasped, "Oh God." She arched her back again and I pressed my tongue into her. She gasped again and I pressed my tongue harder into her. I licked her clitoris and her legs started shaking. She grabbed my head and held me against her. I licked harder and she gasped and squirted in my mouth. She tasted sweet.

Catherine grabbed my shoulders shaking and said, "I want you now."

I rose up on my knees and started taking my shirt off. She stopped me. "No, let me please." She said.

I let her remove my shirt and undo my jeans. I was engorged and she stopped and looked at me there. "It's so big." She said a little frightened. "I have used my fingers, but you are so much bigger than my fingers."

I smiled at her and whispered, "It may hurt the first time a little, but I want you to control it." I lay on my back and grabbed her by the hips and pulled her on top of me. She was tense. I wanted her so bad, I could barely control myself. I pulled her forward and kissed her again. As we kissed, she relaxed and lay on top of me. Slowly, I slid her back until the tip of my erection was against her wetness. I whispered, "Take it as far as you can slowly."

Catherine slowly backed up against my erect penis and let it slide into her. She gasped when I was halfway in and pulled back away. Then she slowly slid back onto me. After several strokes, she started moving faster. I was almost ready to come, when she arched her back and sat up on me. I slid all the way in and we both shook with ecstasy. She collapsed on top of me and I hugged her tight.

"Oh my God Jack, that felt wonderful." She whispered out of breath.

"It was wonderful for me too." I gasped out of breath. "I love you Catherine."

We lay like that joined together and time stopped. I held her against my chest and we both drifted off to sleep.

Much later, Catherine woke up and felt the urge to pee. She slowly untangled herself from Jack and he rolled over and continued sleeping. Catherine got dressed and walked to the edge of the campsite using the glow of the coals in the fire to find her way. She crouched beside a tree and peed. Billy came over and sniffed at her. She pushed him away and stood up. He sniffed around her pee as she walked back to the camp.

As she was approaching their bedrolls, the fire flared up and lit the entire camp. There was a very old Indian man sitting cross legged on the other side of the fire. She bent down and shook Jack awake. "Jack, wake up!" She yelled. Billy started barking at the Indian man.

I jolted awake and grabbed my pistol. Then I looked up at Catherine and saw her staring across the blazing fire. I saw the man sitting there and pointed my pistol at him. He slowly raised his hands and smiled at us. Billy was barking hysterically. The Indian man pointed at Billy, and he lay down and stopped barking.

"Who are you and what do you want?" I asked. I studied the man as I spoke. He was wearing tanned hide clothing with small quill and bead work on the front. He also wore moccasins laced up to his calves. He had long gray hair with a braid on the right side and an eagle feather tied into the braid.

He continued smiling and motioned for me to lower my pistol. He looked non-threatening, so I lowered my gun but kept it ready. Then he spoke.

"Simmu'em, please sit." He said to Catherine. She quickly

sat next to me.

"Skaltumiax, I come in peace." He said to me. I recognized the Salish language for 'woman' and 'man'.

Billy walked over to him and sniffed his hand. The man scratched his ear and said softly, "Nq'q'osmi'." Billy licked his hand and trotted back to Catherine.

Then the man spoke and even though he spoke Salish, I heard the words in English.

"Yetłxʷasq̓t qe y̓amncut u qe es wičstm łu nxʷlxʷiltn ta es hoy qe cxʷič̓łt łu qeqł nxʷlxʷiltn iqs ši?mnwexʷ l es ya? łu l es xʷlxʷilt put u yetłxʷasq̓t łu qe nk̓ʷłaxmintn nk̓ʷu? wilš łu ne qe es lmntmnwexʷ u qe es cuti lemlmtš č es ya? sqlqelixʷ x̣ʷl̓ qe sqelixʷ."

"Today we have gathered and we see that the cycles of life continue. We have been given the duty to live in balance and harmony with each other and all living things. So now, we bring our minds together as one as we give greetings and thanks to each other as People." [1]

I didn't have a clue where this conversation was going, and I looked at Catherine and saw that she had understood what the man had said. She was smiling at him and he smiled back at her.

He continued speaking Salish, but we both understood him in English. He said, "The World has fallen and the People are in disarray. The Coyote and the Wolf tear at the People and leave them in sorrow. The Garden has many weeds and must be cared for."

I said, "I don't understand."

He rose and walked around the fire and knelt before us. "Place your hand in his." He said to Catherine.

Catherine reached for my hand and I held it tight. The man reached into a pouch at his side and pulled out a rawhide strap. He wrapped and tied it around our wrists and said, "Your spirits are one." He got up and walked back and sat down on the other side of the fire. He sat looking at us, and time stopped again.

He smiled at Catherine and asked, "You are a gardener, yes?"

Catherine whispered, "Yes."

He smiled at me and asked, "You are a guide, yes?"

I couldn't help myself, I smiled back at him and said, "I guess I could be called that, yes."

He got a sad look on his face and said, "Your path ahead is full of happiness and sorrow. Your children and grandchildren will unite the People, but first the Gardener must weed the Garden, and the Guide must guide and protect her. Your spirits are one."

"What do you mean?" I asked, but the firelight disappeared as the flames went back to coals and the old Indian man was gone. I looked at Catherine and asked, "Did that just happen, or am I dreaming?"

Catherine released my hand and started to pull it away, but our wrists were held by a rawhide strap. "I think that just happened." She said. "What do you think he meant?"

"I don't know." I said.

Catherine undid the strap on our wrists and kissed me. "I like the sounds of our children and grandchildren though." She whispered in my ear.

We lay back down and made love again. I lay afterwards thinking about what the old Indian man had said and thought to myself as I dozed off. *'I will never leave Catherine. Our spirits are one.'*

CHAPTER 42

Catherine and I took our time on the trip to Bonners Ferry. I have never been so much in love as I was with her. We would stop often and just look at the beauty around us and talk about simple things. The trees were starting to leaf, and the creeks and rivers ran with clear clean water. We camped early every afternoon, and got back into our listening routine. I would glance at her as we sat quietly and see her small smile as she heard a new sound. I started to notice a glow about her and a serenity that took hold of her. I was breathless at her beauty.

Catherine would wake me every morning to make love before we got up, and every evening we would share each other's pleasures before we went to sleep. It was getting to be too much for me, even though I hadn't shared a woman's love for some time. I didn't want to disappoint her, so I made sure she was about to reach her peak before I entered her.

"Catherine, I don't know how much longer I can keep this up." I said one evening. "I'm not as young as you and I don't want to disappoint you. I love you so much."

"Well, you're going have to try 'old man'." She said laughing. "You're going to make up for every time you said 'No' over the last year."

I smiled at her and said, "Yeah, I probably brought this on myself, but you do understand that I had to be sure you wouldn't fall in love with someone closer to your age."

"Jack, you are the only person I will ever love." She said seriously. "You know that."

"I think I do." I said, "And I have never felt about another woman like I do about you."

We continued on our trip and talked about the incident with the old Indian man. We still found it hard to believe that it had really happened, but Catherine still had the rawhide strap wrapped around her left wrist. She said that she would never take it off, because it proved that we were meant for each other. I was still trying to make sense of what he had said to us. I liked the sound of 'our children and grandchildren', even though I thought I was a little late starting a family. *'Or did he mean Lizzy, Pam and Mouse as my children. No, he said your children to both of us'*. I thought.

I asked Catherine, "What do you think he meant by you being a Gardener and me being a Guide?"

Catherine thought for a minute and said, "I don't know, but he referred to weeding the garden and you guiding and protecting me. Maybe the garden is our lives together and overcoming sorrow. He did say our lives would be filled with happiness and sorrow."

"Well, I couldn't be happier than I am right now, with you in my life." I said, "And there is always some sorrow in any relationship. I guess we will have to take it as it comes, and I hope that I am good enough to guide you. I will always protect you."

Catherine smiled at me and rode Black up next to Betty. She leaned over and kissed me as we rode through an open meadow. Zack followed along on his lead rope. Billy was nowhere to be seen, but he always caught up with us by evening.

I laughed and said, "Yep, I couldn't be happier than I am right now."

Catherine smiled and said, "You have always made me happy, since the first day we met."

We continued down the trail to Bonners Ferry for a couple more relaxing days, and started coming across small farms. Most of them were abandoned, and as we got closer to town, we found a few that had been burned down. We were approaching from the south after we had crossed the Kootenay River. I decided that we would circle the town and enter from the north. We rode around about two miles from town and approached across the bridge on the North road into town. There was a wagon pushed across the entrance to town, and a man was standing behind it with a rifle. Billy still hadn't caught up with us, but I wasn't worried about him. He always showed up.

We stopped just outside the entrance to town and I saw that the man was one of those that had been in Elmira with Jim and me. I held my hand up and said, "Aaron, how have you been." Aaron was one of the late additions to our group in Elmira, and I hadn't gotten to know him very well. "What are you doing up here?" I continued.

Aaron got a feral grin on his face and replied, "Oh just taken in the scenery. By the way, Jim is waiting for you down at the hotel." He moved some barrels from the end of the wagon to let us through.

Catherine felt fear deep down in her belly. "Jack we should leave." She said anxiously.

"No, I'll have to face my brother sometime and his hunting us has to stop." I replied. "If we leave now, he will just chase us down and I don't feel like running."

We entered Bonners Ferry and rode slowly down the main street. We came to a bar, and I saw that a bunch of Jim's men were inside drinking. George and Andrew Murphy were sitting on the porch. They gave Catherine a dirty look, smiled and then went inside. Catherine just glared at them, while I ignored them. We passed by businesses and I saw people peeking out of their closed shops. We continued down the street a couple hundred yards to the hotel. Someone had obviously ran ahead to tell Jim that we were coming. Brian stood by the hotel door leaning against its jam. A couple other men that I didn't know were sitting in chairs on the porch. I could see that no one was armed, so I relaxed some. Catherine was very tense though.

"Hi Brian, how have you been?" I asked.

Brian smiled and said, "I've been better. It's good to see you again Jack, but you shouldn't have come here."

Jim came strutting out of the hotel with his hands clasped behind his back. I got down off Betty in the middle of the street and stood waiting for him to come up to me. Jim stopped about ten feet away and glared at me, and then he looked over at Catherine still sitting on Black and gave her a leering smile. Catherine just stared at him.

"Hi Jim, how have you...." I started to say, and Jim pulled a pistol from behind him and pointed it at me.

"About fucking time you brought her back to me." Jim said with an evil smile.

"I didn't bring anyone to you." I said angrily. I was waiting to see where this was going.

"Wrong answer." Jim said and pulled the trigger.

I felt the bullet rip into my chest and blow out of my back. There was no pain, but I suddenly got dizzy and fell over backwards. I heard Catherine scream "Noooo!" and then she was there kneeling beside me.

Catherine was crying and muttering, "No Jack, you can't die, you can't die. Please don't die."

I looked up at her and coughed, and then in a whisper I said, "Catherine, I love you and I will always be with you." I knew I was dying, so I continued, "Catherine, you have to run, now."

Catherine blubbered, "No, I can't leave you. I love you."

I was looking down at my body lying in the street, with Catherine kneeling beside it. I realized that I was still me, but no longer inside my body. Time froze. I had a bright blue glow surrounding me, or what I felt was me. I no longer felt anything physical, but I still felt a deep love for Catherine. I felt a bright white light behind me pulling at me and offering happiness. '**No, I will not leave Catherine**'. I resisted the pull of the light and it released me.

I understood everything. How life began, how the universe

was formed by a Creator, and how life teemed throughout the universe. I understood that all those life forms that existed in the universe had the potential for intelligence or should I say knowledge of self. Each life form that had reached the 'knowledge of self', had a story similar to our Adam and Eve. But I now knew that the apple from the tree of knowledge in the story was a metaphor for the knowledge of self, or intelligence, and full knowledge of our existence could only be achieved through our deaths. That was why they were metaphorically kicked out of Paradise and destined to toil and die in the physical world. Every intelligent species in the universe related a similar story to explain the reasons for hardship and death and the transition to intelligence. But death was only the next step in our existence. We continued as ourselves and retained what we had experienced in our physical lives. All hardships and happiness led us to better understand our existence, or should I say intelligent existence. I had full knowledge of everything that I had ever done, good or bad, and I understood that only the good could carry you to the next existence. The bad weighed down your spirit and you wouldn't be able to reach the next existence. I even understood that those that take their own life chose to end their continued existence.

I became aware of the scene below me again, and realized that the thoughts I had just had took only a millisecond. Catherine was kneeling at the side of my body crying. She was surrounded by a brilliant yellow glow. I could see deep down inside her and I saw two bright blue glowing sparks. On her left wrist, the rawhide strap the old Indian had wrapped our wrists with, glowed a blazing white. If I had eyes, it would have been blinding. I looked at Jim and only saw a darkness surrounding his body. The two lieutenants on the porch had a similar darkness around them. Brian still had a blue glow around his body. I felt the blue glow around me and realized that the two bright blue sparks inside Catherine were our children. I now understood what the Indian man had told us and that at conception when our DNA combined, intelligent life began. Is it blue for boys, yellow for girls? I sent a thought to Catherine, '**You need to run Catherine. Save the children**'.

As I watched Jim walked over and grabbed Catherine by the back of the neck. She stood quickly, throwing him off balance, turned and kneed him in the balls and then slammed her knee into his face when he bent forward. He fell backwards and then the two lieutenants ran towards her off the hotel porch. She pulled her Sig and shot them both, and I saw the darkness that surrounded them dissipate into nonexistence. Catherine pointed the gun at Brian. I thought, '**Don't shoot Brian**'. Jim reached over and grabbed Catherine by the ankle and yelled for Brian to kill her. Brain told him to get fucked. Catherine lowered the gun slowly from Brian and shot Jim twice in the chest. The darkness that surrounded Jim dissipated into non-existence.

I felt sorrow for Jim. '**Brother, I wish you had made better choices in your physical life, so you could experience continued existence and the happiness that everyone deserves**'.

Not the end.

BIBLIOGRAPHY

Jack's philosophy came from my reading Mo Gawdat's book "Solve for Happy'.

Salish Language Reference.
The Salish language in this text is from three sources:

The source for 'woman' and 'man' came from:
www.native-languages.org › American Indian culture › What's new
http://www.native-languages.org/salish_words.htm

The source for 'dog' came from:
Salish Language Animals on YouTube at;
https://www.youtube.com/watch?v=RbcZ8cEA9aw

The source for the text speech came from:
Omniglot, the online encyclopedia of writing systems & languages
https://www.omniglot.com/writing/salish.htm

Made in the USA
Columbia, SC
10 September 2020